TO BELL AND BACK

A Samantha Bell Mystery Thriller

JEREMY WALDRON

ALSO BY JEREMY WALDRON

Never miss a new release. Sign up for Jeremy Waldron's New Releases Newsletter at JeremyWaldron.com

CHAPTER ONE

SCARLETT MOSS HAD THE CAR WINDOW CRACKED AN INCH and the music blaring as she sang along to Taylor Swift's new song. With her head bobbing and both hands on the steering wheel, Scarlett wound her way through the mountainous valley at a fast clip without a care in the world.

It was autumn in the southern California mountains and everything was going right for Scarlett Moss. Nothing could stop her now, she thought as she swerved between the lines on the road, singing her heart out.

Her white Mazda sedan's headlight beams were leading her to a new beginning in a new town. Her few possessions, including her art and paint supplies, were packed into two suitcases in the trunk for what she planned as a self-imposed exile away from worldly responsibilities, like the job and the boyfriend she just left for good.

Soon she came to a stop at the intersection at Mountain Center Market, turned the music down, and reached for her phone. Checking the map for reference to her location, she was only ten minutes from her destination. Turning left, she pointed the wheels north and sped off.

Scarlett was again singing and dancing, grinning at the town lights illuminating the sky orange in her rearview mirror, when she felt her steering wheel suddenly jerk and get ripped from her hand as something large passed beneath the chassis of her small car. Her rear tires squealed and caught on the pavement, causing Scarlett to slam on the brakes. She pulled to the side of the road with at least one of her tires flat and flapping off its rim as she slowed the car to a stop. She knew she had hit something by the sound of the collision but didn't know what. A coyote? A deer?

With her heart galloping, she killed the music and turned off the engine. Checking her mirrors, Scarlett couldn't see into the black abyss that surrounded her. Her car's headlights were her only source of light. When she reached for her phone, she was without service.

"Shit," she sighed, kicking her door open.

Scarlett stepped out onto the empty road, and suddenly was made to feel small and vulnerable by the incredible vast wilderness that surrounded her. Turning on her cellphone's flashlight app, she was thankful to at least have that. She first checked her car for damage. Just as she thought, the front right tire was completely blown. Scarlett dropped to her knees and shined the light beneath the car. A little visible damage beneath, but nothing was leaking or spilling out onto the pavement.

"Okay, a flat tire I can fix," she said to herself as she pushed herself back up onto her feet.

Pointing her light behind her car, she looked to see what she might have hit. She hoped if it was an animal that it wasn't still alive. She didn't want to have to watch it suffer, and she'd never forgive herself.

Scarlett walked slowly, flicking the light from left to right, searching. It was so quiet out here in the country, she could hear herself breathing heavily, and she had a weird sense that she was being watched. Looking over her shoulder and off into the distance, Scarlett felt like she needed to hurry and get back on the road before something worse happened. She lengthened her stride and was surprised to come to two large rocks she assumed she'd hit.

Scarlett stared for a second trying to understand where they'd come from and how they'd got here. She spun around and flashed her light at her car. Her red taillights blinked like dragon eyes and, when she looked over the edge of the road past the guardrail, the hill went down, not up. Thinking they must have fallen off a truck or something, Scarlett moved each rock to the shoulder, before another car hit them.

After wiping her dirty hands clean on her thighs, she checked her phone for service as she walked back to her car. Still nothing. No bars, no matter what she did to try to get a signal. Scarlett pulled her hair back, tied it off into a ponytail, and began changing her tire.

It didn't take her long to pull the spare from the trunk, jack up the corner of her car, and twist the lug nuts free. Her father had taught her to change a tire as soon as she got her license and, though she didn't have much experience, she was thankful for his tedious instruction.

Ten minutes passed and, with the spare tire on, Scarlett lowered the jack and watched the weight of the car press the rubber flat. The tire didn't have enough air in it. Scarlett fell back on her butt and sat and stared, feeling as deflated as her spare tire.

She looked south toward Mountain Center and then north to Idyllwild. It was only about four and a half miles between the two towns, but Scarlett believed she was closer to Mountain Center.

Pushing herself up, she packed only her essentials, planning to walk back to town and get help when beams of light filled her cabin. She turned her head and looked behind her as she heard a man call out from the truck parked behind her, "Everything okay here?"

Scarlett slammed her car door shut and shielded the headlight glare away from her eyes. "Flat tire," she responded.

"You need help changing it?"

"The spare is flat, too. You happen to have an air compressor with you?"

The man said he didn't, then added, "I can give you a ride to town if you'd like?"

Scarlett couldn't see the man's face, only his dark silhouette, but his voice was friendly and nonthreatening. Debating what she should do, Scarlett stared and thought over her options. Either she waited with her broken down car or took her chances with a stranger.

Scarlett said, "I was on my way to Idyllwild."

"C'mon. Get in. I'll have you there in ten minutes."

Scarlett nodded and smiled. She climbed into the front seat of the truck and introduced herself to the man with kind eyes who called himself, Lefty. Then they headed north, into the darkness without a witness to what happened.

CHAPTER TWO

I PEELED BACK THE CURTAINS AND GAZED OUT OVER LOS Angeles as I waited for my sister, Heather, to answer my call. The *Los Angeles Times* had put me up in the DoubleTree in the heart of the city. Formerly known as the Kyoto hotel, it was one block away from the newsroom and had views of City Hall and the criminal court building. The sight alone had my journalism juices flowing. Though I was on west coast time, I was only one hour behind Denver.

"How was the flight?" Heather answered.

I said, "Besides the turbulence we hit over Nevada it was quick and straight forward."

"That's great. Have you bumped into any celebrities yet?"

"I haven't been out. As soon as I arrived, I took an Uber to the hotel." I asked about Mason, my teenage son, and I could practically hear Heather roll her eyes at my question.

"Everything is fine; you haven't been gone that long."

I smiled. Maybe one day my sister would understand my questions and constant worries by having kids of her own, but that day was still beyond the horizon. I heard some voices in the background, glanced at the digital clock behind me, and asked what was happening at my house at such an early hour.

"We had a sleep over," Heather said.

"Are you saying everyone slept at my house last night?"

"That's exactly what I'm saying. We ordered more food and drank entirely too much wine."

I wondered where they—my best friends Susan, Allison, and Erin—all slept, and I was sorry I had missed the party. There was plenty to celebrate yesterday, but a small part of me also wondered if my latest story about Denver Police Chief Gordon Watts may have destroyed privileged access into future investigations.

"At least you weren't celebrating my absence," I teased.

"We had a great time without you. Well, except maybe Erin. She seemed upset that you actually flew to Los Angeles to interview for a job."

Erin Tate was not only a friend but also a business partner. We had started what had become a large crime blog and podcast that journaled our investigations in real time. In a short amount of time, we chronicled a serial killer, a couple of spree killings in the Denver metropolitan area, and had recently lost the trust of the Denver Police Department after breaking a story that blew the lid off of a corrupt crime scheme within the department. We were gaining momentum quickly, just as the industry we loved was shifting beneath our feet. But Erin knew about my interview with the *Los Angeles Times*. It was no secret how they headhunted me for the position I was in California to explore. So I was surprised to hear her mood had shifted after I had left.

"Can I talk to her?" I asked.

Heather said, "Sorry, Sam. You just missed her."

A knock on my door had me saying goodbye. "Tell Mason I'll call him later."

"Not that you need it. But good luck with the interview."

"Thanks," I said. Then I headed to the door to see who it was that was knocking at such an early hour.

CHAPTER THREE

There was another quick rap on my hotel door and I wondered who it was on the other side acting so impatiently. I moved to the mirror, made sure I was presentable, then hurried across the floor to answer the door.

With my hands on the door, I pushed up on my toes and peeked through the peephole with one eye. A tall, lean man stood with one hand on his hip. His fingers were covered in gold rings and he was wearing a gray sports coat over a white tee shirt, hiding his eyes behind a dark shade of sunglasses.

I asked myself, "Now who in the world is he?"

He turned and faced the door. The diamond studs in his ears glimmered in the florescent hallway lights as he ran his left hand casually over his pulled back jet-black hair that was tied off in a ponytail.

Dropping to my heels, I reached for the handle and opened the door. "Yes?"

He stared, chewing his gum, and I could feel him assessing me from behind his sunglasses. "Samantha Bell?"

"That's me," I said with my face between the door and the frame.

He lifted his hand to the door and pushed himself inside my room, taking liberty to peek in the bathroom and in the closet before stopping at the bed.

After I asked who he was, he said, "I'm the cop shop reporter Edgar Diaz." Diaz turned to me and gave me a look that said I should know this. I didn't. Diaz shrugged like he'd make sure I soon knew everything about him and turned to my suitcase which was opened wide on the bed and began picking his way through it.

"Excuse me," I said when he touched my underwear. Quickly flipping it shut, I asked, "Are you from the *Times*?"

Diaz took his sunglasses off his eyes and held them in his hand. "They didn't tell you I was coming?"

I shook my head, no.

"Figures," he said, his eyes still searching every nook and cranny of my hotel room like he would assess a crime scene. "Anyway, you ready to go to work?"

"What about the interview?"

"What do you think this is? A date?"

I couldn't help but look down at what I was wearing. A blue two-buttoned blazer with matching pants.

Diaz grinned, and said, "This is the interview."

CHAPTER FOUR

"C'MON, BON, IT COULD BE OUR LAST GETAWAY BEFORE winter."

"I don't know, John. I kind of just want to stay home."

John Huntress closed his eyes and sighed before swiveling his chair around and looking at his wife. Her feet were planted flat on the floor, a steaming hot mug of tea at her side. She didn't even bother taking her eyes off the book she was reading.

"You can read your book while I fish," John argued, but Bonnie didn't react.

It was the same old song and dance they performed whenever John wanted to get away to fish. But after thirty years of marriage, John thought that his wife Bonnie would be able to read his mind—or at least flatter him by conceding to compromise.

John turned back to his computer and typed in a quick search for Hemet Lake, a reservoir nine miles south of Idyllwild-Pine Cove in the San Jacinto Mountains. It was less than a two hour drive away from their house in Irvine, and he figured if he couldn't sell his wife on this camping destination, then maybe he would go it alone.

Soon, he found himself on the park website and made note of enticing features his wife might like. "Look here," he said to Bonnie, mentioning his idea and how they could make it a long weekend. "We can rent a cabin. You love a cozy cabin in the woods."

"That's true. I do," Bonnie said, her attention still buried in the pages of her book.

"Then what's the problem?"

"No problem. I just feel like staying home is all."

Then it occurred to John that maybe he knew the real reason Bonnie didn't feel like venturing out. None of their adult children or grandkids would be there to keep her occupied. It was autumn and the grandkids were in school. John had tried convincing his children to take a day or two off and when he was unsuccessful at that, he called a few friends, all of whom said maybe next time.

Still dreaming about his fishing vacation, John suggested they rent a boat.

"Just give it up, John. You're making me want to never take a vacation with you again."

John didn't react. He was already navigating the lake on Google Earth, when he stopped on what he thought looked like a submerged vehicle in one of the northwest coves. He clicked and zoomed in on the white sedan.

"Bon, come take a look at this," he said.

"You're not going to convince me otherwise, John. I've already made up my mind."

"No, no. Really. You have to come take a look at this." John briefly explained what he thought he had found.

Bonnie put her book down and pushed herself out of the comfy arm chair and walked across the room to where her husband sat.

John pointed to the screen. "Do you see what I'm seeing?"

Bonnie squinted her eyes and stared.

"Is that not a car?" John's eyes sparkled like he'd found a buried treasure.

Bonnie stepped to the side and reached for the phone.

"What are you doing?" John asked.

Bonnie said, "I'm calling the police to tell them what I just found."

CHAPTER FIVE

WE WERE IN THE ELEVATOR ON OUR WAY TO THE LOBBY floor, when Diaz asked if I was hungry.

"Do we have time?" I asked, lifting my sleeve to glance at my gold watch. "I was told to be in the newsroom ten minutes before ten."

Diaz leaned one shoulder against the wall, swiping his thumb over the screen of his cellphone, acting like he hadn't heard me. Then he said, "I could use a drink, too."

The reporter inside me wanted to ask to see his credentials, because I had a hard time believing Diaz was the *Los Angeles Times's* best. He made an awful first impression, though I kept giving him the benefit of the doubt, hoping his ego would soon prove itself to me, so that maybe I could get on board with whatever he had planned.

"Coffee sounds good," I said.

The elevator car slowed to a stop and the doors chimed open. Diaz was first off and led us to the Justice Urban Tavern inside the hotel. There were few patrons inside, and a lazy staff picking up what little business presented itself on this slow morning. I grabbed a menu on our way to an empty booth and asked Diaz if I should order something to go.

"Get what you want," he said.

Having had little for dinner last night, I was starved. When the waitress came to take our orders, I asked for the Denver omelet with a side of pancakes, and watched with amazement as Diaz ordered a craft beer.

"Watching your diet?" I teased.

Diaz seemed focused on watching the waitress's backside. When I offered to pay, he said, "Don't worry about it. This one is on the paper's dime."

Diaz turned to me and winked, and I felt a shudder work its way up my spine. Neither of us spoke for a long time and, besides, Diaz seemed perfectly happy to be playing on his phone, rather than talking to the newbie interviewing for the open position. I watched him out of the corner of my eye and assumed he was of the new school, the kind of mobile journalists fighting it out on Twitter.

"How long have you been working with the *Times*?" I asked, attempting my hand at small talk. Instead, he turned it around on me and asked about the last story I had just completed working in Denver. Suddenly, my career in Denver flashed before my eyes, and I was reminded of the years I spent covering the most gruesome murders to ever have come out of the Mile High city. "My latest story?"

His eyes showed their amusement, and I wondered if he wanted to hear some of my best war stories. "The breaking news coming out of Denver." He paused. "Your name is on the byline."

"Ah, that," I said, leaning in and bringing my elbows to the table. "It was a case of corruption—"

"Whatever you've seen," Diaz cut me off just as his phone started to ring, "it's ten times worse here in LA."

CHAPTER SIX

DIAZ TOOK THE CALL OUTSIDE AND I WONDERED IF THIS whole situation was real. He seemed to have made up his mind about me before taking the chance to get to know who I actually was. I assumed either he had overheard something really good being said about me, or had dug up something to hold against me. Either way, he was making me fight for his respect.

While I waited for my food to arrive, I pulled out my phone and called Erin. It went straight to voicemail.

"Hey. It's me," I said. "Heard about the slumber party. Didn't realize you all were throwing a going away party without me."

I smiled, thinking how what I really needed was someone to talk to who understood not only the industry, but who could guess why the *Times* had sent Diaz to my hotel room this morning.

"I've got my interview at ten west coast time, but if you get this before then, give me a call. I could really use some support from a friendly voice."

I hung up and glanced toward the kitchen. Then I turned

back to Diaz. He was still on the phone pacing back and forth like a zoo tiger in front of his cage window. I tried to read him from afar, understand his motive for seeming stand-offish and unwilling to listen to the answers to his questions. I assumed he knew everything about me, but I knew nothing about him. That bothered me.

Diaz came back inside just as my plate of food was placed in front of me.

"Time to go," he said.

I hadn't even picked up my fork when I looked him in the eye and said, "At least stay for one drink?"

Diaz flicked his eyes to his dark beer and I watched in amazement as he reached for it and emptied the glass in four swallows.

"I was only kidding," I murmured, not bothering to call him out on telling me not to order my meal to go, or how disgusted I was by what I just witnessed. "At least tell me what's so important that it can't wait."

Diaz turned to the exit and motioned for me to follow. I tossed down enough cash for the meal, as well as his beer, and quickly caught up to him. At the car, he said, "Just received a hot tip on a possible homicide. We'll check it out and then get you back here in time for that promised interview."

Again, I had my eye on the clock. We had ninety minutes to spare. Though I was interested to see more of the under-belly of Los Angeles, I wasn't sure this was my beat, or prerogative.

"Trust me," Diaz said. "With what I'm about to show you, you will thank me later."

CHAPTER SEVEN

Traffic made it impossible to get anywhere fast. I sat back, taking in the sights as we traveled south on the 110, realizing I wasn't prepared to be working in the field on assignment. Compared to Diaz, I looked like a cop. While that had its advantages, I still didn't know what story we were chasing and why.

"We're heading into a dangerous neighborhood," Diaz finally said as we exited the freeway.

Then he glanced over at me as if truly looking at me for the first time today and it was clear he didn't approve of something. But was it the way I was dressed that would be the problem, or that I was an outsider not knowing the lay of the land? I assumed he took issue with both but didn't let it get to me.

"Does this neighborhood have a name?" I asked.

Diaz focused on his driving while he explained, "The Nickerson Gardens. A predominately black housing project. Birth place and home of the Bounty Hunter Bloods gang."

I was familiar enough with Los Angeles gang activity to take his warning seriously. I had entered dangerous neighborhoods before, but not being on my home turf spiked my adrenaline and my senses were working on overdrive.

We arrived to dozens of black and white squad cars, uniformed officers working the scene. Numerous groups huddled around and watched from the sidelines. Diaz found a place to park and told me to stay in the car. "Nothing this neighborhood would like more than to sink their teeth into a white woman like yourself."

He slammed the door shut and I looked around, guessing what had happened. Armed with phone in hand, I kept waiting to hear back from Erin.

Diaz quickly connected with a source, and though I had my window cracked, I was still out of ear shot to catch what was being said. Five minutes passed and he was back at the car saying, "Nothing more for us here."

I hadn't seen anything happen and told him so. He slid the car keys into the ignition and turned to me.

"A twenty-year-old father shot his nine month old infant in the face, killing her instantly."

"Was he arrested?"

"He'll get taken in for questioning. Word is he told police it was caused by a drive-by shooting."

"What about witnesses? Should we get a statement? Someone must have seen what happened?"

Diaz turned his head and looked away. "You just don't get it. But how can you? You're not from here."

"It sounds like you think the father's lying."

"Of course he's lying. Look around; no one here gives a shit."

"So that's it? The story has written itself?"

Diaz started the car and said, "We'll put it up on the web but it will never make print."

I turned and looked back at the scene. A woman was on the ground, hugging her knees to her chest, crying. Apparently even the *LA Times* wasn't immune from the gigantic shift the newspaper industry was experiencing. It wasn't that Diaz didn't want to report the news, it was that he had enough for a clickbait headline that would be replaced and forgotten in a matter of seconds.

Diaz whipped the car around and headed back to the 110 saying, "What? Not the beat you expected?"

CHAPTER EIGHT

WHAT WAS SUPPOSED TO BE AN INTERVIEW WITH ONE OF the country's largest newspapers, felt like my first day on the job—training day. I found it hard to believe this was how the *LA Times* did business, but what did I expect? To be different than the struggles the *Colorado Times* was also experiencing? Readership was changing and so were expectations, but despite the sad state of affairs, I kept thinking about what actually happened to the little girl who was now dead.

Nine months. It was all she had on this earth. I thought about how it was about the age my own son, Mason, started to crawl. And even though we were back on the freeway heading north to the city, I wanted answers. Wanted to dig deeper and learn what happened. I couldn't help but feel we were letting a story go because it lacked substance on the surface.

I turned my head and glanced at Diaz. He had one hand on the steering wheel, his other working his cellphone. Desensitized wasn't a strong enough word for Diaz's attitude. Like the victim's life was only worth his five minutes of time.

I turned my head and watched the world go by, reasoning

with myself by saying it wasn't my city, therefore wasn't my fight. I started to think that maybe that was the true intent of this ride along—to give me just enough of a taste of what to expect, so I would have my answer waiting for the chief editors by the time I sat down for the interview.

Diaz's phone kept going off and I wondered what was so important. I asked him about it and he said, "Just getting the facts straight on Twitter."

He looked at me with a judgmental expression and made the assumption, "I know what you're thinking. That this way of reporting is quasi-journalism."

"That's not what I'm thinking," I said. "Online is the future."

"Ah, yes. That's right. I was told you have a blog."

"Real Crime News is solid investigative reporting."

"And I'll assume it isn't successful, seeing as you're here to interview for an actual *paying* job." I didn't answer. No matter what I said would be wrong. Diaz continued, "Perhaps that's the reason it's not profitable."

"I'm sorry, what?"

He turned his head and looked at me. "It has no entrainment value."

"My job isn't to entertain, it's to report the news. But, isn't that your job, too?"

"People don't want the truth. They want to be entertained."

"So entertain me," I said.

"Have I not entertained you already?"

I laughed. "You wouldn't even allow me to get out of the car."

Diaz's phone rang and he answered as I sat back, not believing the conversation we had been having. Then he pulled the phone away from his ear and handed it to me. "It's for you."

I gave him a skeptical look as I answered. "Hello?"

"Samantha, welcome to Los Angeles. How is everything going?"

It was chief editor Jeffrey Hineman, the one I was supposed to meet for my interview. I told him about our stint in Nickerson Gardens and mentioned how we were on our way back to the newsroom.

"About that. Change of plans," he said. "Something has come up and I'm going to ask that we delay our interview until tomorrow."

"Is everything all right?" I asked.

"Yes. Just fine. I promise to get you in before your flight home. But, in the meantime, I'd like you to travel to Hemet Lake with Edgar."

I didn't know the place, but Hineman briefed me on the details, and the story I was hearing definitely piqued my interest.

"What do you say?" Hineman said. "Have a little fun while you're in California before we sit down and get to know each other better?"

I turned to look at Diaz and thought about the assignment, that I would have to work alongside him. The situation wasn't ideal but I answered, "Sounds great. Let's do this."

CHAPTER NINE

"I DIDN'T THINK YOU'D SAY, YES," DIAZ SAID WHEN I handed his phone back to him.

"Would you prefer I didn't?"

He slid his phone into an inside coat pocket, and said, "I'll plead the fifth."

I couldn't see if there was a twinkle in his eye to know if he was serious or not, but at least he was honest. I wasn't too fond of him either, but maybe this assignment would help break the ice, give us both a chance to prove our worth. Besides, it wasn't like I was going to stay in my hotel room all day and play tourist. I was more interested in getting a feel for the crimes happening around me than anything else. Crimes were a window into a culture and LA had an interesting one.

Diaz turned the car south and we connected to 91 east when Diaz told me more about the submerged vehicle found via Google Earth in the cold mountain lake we were now on our way to see. He smoked while he talked, not bothering to ask if I was okay with it. I powered down my window and concentrated on learning more about what we were heading into. After my small glimpse into gang territory, something told me this was going to be different.

Once I pulled up our location on the map, I learned just how far away we actually were from where we were heading. It was further east than I realized, and now understood why Hineman postponed today's interview. "It says here Lake Hemet is a two-hour drive."

"I'll get us there faster," Diaz said, increasing his speed. He flicked his cigarette butt out the window and added, "It might be nothing, but could be related to a missing persons case from nearly twenty years ago involving a local millionaire."

These were more details than Hineman had offered. He'd left out the part about the local millionaire. I pressed for more information, but Diaz refused to shed light on the subject, saying he wanted me to have fresh eyes on something he might otherwise miss. I assumed it was only an excuse so he wouldn't have to talk to me, but I could hear the potential in both his and Hineman's voices, and I was starting to get excited. At the same time, I couldn't help but feel like there was something Diaz was keeping from me.

The landscape gave way from concrete jungle to desert and rolling hills and I wished I had worn something else. To pass the time, I caught up with emails and waited to hear back from Erin. Something was up with her and I couldn't help but feel like maybe I had done something wrong.

When we arrived at Lake Hemet, we passed through the gate attendant and were surrounded by the majestic beauty of the San Jacinto Mountains that vaguely reminded me of the Rockies. It always amazed me how something as ugly as murder could happen in the presence of such beauty.

Diaz followed the road near the edge of the water and I

listened to the sound of gravel crunching beneath the tires, when I caught sight of a sheriff and park ranger standing near a tow truck, pointing into the water.

CHAPTER TEN

LEFTY STOOD AND ADMIRED THE WOMAN'S FIGURE. HER skin was smooth porcelain and she had the most perfect hour glass figure he'd ever laid eyes on. The way she moved gracefully across the kitchen floor was like walking on water. Graceful, gentle touches. She hummed a soft tune, not realizing she was being watched when Lefty snuck up behind her and grabbed her waist. Her stomach quivered when his hands circled her waist and pulled her tightly against his chest. She giggled and mewed as Lefty planted several kisses across the nape of her neck until finally she spun around and kissed him back.

Lefty retreated and smacked his lips as he peered down into her shimmering blue eyes. He said, "Hot *and* spicy."

"I'm glad you approve." She swayed from side to side as she hung off his neck.

Lefty reached behind her and let his hands drift south. "I very much approve," he said, when suddenly their intimate moment was shattered when two girls, ages five and six, came running into the kitchen.

"Daddy is kissing mommy," the younger one said.

"Yuck. Gross." The older one made a face.

Lefty turned and shooed the girls to the table. He heard his cellphone ring and his wife kissed him on his cheek, saying, "Lunch will be ready in five."

Lefty kissed his wife one last time to the same disapproval from his girls before retrieving his phone in the living room, taking the call from his friend, Rip. Rip said, "We've got a problem."

Lefty, hearing the seriousness in Rip's voice, glanced over his shoulder to where his wife was placing sandwiches on the table, and moved to the den and closed the door. "What kind of problem?"

"Hemet Lake."

Lefty held his breath and tipped his chin back. He didn't need Rip to explain any further. He knew what this meant, why Rip was calling, sounding so concerned. "Who is there now?"

"The sheriff. A couple of his deputies."

Lefty remained calm. "Any media?"

"Not that I see."

Lefty didn't need to hear more, and he certainly didn't want to be discussing this over the phone. He knew exactly what was happening—what would happen next. The forces had been set in motion and there was no turning back the tide. They'd gone eighteen years without incident and now their secret had finally surfaced, thanks to the ongoing drought.

The door opened behind him after a quick knock. It was his wife.

"Lunch is ready," she said with a smile.

Lefty pulled the phone away from his ear and covered the mic with his hand. "I'll only be a few more minutes."

She shut the door and Lefty dropped his smile when he told Rip, "Keep an eye on things, and don't you worry. When they learn who is inside, this will be a thing of the past."

CHAPTER ELEVEN

AFTER STANDING AROUND FOR OVER AN HOUR AND watching the divers get the hook and chain secured, the submerged vehicle was finally pulled from the water. It shimmered beneath the sunlight as it dripped dry.

I glanced in Diaz's direction. He was leaning against a tall pine, smoking. He never told me to stay back, or not do what I considered to be my job. I roamed back and forth, taking in the incredible scenery, noting the manzanita trees and giant oaks, trying to figure out how and when this car might have found its way into the water and if it was related to the case Diaz thought it was. There were no visible clues. The logistics of its recovery were challenging as the wrecker struggled to get the silvery white car up the steep hillside that gave way beneath the pressure of the vehicle's rusted out rims.

The recovery had since drawn a crowd, both on shore and in the water, with boats circling the perimeter, and I canvassed for answers while we waited.

How long have you been here? Were you on the water at any point during your stay? Have you seen any suspicious activity at any point during your stay?

No one knew a local millionaire and I didn't have a name to provide. I asked all the questions and no one knew a thing, not even that it was spotted by someone searching on Google Earth. This car was meant to stay buried—either on purpose or by accident—and everything had me thinking it was the missing persons case Diaz alluded to on our drive here. But he wasn't giving me any more clues.

I turned to Diaz and watched him flick his cigarette butt to the ground and snub it out with the tip of his shoe. He asked few questions and seemed mostly interested in what the sheriff would decide to do with the vehicle now that it was out of the water. I continued to work the crowd and kept searching for a quote we could use for a future story somebody might tell.

"We just arrived yesterday," one young couple said, telling me little about their plans.

Another retiree said, "I come here every year and have never seen anything like this. I wonder how many times I passed it not knowing it was there."

I heard the same story over and over again. Other than learning the lake was a popular camping and fishing spot, not much else was known. No one seemed too concerned about it, just interested to know how it got there and if anyone was caught inside.

The tow truck winch whined and I turned to look. Several stones broke free from the hillside and tumbled into the water with a big splash. I took out my phone, got into position, and began taking pictures. I noticed Diaz had done the same, and though we were here together, we certainly weren't working as if we were on the same team. Maybe we weren't. I sensed Diaz preferred working alone and that was fine with me.

By the time the vehicle was finally pulled onto flat land, it was clear what exactly we were looking at. It was a dirty, two door vehicle that reminded me of a Porsche but wasn't. Diaz made his way to me and asked, "Learn anything new?"

I shook my head, no. "Is that the Millionaire's car?"

Diaz didn't give any indication either way. Maybe he didn't know, or perhaps he just didn't want to tell me. He stared ahead as if he hadn't heard me, and then finally said, "We'll wait a little longer to see if there is going to be a press conference, then we'll hit the road."

I didn't know why his answer surprised me, but I should have seen it coming. Our investigation and reporting seemed incomplete until we knew whose car it was and who might be inside, but Diaz was making it seem like we only came out here for a couple photos we could have easily gotten from someone else. It seemed like such a waste of resources. When he turned back toward his car, something happened that had the sheriff running toward the waterlogged vehicle.

CHAPTER TWELVE

Whether this was Diaz's missing person's case or not, by the reaction I saw coming from the sheriff, I knew we had landed on something big. The coroner, who had only just arrived, quickly wheeled over a gurney and the sheriff was the first to fill her in on their find. I couldn't hear what was being said, but she had a digital camera around her neck and I watched her reaction as the deputies struggled to put up a tent, before too much was revealed to the public.

The crowd of campers and day hikers was growing and I kept waiting for Diaz to leave his car and join me on the sidelines. He must have had the foresight to realize we would be pushed back and sectioned off by crime tape, because he never came.

I kept trying to steal a glimpse into what was happening, to eavesdrop my way into the investigation, but I was surrounded by too much gossip as people guessed if it was an accident or murder.

The sun was tucking in behind the mountains and, though I expected Diaz to tell me we were leaving at any moment, he never did. Apparently, there was enough activity to convince him to stay, and I was happy to do so.

I broke free from the group and scrambled my way up the hillside, hoping to get a better vantage to see what was happening at the vehicle. Once in position, I used the camera lens on my phone and looked for the license number but couldn't find one. The vehicle's make and model were still unknown to me, but it was unique enough to know it wouldn't be hard to figure out, once I was connected to the internet and behind my computer. The coroner's team of investigators was focused on two areas of the car: the driver's seat and the trunk. I couldn't see what had their focus and decided to leave my hideout, when I spotted a man who looked like a cop working his way over to me.

I scurried back down the embankment and made my way back to Diaz's car thinking about what had happened and why, not knowing how many victims were inside, or if that was even what they had found. Then I heard the man who was coming after me say, "It's an Aston Martin DB4."

I stopped when I realized he was talking to me. "Excuse me?" I said.

"The car that was pulled from the water."

"Oh." We met eyes. He was tall, dark, and extremely handsome, but I couldn't decide why he was talking to me if he wasn't a cop. "I'm not familiar," I said.

"It's the precursor to James Bond's getaway car."

"Sounds like you know your cars."

"I know this one." He made his way over to me and extended his hand, introducing himself. "Carson Reynolds. Private detective."

"Samantha Bell, exploring opportunities." That made Carson smile. He had a strong, but not overpowering, grip and I said I hadn't noticed him earlier in the day.

Carson said, "I just arrived."

I thought it interesting how one lost car seemed to pique so many outside interests, but not as interesting as what he said next.

"Let me guess, no bodies only bones?"

"Are you suggesting there are multiple victims inside that car?"

"Only guessing there are bones inside," he said.

"Bones?"

Carson turned his attention to where the investigators were working and seemed to get lost in his own thoughts. I saw nothing to confirm his theory, but he convinced me he knew what he was talking about despite having only just arrived. I watched a floodlight get turned on and started to believe this was the missing person's case of the local millionaire. I was about to ask Carson about it when Diaz honked his car horn, indicating my time was up. Carson gave me a look and I said my ride was leaving.

"You're with him?"

I glanced in Diaz's direction. "Not exactly, but he is waiting for me."

"So that's it?"

"Not my choice," I said, telling him it was nice meeting him.

"You shouldn't go, Samantha."

I stopped, turned, and looked into Carson's deep brown eyes. They were sincere and trustworthy, but he seemed to know who I was even though I was certain we hadn't ever met.

"This is far from over."

I said, "It's not my decision."

He closed the gap between us, handed me his business card, and told me to call him if I happened to change my mind. "This might appear to be over, but the story is only beginning."

CHAPTER THIRTEEN

DIAZ DROPPED ME AT THE HOTEL LATE THAT NIGHT AND I woke early thinking of Carson's parting words: *the story is only beginning*. I got that sense, too. The sheriff's reaction to whatever they found inside the car, the tent that was set up to try to block the public from seeing their investigation unfold. But was it murder? Suicide? Or something else? I didn't know and Diaz didn't want to talk about it during our two hour drive back to LA, but I couldn't get it out of my head.

I supposed that was the reason why cold cases fascinated me. It had a pull on me I couldn't shake. I wanted answers; to know what happened and why. But I wasn't sure I would ever be given the chance since I was set fly back to Colorado later today.

I packed my bags, thinking about the fact that I'd kept Carson's words and their implications to myself on the drive back to LA with Diaz. I assumed Diaz saw me speaking to Carson, so it wasn't like I was keeping a secret. Perhaps he didn't care, or didn't know who Carson was, despite Carson leading me to believe he knew who Diaz was.

After my shower, I called Alex King, the Denver homicide detective I was currently dating. He was quick to answer and ask how my interview went. With a smile on my face, I said, "It got delayed until today."

King seemed surprised and I told him why. He said, "They're not making you work for free, are they?"

"I was only riding along. Besides, it wasn't completely free labor. They did fly me out here."

"As long as they fly you back, I really don't care."

It was so good to talk to him, to hear his voice. I asked about work, how things were going, and he assured me things were slow and he was hardly working. I didn't buy it. King was the hardest working, most dedicated detective I knew.

I asked, "You haven't spoken to Erin, have you?"

"Not since you left. Why? Is everything okay between you two?"

"I'm sure it's nothing," I said. "But she hasn't responded to any of my messages. I think she's giving me the cold shoulder for actually interviewing for the *LA Times*."

"She wants you to go full-time on your crime blog."

"I know." A moment passed, then I asked, "Did I make the right decision by coming out here?"

"Depends what they offer you in today's interview."

King wished me luck, even though I knew he was secretly hoping I would decline whatever the offer was and stay in Colorado to be with him. We hadn't discussed our future in depth, but I sensed that nobody wanted me anywhere but Denver.

After breakfast, I left the hotel and walked to the newsroom and entered through the lobby. I passed a cafeteria and took the elevator up to the third floor, where I was quickly introduced to chief editor, Jeffrey Hineman.

"The famous Samantha Bell in my office," he said by way of greeting.

"Finally," I said. "It's good to be here."

"I apologize for yesterday, but I hope you're day was well spent with Edgar."

A quick snapshot of everything I witnessed yesterday flashed across my mind, and I regretted my moment of hesitation, as Hineman called out his mistake.

"Or perhaps I made the wrong call."

"No, not at all," I quickly corrected course. "I very much appreciated the insight into the area, get a feel for the beat."

Hineman flashed a quick smile and moved behind his desk, motioning for me to take a seat. I sat across from him and appreciated his quiet demeanor. He seemed smart, driven, and keen on reading people's emotions before jumping to conclusions. Though I had just met him, he was easy to like.

He had a dozen or so of his favorite articles I had written spread across his desk, and when he noticed me looking at them, he said, "Let's talk about you."

"What would you like to know?"

Hineman brought up a few of my recent wins and said, "It's clear you have a detective instinct."

"Thank you. My late husband was a cop."

"That certainly explains your résumé."

We talked a little about my deceased husband Gavin Bell, without going into details on how he died, and my early days with the *Colorado Times,* but what Hineman really wanted to discuss, was my work with Erin. "Your blog and podcast are impressive. Tell me more about it."

I didn't know if he was bringing this to the forefront because of a possible conflict of interest, but I assured him it didn't get in the way of my reporting with the paper and wanted him to understand that blogging actually enhanced my readership, by making my investigations come to life in real time.

"I like to keep my audience in suspense," I said, feeling a

slight trickle of betrayal for being here instead of with Erin. Our blog, Real Crime News, was as much her success as it was mine.

Hineman took his eye glasses off and set them on the desk in front of him before saying, "It's the reason you're here. As you're aware, it's all about the internet now. The digital tide is a constant tsunami of information of hourly uploads and television tie-ins. We'll be lucky if there is such thing as a morning paper five years from now. You, Samantha, have the experience we're looking for to bring the digital arm of the *Los Angeles Times* into focus."

By the look he was giving me, I knew if I accepted his offer, I would create tension with Diaz's clickbait reporting techniques. It might be what today's readers responded to, and it might also be what was creating revenue for the paper, but it wasn't a method I could fully get behind.

I listened as he spoke about how the *LA Times* ranked in the country's top ten papers, had a current subscriber base of four-hundred thousand; but I also appreciated his honesty when mentioning why it had turned to me to lead the way.

"It's not just happening here in LA but across the country, as I'm sure you've personally experienced." Hineman leaned forward and I watched the corners of his eyes crinkle. "We're prepared to compensate you handsomely."

They were taking a huge gamble, and not just on me. It was the entire model at stake—a struggle for survival in an increasingly polarized world. I couldn't help but feel some of the excitement he exuded, when thinking about leading the *LA Times* into the future. So I sold my skills and talked myself up the best I could before asking what the *Times* was prepared to offer, besides pay, and what they expected me to give up in return.

"Samantha, around here, you're considered a rising star, and with that comes a bump in pay, office with door, regular byline on the front page, above the fold, on the home page of our website, and, as far as I'm concerned, you're one killer story short of national acclaim."

It was all very flattering, but refusing to get caught up in the glamor, I asked, "But...?"

"You're currently working for the wrong paper." Hineman held my gaze and watched me let the thought sink in. "Please say, yes, Samantha. We're not wasting our time with anyone else. We want you."

I hesitated and held still. "It's a big decision. I have a teenage son who will turn eighteen in a couple years."

"I get it. It's a big move. For you and your family. What can I do to help make that decision easier for you?"

I stared into his eyes and listened to my thoughts tumble over each other, thinking about where I wanted to be in five years. Then, surprising myself, I said, "Yesterday wasn't enough. I'd like to stay a little longer, investigate the Hemet Lake story as a freelancer. I think there might be something there. While I do that, I'll think about your offer to come on fulltime. But I'm going to need a car, a place to stay—"

"Done," Hineman said without hesitation. "You have two days to find something and make your pitch. You can send your spec to Diaz. And, by then, I expect an answer on whether or not you're coming to work for me."

CHAPTER FOURTEEN

"Nora," the shift manager raised his voice. "Table two."

Nora Barnes heard the instruction and turned toward the table closest to the door in the far right corner of the restaurant. She couldn't believe who she saw sitting there. Quickly looking away, her heart started beating faster.

What was *he* doing here, and what was she going to say to him? She closed her eyes and tried to calm her racing heart.

"Well?" her manager said into her ear as he passed behind her.

Nora opened her eyes, stared at the tips of her black sneakers, and felt her fingers swell until her skin stretched tight, throbbing in rhythm with her beating heart.

Her manager was still staring when he said, "Do it, or find yourself working someplace else."

Nora knew not to take his threat lightly. If she didn't serve the customer at table two, she'd be having to look for a new job later this afternoon—which she couldn't afford to do.

She grabbed a single menu from the stack at the front counter and tipped her chin back, steeling herself for the encounter she wished she could avoid. This job was all she had—the best she could get—and something told her *he* was about to ruin it for her. Like he did everything else in her life.

Weaving her way across the restaurant floor, she slammed the menu down on top of the table and said, "What are you doing here?"

Rip scooted to the edge of the bench and reached for Nora's hand, which she promptly reeled behind her back. He said, "I came to see you, babe."

"Don't call me babe."

Rip chuckled. "Have you taken your break yet?"

"Yes," Nora lied.

"Don't lie to me." Rip's smile disappeared. He looked at his watch. "You take your ten minute break at eleven-thirty, smoke two cigarettes, and hope the lunch rush tips you well."

Nora's eyes were wide as she realized Rip had been watching her. Playing it cool, she said, "What can I get you?"

"I want you." Rip hooked his hand on her thigh and yanked her against the edge of the table. The salt shakers shook and Nora swatted at his arm, embarrassed that she was being closely watched by her manager. "C'mon, Nora. Let's go out back and roll in the grass like old times."

Nora got a whiff of alcohol on his breath and managed to wiggle herself free. "Rip, you're drunk. Now stop it before my manager calls the cops on you."

"That's what you would want, isn't it? For me to get arrested."

"What I want is for you to order food or get the hell out of here."

"Or what?" Rip was starting to get angry. He raised his voice and grabbed Nora's wrist. Staring into his eyes, everything inside of her went stiff. Memories came rushing back in a flash. Knowing what Rip was capable of doing, made the trauma and fear unfold inside her chest. He noticed the pain in her eyes and grinned as he let go. He asked, "Did you hear what happened at Hemet Lake?"

Nora nervously glanced from side to side, hoping no one had witnessed her encounter with Rip. Knitting her eyebrows, she shook her head, no, and asked, "What happened?"

Rip smiled as he stood. Leaning close to Nora's ear he whispered, "Nothing happened. Got it?"

With her heart hammering, Nora nodded her head and watched him leave. She refused to cry, locked in the tears that threatened to spill, and considered the implications of Rip's words. When she turned around, her manager gave her a look that said he blamed her for the sudden lost business. But Nora didn't care. She was only happy to have gotten rid of Rip—even if it was only temporary.

CHAPTER FIFTEEN

LEFTY PULLED IN FRONT OF RIP'S HOUSE AND PARKED NEXT to Rip's rig. An hour earlier, Lefty had received a call from a friend saying Rip was drunk and causing trouble. It was the last thing Lefty wanted to hear with everything else going on, but he feared Rip had relapsed from two years of sobriety because of the news coming out of Hemet Lake.

Lefty exited his truck and shut the door. He looked around, scoping the neighborhood before walking to the house. At the door, he turned around to see who might be watching before letting himself inside. Quietly, he stepped through the front door and shut it behind him, then walked through the kitchen. He was greeted by the smell of booze and dirty dishes. Rip lived the bachelor life and, the older they got, the more problematic Lefty knew it would become if they kept up their ways.

The television was on in the living room and Lefty found Rip lying on the couch with his eyes closed, an open whiskey bottle on the coffee table in front of him. Rip snored lightly. Lefty picked up the TV remote and clicked the television off.

Rip stirred but didn't wake, so Lefty kicked him with his boot.

"C'mon. Get up," Lefty said.

Rip tossed, and turned, and groaned.

"Get up." Lefty continued kicking him until Rip rubbed his eyes and blinked away the fog.

Recognizing Lefty's face, Rip rocked forward and murmured, "I was watching that."

Lefty hovered over him on wide pillars for legs, thinking about what to do about Rip. Not only was his drinking going to be an issue, but he looked paranoid and stressed—the signs of a guilty man, Lefty thought.

"Who is here with you, Rip? Anybody in the house I should know about?"

"What? No." Rip squinted, and could barely keep his eyes open.

"You mean to tell me you're drinking alone?"

"What's it matter to you?"

Lefty inhaled a sharp breath and wagged his head from side to side, listening to his joints crack. He found it hard to believe Rip would do anything alone, but he also guessed Rip would overreact and think their secret was out of the bag now that the Aston Martin had been fished from the lake.

Without saying another word, Lefty searched the back rooms of the house and poked his head into the bathroom before swiping Rip's cellphone from the coffee table to see who he had spoken to about this.

Rip protested, saying, "Give that back."

"Who have you talked to about this?"

"What?"

Lefty smacked Rip across the face with an open hand. Getting in his face, Lefty asked, "Who have you spoken to besides me about Hemet Lake?"

"No one." Rip scowled, pressing his hand over the cheek Lefty just smacked. It was hot, red and looked like it hurt.

Lefty stared, knew Rip was lying, but didn't know what exactly Rip was keeping from him. "I told you to keep me informed, and here I am having to come to you after hearing rumors the coroner showed up at the lake last night. Why is that?"

"Heard rumors? From who?"

"Don't blow this for me. You understand? It's going to get heated quickly, and if I think there is even the smallest chance of you ruining this for me, I will kill you myself."

"Should we be worried?"

"You're acting like we haven't done this before," Lefty snapped. "As long as you keep your mouth shut, this *will* blow over."

Rip looked up at Lefty and said quietly, "There were survivors that night."

"And we turned it around. Remember?"

Rip reached for the whiskey bottle, acting like the town had already identified them as being guilty of such horrendous crimes. But Lefty swatted it out of his hand before it ever had a chance of reaching his lips. Rip watched as the bottle crashed to the floor, spilling across his carpet. First he was stunned, then he was angry.

"I need you to stay sober," Lefty said sternly. "I can't have you losing your top over this. Got it?" As he waited for Rip to acknowledge his statement, he noticed Rip's first mistake quietly resting on an end table in plain view for anyone to see.

"What is that?" Lefty said, pointing.

Rip was still staring at the whiskey bottle dripping the last of its contents on the floor when Lefty plucked Scarlett Moss's driver's license off the end table.

Holding it between his fingers, Lefty looked Rip in the eye and said, "I thought I told you to get rid of her."

"I did."

"Then why do you still have this?"

Rip shrugged. "I forget."

"Jesus Christ." Lefty had his work cut out for him. He slid Scarlett's license into his back pocket, hoped no one else had seen it lying around, and told Rip to take a cold shower, drink some coffee, and sober up.

"What are we going to do?" Rip said as Lefty was on his way out.

Lefty turned and said, "Go about your life and appear normal. *If that's even possible.* And if anybody asks, you say nothing. We'll get through this, but only if we play it smart."

CHAPTER SIXTEEN

I EXITED THE NEWSROOM BUILDING AFTER FAILING TO FIND Diaz and thank him for yesterday's glimpse into the future I was now embarking on. I was excited for my opportunity, but also questioned if the two-day deadline Hineman gave me would be enough time to produce anything of value.

A rental car was on its way and as I walked back to the hotel waiting for it to show, I squinted into what felt like the limelight shining upon me as I fantasized about receiving national acclaim. It was something every journalist secretly aspired to; that, and maybe writing a novel.

I believed I could do both, but had never given it much thought until today. But was it the fact of being in LA surrounded by fame, fortune, and glamor, or that I actually believed Hineman could deliver on his promise? Perhaps it was a little bit of both. Hineman sold it well, and certainly had me thinking.

A half-hour later, I changed clothes and checked out of the DoubleTree when I received a call from Denver. I answered, "I was just thinking about you."

"Hopefully to apologize for not saying goodbye."

My long time editor and friend, Ryan Dawson, at the *Colorado Times* always kept me in check. Though I knew he was only half-kidding, I appreciated his excuse to call to see how my trip was going. We never personally discussed it, but he suspected he was on borrowed time; potentially losing one of his best crime reporters to a bigger paper. At least that's what I wanted to believe he was thinking.

I said, "You should have called me yesterday."

"I didn't want to interrupt you in case you were busy."

I knew he wanted to know what I was offered, how the *Colorado Times* stacked up against the *LA Times*. I told him, "I haven't made a decision."

"It must be a good offer then if you're still thinking about it." Dawson let it go, knowing I was never going to discuss my thoughts with him until I'd made a final decision. Instead, he informed me about a homicide and nasty domestic dispute King was working. I knew King had lied about his work, and I also knew Dawson was purposely trying to make me feel homesick.

I asked Dawson, "Who do you have covering my beat?"

"I won't give you any names, but I will tell you they aren't nearly as good as you."

I smiled at the compliment. We made small talk and Dawson mentioned how it wasn't the Denver Broncos' year. Again, our football franchise was struggling to achieve greatness since the owner passed.

My rental arrived and I said I had to go. The driver took my bag and tossed it into the trunk, when Dawson asked when I was planning to be back at my desk.

I said, "I've decided to stay for a couple more days."

Dawson sounded heartbroken. "I knew I was going to lose my best reporter."

CHAPTER SEVENTEEN

I HAD A LOT ON MY MIND AND WAS LOOKING FORWARD TO the long drive ahead of me. As soon as I had my mirrors adjusted, I plugged the location into my GPS and set sail.

Dawson left me longing for home. I noted the way I felt even though I hadn't been gone that long. He made me question my intention for coming out here, even doubt what it was I was hoping to achieve by going after this story. I know he had done it on purpose, not out of spite, but because he was afraid to lose me.

With the city in my review mirror, I reached into my purse on the passenger seat and called Erin only to get no answer. I didn't leave a message. Erin had to be giving me the cold shoulder for having taken this interview. It was the only explanation I could come up, unless she'd stumbled on a huge story of her own.

Either way, I didn't like not hearing from her. If her lack of response was due to me interviewing for a new position, she had to have known anyone offered a job with a paper as big as the *LA Times* would be a fool not to at least explore it.

National acclaim.

Jeffrey Hineman's words were still echoing between my ears. It was the type of recognition our blog and podcast simply couldn't achieve on its own. At least not at the same level and with the same prestige attached. But I questioned *LA Times's* financials as well, hoping this little stunt into the mountains would gain me enough insight to make an informed decision.

My phone chimed on my lap. It was a notification alerting me to Erin's latest podcast—A Killer State of Mind—having just gone live. I connected the Bluetooth and turned up the volume, again finding myself listening to what I was missing back home.

CHAPTER EIGHTEEN

I ARRIVED IN THE LATE AFTERNOON TO A GRAY SKY reflecting off the lake. I parked near where the tow truck had pulled the Aston Martin from the water and looked around before stepping out. The campers, boats, and tents had since dispersed and it was a drastically different setting than what we had witnessed only yesterday.

As soon as I exited the vehicle, I took note of the still air. There were still signs of yesterday everywhere. Stomped down grass, tire tracks and footprints in the dirt, and ruts cut out of the hillside from the Aston Martin's rusted tire rims carving their way to the top of the embankment.

I wasn't surprised to see the lake guests gone. Rumors of murder were easy to believe at the sight of a coroner's van. Who would want to stay? Especially if a killer was still on the loose?

But for me, murder was the reason I came back. It was my beat. The life I chose. It didn't matter if it happened here or in Colorado; I had an appetite to investigate until the truth was told—'til the perpetrator was caught.

I moved to the edge of the flats and scurried down the

steep embankment until I came to a stop at the water's edge. The sky above looked heavy as I crouched down and took a fist full of dirt and sand into my hand. The sand poured between my fingers as I stared at the glass surface, thinking about the car that had come to rest here.

When did it come here? Who was inside? And why hadn't it been found until now?

The questions circled in my mind and mixed with Erin's show. Her new podcast resonated with me and had me thinking about our knack for thinking our way around killers. This case was different for many reasons, but the most obvious was it being a cold case. If Carson was right about who the victim, or victims, might be, was the person responsible still alive? Were there any clues left to follow? And perhaps the most chilling of all, did this person know that the car had been found?

Earth broke free above me and a stone tumbled down to where I stood. I jumped out of the way before getting hit, and felt the splash soak through my pants below the knee. I turned my head and stared at the man who had caused the earth to come crashing down on me. He had a hood pulled over his head and a dog at his side. He was staring through me when he said, "It was no accident."

Did he not see me? Or was he trying to hit me? Then I realized he wasn't talking about sending the rock down into the water but perhaps the car from yesterday.

"Are you talking about the vehicle that was found yesterday?" I asked.

He blinked and looked me directly in the eye when he said, "People in these parts go missing all the time."

His dark reptilian eyes held steady while he stared. I felt the hairs on my arm stand when he said, "These were two of the lucky ones. They were found."

Lucky? There were no survivors. "Two? Did you say two? How do you know that?"

Having caught the scent of something, his dog tugged on the leash and pulled the man off balance. He jerked the leash back and the dog yipped.

Was he right, and if so, how did he know? I called out again. "Did you say two?"

Suddenly, his dog broke free from his grip and took off running. The man spun and sprinted after the dog. Though I called out to him to stop, he didn't respond. I scurried to the top of the hill, climbing over loose gravel, hoping to catch him, only to find him already gone by the time I reached the top.

CHAPTER NINETEEN

I NEVER WAS ABLE TO FIND THE MAN AGAIN. IT SEEMED HE
had vanished as quickly as he came. Like a ghost sent to
reveal only enough to get me started on a story Carson had
said was just beginning.

I figured the stranger went off into the woods somewhere
looking for his dog and wasn't coming back. I searched for his
car, but mine was the only one in sight. There was a network
of trails around the lake, but I wasn't about to get on them. I
just hoped I was making the right decision, and not letting
my only witness get away from me.

I walked back to my car thinking how this man also
suggested what Carson suspected, but had never actually
confirmed. That there were *two victims* inside the submerged
vehicle. At this point in the investigation, it didn't matter if
there were one or one hundred victims. All that mattered was
learning who they were and why they died.

Before exiting the park, I stopped to talk with the camp
host who didn't offer me anything new. The sheriff never fully
closed the park and seemed to be satisfied with yesterday's
evidence collection, to keep camp sites open.

Once back on the road, I dialed Carson's number. When he didn't answer, I left a message. "Hi Carson. It's Samantha Bell." I reminded him who I was in case he forgot and told him I was back in town and that I'd like to talk more about yesterday, if he was still around. I assumed he was. Where did he come from, and what had him so interested in the case?

While I waited to hear back from Carson, Hineman sent me instructions to a cabin tucked in the hillside of the mountain town of Idyllwild. It was a twenty minute drive from the lake and, knowing I'd be here for the next two nights, I scoped out a place to eat when passing through the middle of town, before heading up the hill to settle in my new, temporary residence.

The three bed, two bath cabin was tucked away on a secluded mountainside surrounded by tall pines and small junipers. I parked near the front porch and, as soon as I stepped out, I breathed in the cool air, thankful for being out of the smog.

I found the key, per Hineman's instructions, and opened the place up. It was a small taste of vacation and the perfect place to disappear. An open floor plan with huge window views to the towering pines outside eventually led me to the bedroom in the back of the house. I dropped my bag on the floor and fell onto the bed liked a toppled tree, finding myself once again thinking about my son and friends, when I decided to phone King.

"I heard about your domestic dispute," I said after a quick greeting.

King was quiet, seeming to want to not talk about work, so I turned the conversation back to me and told him I was staying a couple days longer than intended.

"Your job offer was that good, huh?"

"It was pretty good," I said. "But really, it's just this story I stumbled on that might lead to something big." I gave King the details, told him the offer I made to freelance, while I considered jumping on fulltime. King seemed relieved to know I hadn't made a commitment, without first discussing it with him.

He said, "I'll be a consultant on the case, if you need one."

It made me laugh. I heard a beep in my ear and checked the display screen to see who was calling me. "I'll keep you informed, and I hate to cut our call short, but I have to go," I said, seeing Carson was calling me back.

"Stay out of trouble."

"I'll try my best," I said, knowing King wouldn't be there to save me, if I needed it.

CHAPTER TWENTY

I PARKED IN THE BACK OF THE BAR AND GRILL OFF Highway 243 and found Carson perched on a stool at the counter watching the Monday night football game. It was the Niners versus the Rams and it seemed, by the way he cheered, that Carson was rooting for the Niners. He hadn't seen me come in and I took the chance to study the man I knew little about.

The Niners's quarterback dropped back for a pass and scrambled out of the pocket avoiding the pass rush. He dodged a couple tackles and took off running, hurdling over a defender that had Carson jumping to his feet and high-fiving the pretty bartender serving him drinks.

There was a familiarity about Carson that reminded me of someone I knew when I was younger. I had noticed it yesterday too, but seeing him respond to the football game, was like watching my late husband cheer for the Broncos in the not-so-distant past.

I joined Carson at the counter, and he leaned back and asked, "Have you settled on an opportunity yet?"

"I guess that depends on what you have to share with me tonight."

A glimmer caught his eye, but he didn't act on the comment that came out sounding more suggestive than I intended.

Carson asked, "Are you a beer drinker, Samantha?"

"Only if it's dark and heavy."

My answer surprised him and he seemed delighted to order me a chocolate stout. He asked me, "You're not from LA, are you?"

The pretty bar keep brought me my pint and I said to Carson, "What gave me away?"

He watched me sip my beer, and then gently alerted me to my foam mustache. We both laughed. He said, "You don't come across as a cosmopolitan or martini type, but it wasn't your choice in microbrews that had me guessing you're not from around here."

"Then it must be my accent."

Carson gave me a look that said, *what accent?* "It was the rental I saw you driving."

I paused and asked myself when he might have seen me today. "You saw what car I was driving?"

He nodded and flicked his gaze quickly to the game. "I saw you arrive." He turned his head to me and winked. "P.I. Remember?"

Carson was smart, playful, and charming. Talking to him was like reuniting with old friends, and I could tell he wasn't just this way with me, but with everyone he spoke to. He made friends easily and I witnessed it myself with the female bartender who kept refilling his plate of tater tots for no additional cost.

"How did you find yourself working as a private detective?" I asked, making small talk, wanting to get to know who he was, why he was here.

"Long story," he said.

"I've got time."

Carson turned to the television and watched the Niners make a complete pass for another first down. He said, "First tell me what you were doing with that reporter from the *LA Times* yesterday."

"Like I said, I'm exploring opportunities."

He took his eyes off the game and gave me a sideways glance, like he didn't believe me. Or perhaps Carson didn't approve of who I chose to hang out with. Whatever it was, I told him, "They're recruiting me to lead their digital arm of the newspaper."

He turned his head, looked forward, and brought his glass to his lips like he was deciding whether or not he liked what he heard.

I asked, "Does that change things between us?"

Carson was slow to respond, choosing his words carefully. As I watched him think, I wondered if he expected to be part of my story to enhance his PI gig, or if his hesitation was something else entirely. He turned his head and stared.

"No," he said. "That means you know what you're doing and I'm going to need all the help I can get."

We locked eyes and it was like looking through a portal into the past. He had the same coffee bean eyes that Gavin had. The same determined look to solve a crime he held close to his heart. It was crazy of me to think, but it felt like the world had brought my husband back and that we somehow found each other once again, working a case. Beyond that, I suspected Carson had a former career in law enforcement, and a hunch that this story was something more than a submerged car hidden away in a mountain lake.

I kept touching my ring finger without meaning to, searching for the same wedding band I had only recently taken off. I murmured, "I was told it has to do with a missing persons case."

Carson looked me in the eye and said, "And whoever told you that would be right."

"My gut also tells me it's now a homicide case."

Carson cast his gaze to my hand and held his eyes on my empty ring finger, making me feel slightly embarrassed by the way I was reacting to someone I had just met.

"Am I right? Is it a homicide case?" I asked.

Carson lifted his gaze and said, "Do you often work off of hunches?"

"There's no other reason to explain you being here."

Carson's gaze dropped as if thinking of something else. He whispered, "You're right. I'm here because I think it was murder."

CHAPTER TWENTY-ONE

As soon as he saw her exit the bar and grill, Lefty flashed his lights to signal his position. The woman waved her free hand and jogged across the street, avoiding traffic.

Lefty watched intently, admiring the way the woman's cascading curls lifted off her shoulders as her breasts bounced beneath her tight shirt while she ran. She highlighted her features as well as any woman who lived off of tips would, and Lefty appreciated every inch of what he saw.

She had thick thighs and youth on her side and he adored everything about her, including her naiveté to give him anything he asked of her. When she drew close, he powered down his window and greeted her with a smile. "Hey, sweetheart. What do you have for me?"

She held up a to-go bag. Lefty reached out for it, took it into his hand, and rested it on his lap. He opened the bag and peeked inside. The front cab of his truck was quickly engulfed with the thick scent of a double cheeseburger and fries.

"Are you sure you don't want to come inside?" the woman asked him. "I've got the game on."

Lefty closed the bag and turned to, once again, admire her high-cheekbones and subtle application of makeup.

"Niners are on the goal line." She smiled.

"I'm a Rams fan," Lefty said with a crinkle of the eye.

The woman flicked her hair off her shoulder and said, "Your loss."

"Besides, there's a plumbing issue at one of the houses and, by the sounds of it, the job might take me well into the night." Lefty held her eyes as he spoke. "What do I owe you for dinner?"

"Make it thirteen even or, if you're feeling particularly generous, you can knock off a week's worth of rent and have it for free."

Lefty opened his wallet, retrieved a twenty and said, "Keep the change."

The woman folded the bill in half and tucked it into her back pocket.

"I still expect rent to be paid on time."

"You know I'm good for it."

Before she left, Lefty said, "Hey, can I ask you something?"

"As long as it's not personal."

"Were you working the restaurant earlier today?"

"You know I was."

Lefty chuckled, but only because he liked her. She was easy on the eyes and had a gorgeous full-lip smile that sent a tickle up his spine. Plus, he could easily manipulate her, like a pawn on the chess board.

The woman rested her elbow on his window sill, leaned into his truck and said, "It's true. I saw him there. He came to see Nora."

"Do you know what they talked about?"

"I don't. But I did hear he was drunk and she seemed upset with him being there."

"I heard about him drinking, too," Lefty murmured as he cast his gaze across the street toward the bar. "I've already spoken to him about it."

"I hope he doesn't relapse," she said. "He gets awfully mean when he drinks. What's this about, anyway?"

"Oh, just some shit you don't need to worry about."

"I better get going then."

"Thanks for the burger."

"Next time come inside. Stay for a while."

"I will," Lefty said.

"If there is anything I can do to help, with you know... well, you know where to find me."

"You've already done plenty," Lefty said, holding up the bag of food.

She blew him a kiss as Lefty powered up his window. He was worried about Rip, and certainly didn't like how he was drinking again. But he was furious to learn Rip had lied to him about who he had spoken to about Hemet Lake. Nora Barnes was another variable Lefty had to keep a close eye on. Just like that, Lefty had two wild cards at play.

He started his truck, took a quick bite of his burger, and watched his source go back to work in the bar. Shifting into gear, he pulled out onto the street and turned left. Passing in front of the bar, he looked through the front windows and couldn't believe who he spotted sitting at the counter.

"It couldn't be him, could it?"

Lefty took the next right and circled back around, thinking it might be possible. It had been so long since he'd last seen him, he wasn't sure he'd be able to pick him out of a lineup if he tried. But there weren't too many Black people in Idyllwild, and certainly not many that looked like cops.

This time, Lefty slowed to a stop out front and waited for the man to show his face. Then Carson Reynolds turned and Lefty knew that his being back in town wasn't good for business. He'd have to do something about it, before it did something about him.

CHAPTER TWENTY-TWO

CARSON'S LOOK CHANGED. I WATCHED HIS NICE SMILE FADE and it felt like the air in the room had been sucked out. I waited for him to say something and, when he didn't, I wondered if I had said something wrong.

"Let's get a table outside," he finally said, sliding off his stool.

I followed him to the patio and we took the first open table we came across. Carson sat with his drink in hand for a long while without talking, and I let him gather his thoughts before I said, "Yesterday you assumed there were multiple victims in the car. Do you still think that's true?"

Carson nodded, and I told him about the dog walker I came across at the lake who also said there were two. Carson was suddenly curious to know everything I knew about the dog walker. What he looked like, approximate age, hair color, shoe size, everything. I answered him as best I could, but I didn't know much.

Carson didn't seem upset with the little information I had, he only asked, "What is the *Times* saying about this?"

"Nothing that I know about," I said. "I asked to come here on my own."

"You requested to be here?"

I confirmed with a single nod. Carson's look said he knew more about the case than he was willing to share, but he didn't open up. I asked, "Do you know who the victims might be?"

Carson reached for his glass even though it was empty. He set it back on the table in front of him and brought his hands back to his thighs, as he told me a story about a missing persons case from 2002 that he happened to find himself involved with.

I listened closely to what he had to say and guessed he wasn't too much older than me, maybe by about ten or twelve years, which would put him around fifty.

Carson said, "I always suspected it ended here, but never could prove it."

"Where did it begin?" I asked.

"Here."

I turned my attention to the street and watched the cars slowly drive past. The pace was slow, typical of mountain towns, which relied heavily on an economy of people escaping their daily grinds.

I said, "So it's murder, and you're back because...why? You want closure?"

Carson said, "I've thought about this case for the last eighteen years, and if it weren't for Google Earth and a couple looking for a place to fish, I'd probably still be wondering what happened to that car."

When I asked what he knew, he told an elaborate story of an aging multimillionaire by the name of Barry Tate, "A man hated by virtually everyone in Idyllwild," who had a mansion on the mountain.

The last name got my attention. It was the same last name as my friend and colleague Erin Tate. But did Carson know that? Was it possible he knew who my business partner was and was messing with me? Or was I thinking too far into this story hoping to link me to a case I knew little about?

I took note and kept listening to what Carson had to say, reminding myself I knew nothing about Carson Reynolds, other than the fact it seemed we were both interested in cracking this case, when no one else cared.

"People wanted it to be Barry," Carson said, "because life without Barry was better, or so I was told back in '02."

"And you think one of the possible victims might be Barry?"

"Only Barry had a car like that."

"Let's say there are in fact two victims and one of them is him. Then who is the second victim?"

"I don't want to make any assumptions, but if anybody knows, it's a woman named Nora Barnes."

"Have you spoken to her?"

"She stopped talking to me a long time ago and certainly won't talk to me now." Carson shook his head. Then he locked eyes and said, "But maybe she'll talk to you?"

I held his gaze, trying to make sense of it all. Carson produced a business card from his pocket and pushed it across the table, giving it to me. It had Nora's full name, phone number, and place of work typed neatly across the middle with an address in Idyllwild. When I flipped it around, there was Nora's picture.

"She lives here?"

"As far as I know, she never left."

"Why would she talk to me if she won't talk to you?"

Carson pushed back from the table, stood, and raised his brows. "I don't know if she will. But before you go looking for her, I must warn you, Samantha: last time I started looking into this case, weird things started happening to me."

"Like what?"

"Find Nora." Carson pointed to the business card. "Ask her what she knows, and then get back to me. After that, I'll tell you everything you need to know."

CHAPTER TWENTY-THREE

ERIN PARKED HER RED BRONCO AT THE CURB IN FRONT OF Samantha's house in Denver, Colorado, and rang the doorbell. When Samantha's son Mason answered, he said, "Hi Erin. Can't party here tonight. Sorry. It's a school night and you know my mom would be upset if she found out."

"Funny, mister." Erin laughed. "Is your mom home yet?"

Mason scrunched his face and said, "She didn't tell you?"

Erin looked him in the eye and asked, "Tell me what?"

"She extended her trip, decided to stay."

Samantha's dog Cooper nudged his way past Mason and jumped on Erin, with his tail wagging. "I guess I hadn't heard that," Erin said. "Is Heather still here?"

"In the kitchen," Heather called to the front of the house.

Mason pulled Cooper down to all fours and called him to the couch, where Mason was watching the football game. Erin followed Mason inside and dropped her handbag on the table as she entered the kitchen.

Heather was doing dishes, cleaning up dinner, when she asked, "Did you eat? There are plenty of leftovers."

"That's all right. I'm not hungry, but thanks anyway."

Erin pulled out a chair and sat at the table. Heather held up a bottle of red wine, and Erin nodded. Heather walked to the table and poured them both a glass before sitting across from Erin at the table.

Heather said, "She asked again about you today. She said you're not responding to her calls. Want to tell me what that's about?"

"It's nothing," Erin said, staring into her glass.

Heather raised an eyebrow. She didn't believe Erin. "Really?" When Erin didn't respond, Heather said, "You're afraid of losing her."

"I'll be fine once I know she's back in Denver."

"You'll have to wait. Samantha said she's staying a couple more days."

Erin said, "I heard, but I don't know why."

"She caught wind of a story she's pitching to the *Times*."

"They have her working already?"

"You really should call her." Heather sipped from her glass.

"What's the story about?"

Heather shrugged. "You know my sister. She never reveals her hand until she knows how it will play out, but it sounds like a cold case of some sort."

"What's King have to say about all this?"

"Not sure. Haven't seen him since she left."

Erin thought King's absence strange, considering the role he played in Mason's life. Erin stayed and visited for a while. After she finished her glass of wine, when she finally got up to leave, she said her goodbyes and promised to call Samantha as soon as she got home.

"Don't make this personal," Heather said to Erin on her way out the door. "If there is anything I can guarantee about Sam, it's that she always puts other people first."

CHAPTER TWENTY-FOUR

AFTER CARSON LEFT THE BAR, I STAYED AT THE TABLE AND just sat watching the world go by as I thought about what it was he was asking me to do. I was happy to take the lead but I was also a little suspicious as to why it had to be me and not him to go after Nora Barnes.

I headed inside and closed out my tab with the bartender, surprised to have found Carson had paid for a meal to-go and the beer I had already had. The bartender must have seen my look of surprise because she said, "That one is a keeper. I wouldn't let him get away if I were you."

"It was only a business meeting," I assured her.

"Your loss," she said, taking her energy to a customer down the line.

I took the to-go bag into my hand, grateful for Carson's gift, but why hadn't he said anything about buying me dinner? Did he consider it a favor for asking me to talk with Nora, assuming I would go along with his plan? I suspected he did.

I headed to my car with thoughts circling back to what Nora might know and the reasons Nora wouldn't want to speak with Carson. I assumed it had to do with his initial involvement in the case eighteen years ago, but what had happened between them to get her to stop talking? It had to be something big for her to not forgive and forget.

Nora was all I could think about my entire drive up to the cabin. I couldn't stop seeing her face and kept making mental notes of what Carson said and how I wanted to go about this investigation. I didn't have much time to get this right. Two days was all Hineman gave me. After that, if I still had nothing, I was on my own.

I was the only one on the road and I kept looking out for animals threatening to run out in front of my car. As soon as I rounded the next bend my cellphone rang from inside my purse. Keeping one hand on the steering wheel, I retrieved my phone with my free hand and noticed it was Erin who was finally calling me back.

"Hey," I answered, thinking about what Carson said about Barry Tate.

"I was just at your house and heard you're staying longer than intended."

"Just a few more days."

"There must be good reason for it."

I focused on my driving, afraid to speculate on what Carson revealed to me tonight until knowing the full spectrum of this strange coincidence I had stumbled upon. I knew little about Erin's parents, her family, and her life before we crossed paths and began working together. I wasn't able to hide my hesitation well. I said, "So, now you care enough to call me back?"

"I've been meaning to, but didn't want to get in your way."

"The interview went well but I haven't accepted their offer yet," I said, filling her in on the important details of Hineman's sales pitch. Erin didn't respond right away and the silence was killing me.

Finally, she said, "That's great, Sam, but what about Real Crime News?"

Her frustration with me was seeping through the line and I understood what she was feeling. I would be worried about the decision I was having to make too, if in her shoes. We spent the last couple years building Real Crime News into a reputable source of information, and a single decision was about to derail everything we had built. And for what? National acclaim?

Erin asked, "Is this story something we can both benefit from?"

I knew the answer was a resounding yes, but I couldn't tell her that without first knowing more about Barry Tate. Erin knew I was struggling to find a way to not have to answer her question and she was suspicious because of it.

"I enjoyed your show today," I said, feeling our connection loosen. "Are you there?"

When Erin didn't respond I turned my phone screen-side up and saw that I had lost our connection. I hated how I couldn't be completely open with her about the story I was working. It was so unlike me to have to keep secrets from her. If only she had answered when I called yesterday, she would have known everything.

I brought both hands to the steering wheel and couldn't stop thinking about the coincidence of Erin sharing the last name with Carson's suspected victim. It was total speculation at this point that Erin might be related to Barry, but the chance of it being a relative of Erin was enough to not mention it until I knew for sure.

"A shared last name. Perhaps that's all it is," I said when headlights appeared in front of me.

I squinted into the lights, trying to stay on the road, after realizing they were drifting into my lane. I flicked my lights at the oncoming car, hoping to get them to slow down, but they only seemed to be coming at me faster.

At the last second, I realized they weren't going to leave my lane. I jerked on the wheel and fishtailed on the loose gravel before spinning the wheel back the other way and slamming on the brakes, just before I crashed into the ditch.

CHAPTER TWENTY-FIVE

As soon as the car stopped, I closed my eyes and put my hand over my racing heart. I wasn't hurt; my seatbelt had done its job and tightened upon impact. I freed myself from the restraints and exited the car to have a look at the damage.

Besides the hillside my headlights were pointing at, everything around me was pitch black. It was just me in the quiet woods, staring down the empty road for the truck that flew past me. It never stopped, never even slowed. The driver must have seen what they had done.

Were they just not looking? Or had they done it on purpose?

Thankful to walk away without a scratch, I flicked on the flashlight app on my cellphone and moved to the front of my rental to check for any damage. One tire was in the ditch and, though the front right corner was kissing the dirt, there didn't appear to be any visible structural damage. I'd hit my brakes just in time to avoid having to get towed.

I got back into the car and reversed onto the road without any trouble. I drove the rest of the way without seeing another vehicle and was thankful to get back to the cabin safely. I didn't appreciate that I had forgotten to leave a light on.

"I always leave a light on," I whispered to myself, knowing I hated arriving home to a dark house. I thought I had, but maybe I forgot.

I stepped out into the dark and instantly flicked on my flashlight app once again. On my way to the house I noticed tire tracks, whose treads were too big to be mine, punched into the dirt.

I glanced towards the cabin before crouching down to trace the tracks with my finger. They were from a large truck or SUV, a clear sign someone might have come to visit me while I was gone. But I couldn't say for sure. Who would want to visit me? Who else besides Hineman knew I was here?

When a distant coyote howled, I glanced over my shoulder and looked behind me. Thick tree trunks stood like ancient pillars casting long, dark shadows across the moonlit ground. The stars above me twinkled in the clear air and it was noticeably colder here than it was in town.

I tried not to think too much into my vulnerability or how ill prepared I was for this trip. But it was Carson's warning that weird things started happening to him once he worked his way into this investigation that rang loudest in my ears and wouldn't stop. Though I knew when I arrived this morning, that the cabin was isolated, it would be my head that would get to me before anybody else did.

I climbed the porch stairs and fumbled my keys when unlocking the door. I never did see Carson leave the bar and didn't know what kind of car he drove. Though I doubted it was him who had been here, I didn't count it out either, even if I couldn't explain it.

The dead bolt clicked over and I pushed the door open. It squeaked on its hinges as I stepped inside and I immediately hit the lights. I looked around the house and listened for any strange noises. There were no visible signs anybody but me had been here. It was quiet, if not quieter inside than it was outside. Satisfied that I was safe—and alone—I turned on the lamp on the end table near the couch and found myself staring at my own reflection in the window.

The woman who stared back at me looked visibly shaken —dead tired. But it was clear she was also asking herself what she was doing here by herself instead of back home, surrounded by the ones she loved.

I looked away before self-doubt and personal demons crept too deep into my thoughts. Instead, I booted up my laptop computer thinking about Carson. He seemed to know what he was talking about when it came to who owned the Aston Martin and who might be inside. But who exactly was this charming man I had drinks with tonight? Why did he seem so interested in working the same missing persons case he couldn't solve eighteen years ago?

CHAPTER TWENTY-SIX

CARSON HAD AN IMPRESSIVE ONLINE RÉSUMÉ AND I quickly got sucked into learning everything I could about him. He had a way about him that was both genuine and rare. Perhaps it was his cool confidence I had noticed the first time I met him, or how he made friends easily. Whatever his attraction was, I felt it again when stalking him on social media.

None of his accounts were set to private and I was both intrigued and surprised by his decision to make everything public. Why did he allow anyone to peek into his life like this? Did he not have anything to hide? Even if he didn't, wouldn't he want to be cautious, considering the line of work he was in?

I clicked around, read his posts and looked at his pictures, noting how his life seemed absent of any kind of woman. That went for family, too. Carson was alone. He came across as a career man too busy for any outside relationships that might get in his way.

I took my eyes off the screen for a moment to think back to the first encounter I had with him. It was an immediate attraction, but there was also no denying I wasn't the only one who found him charming. The bartender tonight did as well, and I was sure there were others I didn't know about who wished to fill that void in Carson's life.

How was it possible this man was single? Things just didn't add up.

According to his profile, Carson was originally from the Oakland bay area and had spent some time working as a beat cop before taking his skills private. But no matter how deep I dug into him, I couldn't find any hint to why he seemed personally invested in the case.

What was he hiding? There must be something. Nobody was this perfect.

As the hours passed, I eventually gave up on finding Carson's secret and soon turned my focus to Barry Tate, hoping to find a link to Carson.

Barry was everywhere on the internet. I scanned past articles about lawsuits he settled, read news about the charity events he attended, and even found a story explaining his connection to the California political class. It was all very interesting, but there was little said about his life in Idyllwild and nothing about how the town had an extreme distaste for the man. Or if he had children. I wondered why that was and where Carson was getting his information from.

Then I found an article about how, at one time, Barry ran for the position of Riverside Sheriff. No one took him seriously and the media and the people of Idyllwild were quick to call out his flaws, which, according to them, were many. But was this what Carson was referring to? I assumed it was, but it didn't explain what happened the night he disappeared.

Next, I found an article printed only two months before his disappearance that said Barry was frequently enamored with whiskey and guns, and had lost his mind on the hillside of Idyllwild. But then, on the next image I clicked, Barry had his arm slung around a little blonde haired girl who shared a resemblance to a much younger Erin Tate.

I zoomed in on the image and I had a hunch that I had found Erin's father. But if that was the case, why didn't Carson mention knowing Erin? He must have done his research on me. Did Carson not know Erin and I had a podcast together? I assumed he didn't, otherwise he would have said something, right?

I sat forward and put my laptop on the coffee table thinking about what I had found. Was it possible Erin had hidden this from me? And if she did, why? Then I turned to face the window and, once again, stared into my reflection, deciding what to do next.

CHAPTER TWENTY-SEVEN

IT WAS TEN MINUTES BEFORE EIGHT THE FOLLOWING morning when I dialed Nora Barnes's number for the first time. I was hoping to catch her before she began her work day. I didn't know what to expect from her, other than I hoped she'd cooperate by telling me what she knew about Barry Tate and what might have happened that night he died.

The line rang and rang and finally clicked over to voicemail.

"Nora, my name is Samantha Bell and I'm a reporter with the *Times*." I didn't specify which *Times* but it was safe to assume she would guess it was the *LA Times*. I thought it best to keep it that way. "I'm calling to ask your thoughts on the car being dragged out of Hemet Lake this weekend. If you could please give me a call when you get this."

The kettle whistled and blew hot steam into the air. I turned off the stove and made my coffee in a French press. When it was ready, I took it outside. I breathed in the cold morning air and prepared myself for the day ahead.

There were a few scattered clouds drifting overhead as my thoughts turned to Erin. It had to be her in the photo I found online last night. Though I wanted to ask, I found every excuse to not bring it up until I knew for sure.

I still had no solid evidence Barry was her father and, as far as I was concerned, the sheriff was keeping the media—and town—in the dark. But if it was Barry, and Barry was in fact Erin's father, who was he with? Carson had never answered that question, but I assumed he must have an idea.

I moved to the edge of the porch and cradled my mug with both hands. I couldn't ignore how both Carson and the dog walker suspected there were two victims inside the car. I hated myself for letting the dog walker get away before I could ask follow-up questions.

When my eyes landed on the tire tracks in the dirt, I paused. The daylight gave new clarity to what I had seen last night. There was no doubt they were fresh and not mine. But whose were they, and could it be possible this was the beginning of the weird things Carson had warned me about? Or was getting run off the road last night only a fluke?

I stepped off the porch and found myself crouched down in front of my rental. I brushed my fingers across the scratched paint, thankful my accident hadn't been worse, wondering if I should report the damage today or wait. And, as I followed the lines of scratches with the tip of my finger, I thought about who Hineman might have told about me staying here.

I stood and stared at the house, listening to the pines rustle in the breeze. Diaz was the first person who came to mind, but I didn't see him caring about anything—especially me. The only other person was Carson, and I could easily cross him off the list, as I was certain he didn't have any affiliation with the paper.

After I finished my first cup of coffee, I poured myself another and sat at the kitchen table checking emails before searching what I could find on Nora Barnes.

Carson made me believe she held the key to the puzzle. If she did, I wasn't going to find it online. Unlike Carson, Nora had her security settings snapped up tight. I couldn't see anything other than her profile picture that was now over a year old. It was a smart move on her part, but did little to help me.

Then I thought about Barry Tate running for sheriff back in the day, and had another idea that might allow me direct access into the investigation without having to go through Nora.

CHAPTER TWENTY-EIGHT

I PARKED OUTSIDE THE CONCRETE BUNKER IN VALLE VISTA, about thirty minutes west of Idyllwild, and entered the Riverside County Sheriff's Department, hoping to trade information for access to the Hemet Lake investigation.

An older lady with silvery, long hair worked the front desk and greeted me with friendly, blue eyes. Assuming this was the office that had responded to the call, I said, "I'd like to speak with someone inside the Major Crimes Bureau."

"May I ask what this is about?"

"The car that was recovered from Hemet Lake."

I was told to take a seat and, when I turned my back, I heard her make a call, but couldn't hear what she was saying. Too anxious to sit, I paced the slate tiles, reading fliers posted to the wall and pamphlets tucked into bins. I heard the front desk woman get up and I peeked around the wall to see her disappear behind the wooden door in the back.

I tucked the domestic abuse counseling flier back where I had found it and took note of the heavily fortified building. Big heavy locks on doors and bulletproof glass in full view of security cameras mounted to the ceiling, next to an air filtration system that blew much too cold air into the room. The woman came back to her desk and only smiled as she took her seat. Finally, I did the same.

The time passed slowly. I stood. I sat. And we kept exchanging friendly glances as I kept a close eye on the time. An hour passed before I wondered if I was wasting my time by being here.

"Is there anybody who can help me?" I asked again.

The front desk said, "I will remind them you're here."

"Please remind them I have valuable information pertaining to the case. It's important."

I didn't mention I was a reporter because I didn't want to get redirected to the Media Information division, assuming they would only stonewall me when I asked for information. Instead, I took my chances with working my way up the ladder and continued to wait.

It hadn't been since my rookie reporting days, that I'd been involved in a small town investigation, and I welcomed the change of scenery and pace this community offered. On the surface it was simpler, didn't have so many layers, but underneath the top soil, there was the same criminal grime and oily underbelly of any modern town. That was what I was after—the dirt.

I felt my phone buzz with a call before it rang. When I checked to see who was calling, I recognized the number and stood. It was Nora.

"Thanks for calling me back," I said in a tone just above a whisper.

"I don't know how you got my number but I have nothing to say to you."

I made eye contact with the front desk woman and indicated I'd be right back. She nodded her head and I turned to the exit, encouraging Nora to meet with me in person.

"I have nothing to say to you or anybody else about what they found in Hemet Lake."

"Did you know it was Barry Tate's car they found?" The line was silent, but I knew Nora hadn't hung up. "You knew him, didn't you?"

"Did they say that?"

I didn't know who she was referring to, but knew I couldn't afford to lose her. I said, "I know you know what happened." Nora went quiet again and I continued, "Tell me, Nora. I just want to know. Who was Barry with the night he went missing?"

"Who said he was with anybody?"

"Was he?"

Another pause hung on the line. "I told you, I don't know what you're talking about."

I knew she was lying by the way she said it. But who was she trying to protect? Herself?

"Where are you?" I asked. Nora wouldn't say. "Let's talk in private. We can go somewhere of your choice. No one has to know about it."

"You don't know this town. Everyone knows everything about everyone."

"This isn't going to go away, Nora, and the sooner you get it off your chest, the sooner you can go back to living your life."

"What do you think I've been trying to do for the last eighteen years?" Nora scoffed. "Now don't call me again."

The line went dead.

CHAPTER TWENTY-NINE

I STARED AT MY PHONE'S SCREEN, REPLAYING MY conversation with Nora in my head. Now I was beginning to understand why Carson might have given me the task of speaking to Nora. She was going to be a tough nut to crack, as she made it abundantly clear she didn't want to be involved.

I thought about the old saying in journalism, *seduce and betray*, as I headed back inside the sheriff's department. Nora might be determined to stay quiet, but I had the determination to persist until I got what I was after.

Did Carson know that about me, too? I assumed that by the end of the first conversation with me, everyone knew I wasn't one to give up easily. I liked to think Nora knew it now, too, because she knew something about the case—a secret she had kept for the last eighteen years, as she tried to get her life back.

I was about to take a seat when the door to the sheriff's office opened. I watched a Forest Service Law Enforcement Officer step out and nod to the front desk before turning to me.

We locked eyes and I recognized his face from the day at the lake. He was late forties and had a black handlebar mustache that was beginning to gray. He nodded cordially, and I managed to catch the name engraved on his nameplate —Tom Rhodes—which I filed away with a note to check into later.

Rhodes left the building and I wondered why he was here, what he and the sheriff might have been discussing behind closed doors. It had to be something about the case.

After making eye contact with the front desk, I pointed to the sheriff's open door and asked if I could now go in. She picked up her phone and I heard the sheriff's line ring. He picked up a second later and I listened to them discuss my need to speak with him. Then I heard the sheriff say, "Send her in."

The front desk said to me through the glass, "The sheriff can speak with you now."

My toes were already pointing in that direction and I knocked on the sheriff's door as I entered. He didn't bother getting up to greet me; instead, he told me to sit and tell him why I was here.

I settled in and noted the heavy dark bags beneath his eyes. I didn't notice them the other day and assumed this case was giving him hell. I caught his name plate, Sheriff Matt Graves, and said, "Sheriff my name is Samantha—"

Sheriff Graves held up his hand and stood, telling me to hang onto that thought. He scooted past me and I turned in my seat and watched him exit the small box of an office he called home. His heavy steps echoed down the hall before disappearing completely. I didn't know where he went, or what to think of my visit here today, but I turned to his desk and began looking for hints at what he might be up to.

Keeping one ear on the door behind me, I sifted through papers, peeked under folders, and glanced at his computer. It was like raking leaves as I searched his desk, but then I landed on gold when I found the coroner's report for the Hemet Lake case.

I slipped my phone into the palm of my hand and began snapping photos as I flipped through the pages. I knew I didn't have much time but I didn't want to let a single second go to waste. When I was convinced I had enough information, I tucked my phone away and read the report with my own eyes.

"Unbelievable. Carson was right," I whispered when reading how it was confirmed two sets of bones were found inside the car. Though the names of the victims weren't yet known, they were working on identifying them.

I heard the sound of the sheriff's heavy boots start up again and I quickly closed the report, sat back down, and tried to hide the fact that I now knew what Carson had only assumed yesterday.

CHAPTER THIRTY

THE SHERIFF STOPPED AT THE DOOR.

I kept my back turned and stared at his desk, hoping I'd put things back in place. When I was certain I had, I turned around to face him. His dark eyes were locked on the coroner's report and I quickly distracted him with a question.

"Is everything okay?" I asked.

He blinked and shifted his gaze to me. "Where were we?"

"I was about to tell you my name, Samantha Bell, and tell you about some information I have about the Hemet Lake case."

He edged around me and took a seat. I wondered if he would even be interested in hearing what I had to say now that he had the coroner's report. Shuffling papers into neat piles, he said, "I saw you at the lake."

"Yes. I was there." There was no reason for me to hide it, and I appreciated his ability to observe and remember faces from the crime scenes he worked.

Sheriff Graves raised his gaze and said, "Then perhaps it would be best for you to speak with the public information officer."

I knew where this was going, but what I didn't know was how he knew I was a reporter. Perhaps he knew Edgar Diaz and had seen me with him. I quickly responded, "I'd like to speak with you."

"That may be, but I'm not interested in speaking with the media." He looked me directly in the eye and I watched his gaze sharpen. "You're a reporter, right?"

"Yes." I stared back without blinking, tracing his lines of stress with my eyes. They were like a treasure map of past clues, and it was clear he was worried about the optics of this investigation. If I were him, I would be worried too. From where I sat, it looked like he had a failed investigation on his hands without any solid leads to go on. So I offered my help by stating, "But that isn't why I'm here."

Still holding the coroner's report, he leaned back in his chair, opened a drawer on the wall behind him and filed it away. I was certain he didn't know I had taken photos of the report but his actions certainly suggested he didn't want to take any chances, either.

I said, "You're not the least bit curious what information I have to share?"

"I've been around long enough to know once reporters get hold of a story they do more harm than good."

I was mildly surprised by him not wanting to at least hear me out. His remark made it perfectly clear how in over his head he was with this case, and I only felt bad for him.

I offered, "Even if what I have to say can help you solve this case?" A skeptical look crossed his face, but this time he didn't shoot me down. I said, "What if I told you I could personally connect you with someone who knows the car's owner?"

"I'd ask you how."

I told him about Real Crime News and said, "I manage the blog with my partner, Erin Tate."

His eyes widened a fraction and, when his entire demeanor changed, I was hopeful my plan might actually work. The sheriff angled his head toward the report he just filed away and seemed to be thinking about his options.

"You'd like to speak with her, wouldn't you?" I said.

"Why would you think that?"

It seemed he wanted to dance around the situation a bit before jumping into the deep end with me, so I played along, appreciating that he hadn't yet denied knowing who Erin was. Guessing I was on the right path, I kept going.

"Because it was her father you discovered in the car, wasn't it?"

Sheriff Graves tipped forward and brought his elbows to his desk, continuing to stare me down as if wondering how I knew what he had only just found out.

"Have you spoken to her about it?" I asked.

"I'll make a deal with you," he said, looking me straight in the eye. "You put me in contact with Ms. Tate, and I'll let you in on what we know. But until then, you can keep an open line of communication with our Media Bureau. I'm sure they'd be happy to answer your questions."

CHAPTER THIRTY-ONE

I LEFT THE SHERIFF'S DEPARTMENT FEELING LIKE I SCORED A victory. The sheriff's deal gave me the confidence to go forward—certain I had found the missing link connecting Erin to Barry Tate. I even enjoyed his sarcasm about keeping an open line of communication with the Media Bureau who would never answer my questions.

Now I just needed to get Erin on board and let her know that her father had been found. I wasn't sure how she'd react to the news but I had a lot of questions for her myself. Like, how did she receive his inheritance if Barry was only now being found? Erin had funded the startup costs of our blog and podcast with that money and, even to this day, I didn't know the specifics. Now I was thinking I should.

The sun was beating down on me as I approached my car. I was thinking about my next step, and how I could go about speaking with Nora Barnes when Carson called my phone.

"Did you know Erin Tate was my partner?" I asked.

"Not until this morning."

It appeared we'd both done our research after last night's

dinner. I liked that we thought alike. Perhaps Carson was just as great as he thought I was when it came to investigating.

"It's why I'm calling," he said.

I paused, lifted my head, and looked around. Was he here? His tone had me feeling like there was a chance he was. But maybe I was jumping ahead of myself. I said, "Because it's her father who was killed?"

Carson never answered my question. Instead, he said, "You shouldn't be here, Samantha. If people learn your connection to Erin, no one will speak to you."

I unlocked my car as I approached and thought how Carson was wrong. The sheriff was willing to talk, even with my connection to Erin.

"You mean, I'll lose my leverage, the same influence you were hoping to exploit yourself," I said.

Carson went quiet. I opened my car door and got behind wheel.

Carson asked, "Who have you told?"

"Told?"

"Does anyone in California know you're association with Erin?"

Carson was losing his patience with me and that had me worried. There was something he wasn't telling me. There were a handful of people who now knew. A couple people at the *LA Times* and now the sheriff, too. None of whom I was worried about.

Carson said preemptively, "It doesn't matter. People will learn it soon enough."

"The sheriff. I told the sheriff," I said, quickly explaining why.

Carson cursed and it was clear he was upset but I didn't fully understand why. "Don't do it, Samantha. Keep Erin in Colorado."

"Why? What does it matter?" I asked.

"Erin was a suspect in her father's disappearance and, if one of the victims was Barry, like I suspect, the sheriff will want to sweep this old story under the rug as quickly as possible, using Erin as his scapegoat." Carson paused to catch his breath. "Did you hear what I said, Samantha? No matter what you do, don't bring Erin to California."

CHAPTER THIRTY-TWO

ERIN WOKE EARLY AND SPENT HER MORNING IN HER HOME office searching digital archives, hoping to track down the story Samantha was working for the *LA Times*. She suspected something was up, but no matter which archive she dug through, she kept coming up with nothing.

"What are you up to, Sam?"

Growing increasingly anxious, she glanced at her phone and thought about calling Samantha back. She didn't like how they were disconnected on their last call, but she also suspected Samantha wouldn't tell her any more than what she already had. So, Erin had another idea.

After a short drive across town, Erin found herself weaving her way to the homicide unit of the Denver Police Department to track down Samantha's boyfriend, Alex King.

"Knock knock," Erin said when finding him.

King was busy working a domestic dispute turned homicide at his desk with his partner, Detective John Alvarez, pushing papers and following up on leads. He closed out his computer and turned to face Erin.

"I already talked with Samantha," he said, making the assumption as to why Erin was here.

Erin said, "She's going to take the job."

King gave her a look. "Did she tell you that?"

"No," Erin said, as King visibly relaxed. "It's just the way she's talking."

"Look, I spoke to her about it yesterday. She landed on a story and, when it's done, she'll come home."

"That's just it. She's not telling me what this story is about."

"There must be a reason for it," King said.

"But you know about it?"

"I do."

"Alex, please tell me," Erin pleaded. "It's the reason I'm here. I need to know."

"Why is it so important to you?"

Erin stared. She wasn't able to come up with a good reason for him to share Samantha's secret.

"Sam will be home before you know it. I'm sure she'll be happy to tell us all about it then."

Erin said, "What if she doesn't come home? What if this story is bigger than what she's leading you to believe it is?"

King looked Erin in the eye and said, "It's a cold case. There was a car found submerged in some lake near a small town two hours east of Los Angeles. She offered to investigate and report on it for the *Times,* while she thought over their offer, and they agreed. That's all I know, now if you'll please excuse me, I have a murder to solve myself."

Erin asked, "What small town? Did she say?"

"I don't know. If she told me, I don't remember. Please, just call her and ask her yourself."

Erin didn't budge. She knew Samantha was keeping her in the dark on purpose. And now she had an idea why.

"Last question before I leave." King raised his eyebrows. "Did Sam ever mention my name when briefing you about this story?"

"No," King said. "Your name never came up."

CHAPTER THIRTY-THREE

I SAT IN MY CAR FOR A COUPLE OF MINUTES AFTER CARSON'S phone call, thinking about what he had said and the tone in which he said it. There was more to this story than he was telling me, but whatever he knew, or wanted me to think he knew, I refused to believe Erin had anything to do with her father's disappearance and death.

I started the car and glanced at the time. It was four minutes after eleven when I turned back to the sheriff's department and caught Sheriff Graves staring at me from the front window. Through the glare, I could see a skeptical eyebrow raised as if questioning whether or not I was sincere in my offer.

"What is this town hiding?" I asked myself as I plugged in the address to Nora's workplace in Idyllwild, and pointed my wheels east.

As I drove back into the familiar canyon, I thought how this was Carson's second warning that something wasn't right, and that I should be careful who to trust when speaking about this case. But his intention was still unclear, and that had me naturally skeptical of him, too.

Why did he care? What was at stake for him? Why didn't it seem like he wanted to get his hands dirty? Was his charm and perfect profile only a front to the man he really was?

The questions never stopped. They kept rattling around inside my head the entire thirty minute ride. By the time I arrived at the tiny breakfast and brunch restaurant on the south end of town, I was ready to shift my focus to Nora. But first, I needed to read more into the coroner's report I had found on the sheriff's desk, with hopes of finding something that would get Nora's attention and get her to open up.

I opened my phone's gallery and navigated to the photographs, pinching my fingers on the screen to zoom in on the text. The pixels came to focus and I once again read about the two sets of bones found in the Aston Martin. One set was in the driver's seat, the other in the trunk, and only one of them had fractures of the hyoid and thyroid, indicating a possible homicide had taken place.

I looked up and stared at the smoke stack spewing thick clouds of steam into the air from the kitchen. From past murders I had worked, I remembered Denver's Chief Medical Examiner, Leslie Griffin, once tell me the fracture of the hyoid was most common in manual strangulations and how about thirty-four percent of those same victims also had a fractured thyroid. With that information, there was no doubt in my mind, that the person in the trunk of the Aston Martin had been murdered.

A silver Toyota Rav4 parked next to me and I watched the middle-aged couple get out of their car and walk into the restaurant. The small town charm had vanished and, as I sat there thinking about the case, I read into every glance in my direction—looks that suggested they knew who I was and what I was after. Whether it was Carson's intention or not, I was feeling mildly paranoid about my being here.

But was this secret buried in the Aston Martin, Erin's, or

someone else's? I didn't know. The only thing made certain was that secrets never died, especially not in small towns, where everyone knew everyone else's business. And, for better or worse, I was the unwelcomed outsider hoping to bring the past to light.

This was no longer a missing person's case, but a homicide someone would want to keep quiet. Who was that someone? Were they still alive? Still running around Riverside County after all these years, thinking they got away with murder? Or was this a murder-suicide like the evidence might suggest? There was still a second victim and nothing in the report indicated they, too, had been murdered.

My pulse was knocking in my wrists, and suddenly I wanted this story even more than when I first woke up. But my biggest fear was that Barry might have killed someone and put them in his trunk, possibly with Erin's knowing. As much as I didn't like thinking it, it would explain her reason for refusing to ever discuss him with me.

The front door to the restaurant swung open and a middle-aged woman stepped out. When she looked up, I knew immediately it was Nora Barnes.

CHAPTER THIRTY-FOUR

As soon as I saw Nora, I kicked my car door open and hurried to catch up to her. She rounded the corner and seemed to be in a hurry. I wondered where she was going, if she had been tipped off to my being here. I quickened my pace and watched her start to climb into a silver compact car parked beneath a large ponderosa pine.

Before she could get away, I called out, "Nora Barnes?"

She stopped, mid-swing, and gave me a curious look like she was trying to place who I was. I waved and gave her my best smile, hoping she hadn't recognized my voice from our phone call earlier.

"Is everything all right?" she asked.

She seemed to think I was a customer chasing after her to correct a bill or personally leave a tip. I shattered that expectation when I said, "I'm Samantha Bell. I called your phone earlier."

Her lips pinched as she flicked her gaze to the closed back door of the restaurant just behind my right shoulder. We were alone and I assumed she wanted to keep it that way.

Lighting up a cigarette, she said, "Like I told you before, I have nothing to say to you."

"To me, or to anyone who asks you about what happened at Hemet Lake?"

"Look," she said in a sharp tone, "I don't know anything about Hemet Lake."

"But you have heard what was found there over the weekend?"

Nora was in her late thirties, probably about my age, and seemed nervous to be seen speaking with me. She kept flitting her gaze from side to side, keeping watch of what was going on behind me. I watched her inhale a deep drag before blowing out a thick pillow of smoke in my direction.

"I heard they found a car in the lake," she said, without looking me in the eye. "Everyone is talking about it."

"Anyone saying anything else?"

She met my eye. "You tell me. You're the reporter."

"You're right. I am. And that's why I'm here asking you."

"I'm not interested in being part of your story."

"I heard you might know the victims who were found inside the car."

"I don't even know what kind of car was found."

"An Aston Martin."

Nora locked eyes and I could have sworn she stopped breathing. I said, "Early reports indicate there were two victims found inside. One of them was found in the trunk. Any idea who might have put them there?"

She took a deep drag and I watched the cherry light up and burn off the ash, as she shook her head no.

"You don't seem too surprised by the news."

"Because I'm not."

"Because you were there the night it happened?"

Nora's face turned angry. "Because I suspected it. Everyone in this town thought this nightmare was over."

"But you didn't?"

Nora shook her head. "All you had to do was pay atten-tion. Barry's body was never found and he was the cause of everyone's anguish. He was the only one who owned a car like that, and it wouldn't surprise me if you told me he murdered someone, either."

"But if the report comes back that it was Barry Tate inside the car, would that calm your worries?"

My cell beeped with an incoming text. I ignored it, but it got Nora's attention. She stared at my hip as if waiting for my phone to come alive. Then someone came out of the back of the restaurant and called for Nora, saying her break was over.

Nora blinked and flicked her cigarette butt to the ground before snubbing it out in the dirt with the toe of her shoe. She closed her car door and locked it up.

"I've got to go," she said as she brushed past me.

"Here's my number," I said, handing her my card. "I'll be in town for the next couple of days and would love to take you out for dinner. Finish the conversation we started."

Holding my card in her hand, she backpedaled away, saying, "I've already said more than I should have. I'm telling you, it's in your best interest to let this go."

CHAPTER THIRTY-FIVE

LEFTY TURNED OFF THE HIGHWAY AND WOVE HIS WAY BACK to a horse trail and park a few miles outside of Mountain Center. Being a weekday morning, the park and stalls were empty and Lefty parked on the north end, avoiding the houses across the way to the southwest.

He stepped out of his truck and tugged on his pants, looking up at the jagged ridgeline looming overhead. The grass was tinder dry and a murder of crows was circling, when he heard Rip's truck turn into the parking roundabout.

Lefty watched Rip's driving with a careful eye, making sure his wheels were straight and even. After what he witnessed yesterday, he wasn't willing to chance it happening again.

Rip parked behind Lefty's truck and Lefty walked to his door and opened it for Rip.

"Get out," Lefty said.

Rip climbed out but, before his second foot hit the dirt, Lefty lunged forward and slammed Rip into the side of his truck, pinning him against the metal.

"What the hell is your problem?" Rip yelled.

"My problem is that you didn't tell me the complete story when I asked you." Lefty pushed more of his weight into Rip. He was about three inches bigger, standing at six foot three, and had about thirty pounds more muscle than Rip, too.

"What are you talking about?"

Through clenched teeth, Lefty said, "Nora."

"What about her?"

Lefty wedged his forearm deeper into the back of Rip's neck until Rip winced. Sticking his nose near Rip's ear, he smelled to see if he had been drinking. He hadn't. "You went to speak to her when you were drunk," Lefty said.

"Just to see what she heard. If you're worried she's going to talk, she won't."

"How can you be sure about that?"

"Because she is as guilty as we are."

Lefty pushed off Rip and spun around. He heard Rip flop around onto his back and cough as he tugged on his collar, catching his breath. Lefty stared through the trees, across the empty lot and into the neighborhood of houses nearby. As far as he was concerned, it was just them and the birds.

"The cops are sitting on this case," Lefty said confidently. "They aren't even interviewing people."

"That's great," Rip said, entirely too excitedly.

Lefty turned to face Rip and produced a hard glare that had Rip second-guessing his tone. Lefty said, "But Carson Reynolds is in town." If Rip knew this, he didn't give Lefty any indication he did. Lefty asked, "Did you see him at the lake?"

Rip cast his gaze to the ground and stroked the stubble growing out of his chin. He seemed to be thinking awfully hard about it when Lefty said, "You keeping these secrets from me is what is going to get us caught!"

"Lefty, I didn't see him. I swear. If I did, I would have told you about it."

"Then what the hell took you so long to decide if he was there or not?"

"There were a lot of people there. People I didn't even know." A thought crossed Rip's mind and he asked, "Wait a second, do you think the police have already identified the people in the car?"

Lefty kept glancing around to make sure they were still alone. He didn't want their conversation to be overheard and misinterpreted. "The way this county works, doubtful," he said. "But only one person around here owned an Aston Martin and that same person went missing and hasn't been found. It will only be a matter of time before Carson learns who was inside with Barry and, when he does, we can only pray he finally lets this case rest."

Lefty opened his phone and showed Rip a picture he'd taken outside the bar and grill. After he told Rip where he took it, Rip asked, "Who is that he's with?"

"Her name is Samantha Bell. A reporter who runs a popular crime blog and podcast out of Denver, Colorado."

"Wait," Rip said, taking Lefty's phone into his hand. "I think I saw her at the lake. Yeah. That's right. She was definitely there."

"I'm not surprised you did."

Handing the phone back to Lefty, Rip asked, "What is she doing out here, and how did she get from Denver to Riverside so quickly?"

"I don't know. But something tells me it's no accident she's here." Lefty swung his gaze to Rip and said, "But it gets more interesting. It just so happens she runs her little crime business with none other than, Erin Tate."

"Oh, shit." Rip went pale as he swiped a hand over his head.

"Yeah." Lefty sighed, knowing it couldn't be coincidence.

Then a diesel dually and horse trailer pulled into the

parking lot, indicating their time was up. As Rip climbed into his truck, Lefty said, "I've already figured out where she's staying and I'll keep an eye on them both. But remember, we planned for this, knowing this day would eventually come."

"About yesterday—"

"Forget about it." Lefty waved Rip's mistake away. "No one knows anything."

"And if Nora talks?"

"We'll put her into the dirt with the rest of them."

CHAPTER THIRTY-SIX

AFTER I WATCHED NORA DISAPPEAR BACK INTO THE restaurant, I headed to the cabin with a lot on my mind. Several hours had passed, mostly filled with research, and soon I found myself outside pacing the front porch waiting for Carson to arrive.

The more others told me to let this story go, the more I wanted to get my hands dirty. I needed to know what happened, what the secret was, and how Erin might be involved.

I still didn't believe she had anything to do with her father's death, but I didn't have it in me to call her and discuss the story with her, either. Instead, I phoned Carson, right after I spoke to Nora, and asked him to join me at the cabin to discuss the case. It was time he opened up and pulled back the curtains on everything he knew. I was only working with half the story and my shortcomings today proved it.

I kept an ear on the road and anticipated Carson's arrival any minute. He was running late and I hoped my instructions were clear and he hadn't gotten lost.

Another thing I realized today was that two days wasn't going to be nearly enough time to make my case and convince Edgar Diaz, of all people, to let me stay on the story that seemed to be going nowhere. But my biggest mistake was naïvely thinking I could trade access with the sheriff by pawning off one of my best friends. I regretted it deeply.

I stopped shuffling my feet over the wood planks and listened to the silence. There was a cold nip to the air that had me wrapped up in my arms. When I stopped moving, I was reminded of my isolation. The silence was as disorienting as investigating a crime in an unfamiliar town.

Headlights came into view, and the rumble of an engine followed, as I watched the SUV wind its way to the cabin and come to a stop out front. Carson was behind the wheel and waved as I made note of the vehicle he drove. A Toyota FJ Cruiser with tires wide enough to possibly have been my guest last night.

"Nice place," Carson said as he got out. "I hope it's on the paper's dime."

"Part of the deal," I said, gently smiling.

"What else is on that deal of yours you negotiated?"

It wasn't that I didn't think I could trust Carson with that information; it was only that I was feeling impatient and a bit worried about Erin, that had me jumping over the small talk and diving straight into why it was I invited him here tonight. I said, "Why was Erin a suspect in her father's disappearance?"

"You want to talk about this inside?"

I paused a beat and debated how long this might take. We could discuss this on the porch, but it seemed silly. "What? Can't stand the cold?" I teased.

Carson followed me inside and we settled in, him in the arm chair and me on the leather sofa. He acted like this was his first time to the cabin and that settled my thoughts about him being my visitor last night.

"How well do you know your friend?" Carson asked.

"Well enough to know she's not a murderer."

Carson flicked his eyebrows in a sign of doubt. He turned to me and said, "Erin received a very *large* inheritance after her father's disappearance."

"I'm aware."

Carson leaned forward and said, "Do you actually believe the sheriff will trade access in exchange for your friend?"

"If it's Erin's father who was found inside the car, shouldn't she know?"

Carson held my gaze; the tension between us was high. It felt like we were fighting and I didn't understand why. I said, "Nora definitely knows something but she's too scared to say much."

"I'm not surprised." Carson rubbed his thighs, turned his head, and stared out the window.

"Tell me: what the hell am I walking into? Why should I bother staying to find out?"

"Are you thinking about leaving?"

I mentioned my two-day window, how I had until the end of the day tomorrow to make my proposal, and told him I didn't have plans after that. Then I said, "I need to know everything you know about this case. You asked me to speak to Nora and I felt completely ill-equipped to be out in the field today with only half the story."

Carson said, "No one told you to go to the sheriff's."

"If you would have told me sooner—"

"Erin's reputation wasn't too different than her father's," Carson interrupted. "She was labeled by members of the town as greedy, grasping, and after her father disappeared, she pushed the case to be closed so she could receive her father's millions."

I listened carefully to what he had to say and asked myself if I knew Erin as well as I thought. Was it possible this was who she was, and that the person I knew now was someone entirely different? People changed, but this person Carson was describing was someone I didn't recognize.

I said, "And that made her guilty in the eyes of the town?"

"That made her a natural suspect." Carson told me about a California law that said if a person was missing for five years or longer, certain family members could file for a petition with the court requesting that the person be "presumed dead."

"So Barry was presumed dead and Erin received her inheritance," I said.

Carson nodded. "But a body was never found, and it was said Erin might have murdered him for his money."

"And rumors are fact now?"

"Only when the presumed dead was thought to have planned his disappearance with his daughter."

"You're saying Erin is part of a conspiracy to fake her father's death so she could inherit his wealth?"

"That's the story, and there are many people who believe it's true."

Carson seemed to believe it, too. At least enough to investigate its merits. "But Erin never lived in Idyllwild," I said, thinking how presumptuous of the town it was to make so many conclusions about a young woman no one knew.

"No. Not to my knowledge."

I thought about Erin's past, how she attended the school of journalism, and her working on the east coast as a documentary film maker. Everything that eventually brought her to Denver where we finally teamed up and worked our first case together—The Lady Killer.

"I just can't believe the irony of you being here at the same time Barry Tate's car is found," Carson said.

"Me neither."

Carson looked me directly in the eye and asked, "Is it possible it was purposely done by the *LA Times's* editors?"

I almost laughed, but didn't. "That would mean someone at the paper knew the car was going to be found. I just don't think it's possible to predict the future like that."

Carson agreed, then added, "Hollywood. Where life is often stranger than fiction."

"But you suspected there were two victims." Carson nodded, sure of himself despite me not having told him about the coroner's report I happened to come across today. "Then why are we speaking as if Barry was the only victim?"

"Because I think Barry killed the other victim and then asked Erin to help him plan his disappearance."

Carson had his reasons why, and presented the facts as best he could remember them, but I still found it hard to believe Erin had anything to do with this. I asked, "If that *is* true, who did Barry kill?"

Carson had a deadpan look on his face when he said, "My daughter. Jocelyne."

CHAPTER THIRTY-SEVEN

I wasn't ready for the news Carson had shared with me. How could I not have known? It made total sense the second victim was someone close to him. But what had me reeling even more was knowing in my heart Erin couldn't have known about this. If she did, there is no way she would let her father get away with it.

Carson's head was bowed and he sat extremely still. As I watched him, my heart broke and I thought about my son. Now I understood Carson's motivation to solve this case; why he deflected yesterday's question when I asked who might have been inside the Aston Martin, not wanting to confirm through admission, his daughter might be dead.

I unfolded my arms, stood, and sat next to him. I put my hand on his shoulder, feeling his hard muscles flex through his shirt against the heat of my fingertips. He reached across his chest and blanketed his big hand over mine, but kept his head bowed, not wanting to show me his face. He didn't have to. I could feel his pain coursing through his hand, and felt the tears he refused to shed bubbling up inside of him.

I felt my eyes water with grief, but also refused to cry. We fell into rhythm, breathing the same. The sounds of our breaths filled the empty void that suddenly filled the house. I stared at the contrast of our skin tones while letting the tsunami of memories of Gavin come crashing down on me.

Carson turned his head and forced a smile. Our eyes met and a spark flashed in his pupils, that made me pull away. I quickly stood and worked to catch my breath, trying to make sense of him—of this entire investigation. I was having all sorts of feelings for him, and something told me he was having them for me, too.

An awkward silence followed and neither of us knew what to say or how to break the ice.

Carson leaned back into the couch and rubbed his face with both hands.

Though I had already given my heart over to King, there was something in Carson I couldn't deny, no matter how I tried.

Finally, Carson stood and said, "I'm sorry."

But it was me who needed to say sorry. "I wish you would have told me sooner," I said.

He gave me a look that said, *how could I?* It was a tragedy all around, a misfortune that had, for whatever reason, brought us together. Turning my focus back to the investigation, I asked, "Was Nora a friend of Jocelyne's? Is that why she won't speak to you?"

Carson moved to the kitchen, filled a glass with water, and drank it. I waited for him to return and, when he did, he said, "There was a party at Barry's place that went terribly wrong. Nora was there that night. That's why Nora needs to come out. She knows what happened and might be the only one who does."

My mind jumped back to when I surprised Nora outside the restaurant and how she told me I should just let this go. Now I wished I would have pressed harder, made her tell me everything, when I had the chance. I hated to think how I might have missed our only opportunity. Seeing the deep pain swirling in Carson's eyes, had me regretting my decision to wait, thinking I could get to her next time. Assuming there would ever be a next time.

"Who hosted the party?" I asked. "Barry? And you're sure Jocelyne was there?"

"I was never able to confirm if Barry hosted it or not, but what I've been told is that something in Barry snapped that night and he kicked everyone out of his house, everyone except Jocelyne."

My heart was racing and I could easily see how bad of a situation Jocelyne had found herself in. Alone with a man said to be infatuated with guns and alcohol, a person hated by the entire town. "Why?" I asked. "Why keep Jocelyne and let everyone else go?"

Carson raised his chin and said, "She was either passed out drunk or selected by Barry himself. I really don't know."

Carson choked on his words and I reached out to hold his hand, which he accepted graciously, grabbing hold with a firm grip.

"I wish I had known she was there; I would have retrieved her myself." Carson gave a small glimpse into what kind of father he was, someone never to get angry. "I just wanted my baby to be safe."

Did Erin know this? Was this the reason rumors started about her helping her father disappear? Did Erin kill her father after she discovered he killed Jocelyne? Several worst case scenarios played out inside my mind before asking, "What happened to Nora? How could she leave Jocelyne there alone?"

"Nora knows what happened and is too scared to speak."

"You're sure of this?" Carson said he was. "Perhaps she

feels guilty for leaving Jocelyne there that night, alone with Barry?"

Carson released my hold and leaned against the counter, arms crossed. "I've talked with everyone I could over the years and I keep getting the same conclusion."

"Which is?"

"Barry killed Jocelyne."

"There's something I need to show you," I said, having Carson sit on the couch before handing him my cellphone. "I discovered this today on the sheriff's desk."

Carson read through the report on my phone and I watched his face fill with anguish. The first tear fell from his eye, when he whispered, "It's them. It has to be," Carson said of the two victims found inside the Aston Martin. "That coward killed my daughter, and put her in the trunk before killing himself."

CHAPTER THIRTY-EIGHT

THERE WAS NO REASON FOR LEFTY TO WORRY, BUT HE needed to remain cautious. That meant having to check in on a couple of loose ends to make sure the thread to his original plan hadn't frayed.

It was something he did somewhat regularly. These were the thoughts Lefty was having as he exited the Memorial Highway and wove his way to the far reaches of the trailer park neighborhood.

Cautious was a word Lefty preferred to what it was he was actually feeling, which was paranoid. He didn't like having Carson Reynolds back in Riverside County, and that gave him reason to be concerned. But being paranoid was also what kept him from getting caught. And caught wasn't a word in his vocabulary.

Lefty turned his headlights off as he pulled to the side of the road and parked in a clearing between the trees. He sat in the dark for several minutes, looking around, flitting his gaze between the deep shadows of the trees, making sure it was safe to proceed.

This part of the forest was thick with pine that created a

natural fence between the long, narrow homes that made up the block. He kept thinking about Samantha Bell and her relationship with Erin Tate, questioning the coincidence, if it was possible Erin sent Samantha in her place with hopes of hiding her connection to the case. It was possible, but Lefty was smarter than to be fooled by such an easy connection. He had done his research, knew who everyone in the county was, even those just visiting for a long weekend.

When the time came, he silenced his cellphone and locked it up in the glovebox. Lefty put a knitted black ski cap on his head, slid his fingers into a pair of tight fitting leather gloves, and grabbed his Maglite flashlight as he exited his vehicle.

He looked left, then right. Not a sound around, he moved through the woods like a mountain lion on the prowl. Smooth and steady. The dry rocky soil crunched under his boots, but Lefty moved fast, knowing which backyard he needed to get to without being spotted.

The sliver of moonlight poked over the distant horizon and peeked between the trees. Lefty stuck to the shadows and a quick jog brought him to the white-sided mobile home whose porch and inside lights were off. He crouched by a nearby tree and caught his breath as he surveyed the perimeter.

A familiar silver subcompact sedan was parked out front. Its roof reflected the bright moon glow and shone as brightly as any flashlight. Focusing on the back door, he pulled the ski mask over his face and sprang into action.

Lefty knew these woods better than anybody. He'd grown up here, gotten his start in life, and where he became a man. These woods and mountains meant everything to him, and he wasn't about to let an outsider come and take that away from him.

When he reached the house, he stopped and crouched,

once again hiding in a dark shadow to remain invisible from the world. No one could touch him. They never had been able to stop him. He did what he wanted, when he wanted, how he wanted. Riverside was his.

Lefty pressed his body against the side of the house and glanced through the windows. A single hanging bulb in the kitchen was on, but he didn't see any movement inside.

He circled the house and tested each window and door, hoping to find one unlocked. To his misfortune, they were all snapped tight, so Lefty went around back and produced a key he had on file. He unlocked the top deadbolt, then the bottom lock clicked over, and he was in.

The refrigerator hummed softly as he moved through the living room. He came across a purse on the kitchen counter and opened it up to search for valuables. Inside, he found the usual items; a wallet with no cash, makeup paraphernalia, keys, credit cards, and a California driver's license.

None of it was important to Lefty. He turned his attention to the bedroom. He moved quietly on his feet. Each step lighter than his last until he pushed the bedroom door open with a single finger. In the dark room, he could make out the figure of a woman sleeping.

There you are, sweetheart. Alive and alone...but not for long.

Lefty flexed his fingers and thought about how, soon, they would be wrapped tightly around the woman's neck, as he squeezed the life from her. He envisioned the way she'd look as she squirmed and fought beneath him. Killing reminded him of his own mortality, a simple meditation on death.

One step closer and he lunged forward and ripped off the covers, preparing to lunge on his victim. The bed was empty. There was no one there. Only a body pillow where Nora usually slept.

This time she had escaped. Next time she wouldn't be so lucky.

CHAPTER THIRTY-NINE

I WAS UP EARLY THE FOLLOWING MORNING AND DECIDED TO go for a run, hoping it would be enough to get my mind off of Carson's pain. I pushed hard, sprinting up hills and keeping the pace up for nearly an hour only to arrive back at the cabin, with little change to how I felt.

Jocelyne was all I could think about. A young woman just starting out in life who was suspected of being murdered.

I knew what Carson was going through as I had experienced this pain before. The hidden depression, the feeling of getting sucked into a blackhole with no escape. It was a feeling that never seemed to go away. A dark cloud that followed you wherever you went. I knew this because it was the same way I felt when I had lost Gavin—the first man I truly loved.

That was what was strange about being around Carson. He reminded me so much of my late husband Gavin that sometimes my mind fooled me into believing it was actually him.

The temperature had dipped into the forties last night and with overcast gray skies it was feeling like fall. I stretched on the front porch and kicked my shoes off at the door. After a quick shower, I made coffee and had eggs with toast from supplies I picked up in town. I went over my notes as I ate and I kept coming back to one question I couldn't find an answer to.

If Barry was dead like we all thought, why was Nora still scared to talk? Did she know something we didn't? Was Barry actually alive? And if he wasn't dead, then who was with Jocelyne inside the Aston Martin?

When I finished my first cup of coffee, I opened my laptop and began typing up notes on the coroner's report before drafting my first story proposal to present to Diaz. When I finished, it wasn't as strong as I hoped, but maybe I could sell him on the idea of giving me more time to get it right.

I pushed back from the table and put my dirty dish in the sink.

As much as I didn't want to stay away from my son any longer than I had to, I knew I couldn't just go home, either. This story had legs and was more than the national acclaim Hineman dangled in front of me. With Erin's father directly linked to the case, I felt personally responsible to see it to the end.

I turned back to the table when I heard my cellphone buzz. It was a message from King.

Thinking of you.

Attached was a picture of him smiling into the camera. From what I could see behind him, I knew he was at his homicide desk.

Loneliness hollowed my core and King's simple text message only made me miss him even more than I already did. A part of me felt guilty for having an attraction to someone I only just met, and I was thankful for Carson's restraint last night when things could have gone in a completely different direction.

I messaged King back. *Miss you like crazy.*

Though I didn't expect a response, King had me questioning why I couldn't just hand this story off to Diaz. I had everything I was being offered by the *LA Times* neatly packaged into a single website we rightly named, Real Crime News. And, to top it off, I was able to do the work with a friend who I loved and respected dearly.

Erin is suspicious of your story, King typed back. *Care to share why?*

I thought about taking the story for ourselves, splitting our time between Denver and here. It would burn my bridge with the *Times* and taint any future propositions, but Erin deserved to know what I had found.

My thumbs hesitated over the screen as I thought about what to say next. Unable to find the words, I couldn't make a decision on when I should tell Erin. Making assumptions was dangerous enough, and I needed to be certain Barry was not only dead, but also inside that car, before getting Erin involved in what would certainly be an emotional investigation.

I took my eyes off the screen and glanced at the window. Did Erin know about the story unfolding, or was it only her intuition that I was onto something big?

Then a thought struck.

I responded to King—*I'll call you later*—and rushed out the door.

CHAPTER FORTY

TWENTY MINUTES LATER, I FOUND MYSELF AT THE IRON clad metal gate, the entrance to the house I believed once belonged to Barry Tate. Carson had mentioned the location last night at one point in our conversation and I committed it to memory. There was an intercom system attached to the stone pillar and a button to call the house. When I pressed it, nothing happened.

Was it not working? Was no one home? I wasn't sure.

The driveway wound its way through the trees, up the hillside, and disappeared over the knoll. I thought maybe if I saw the house myself I could better understand what type of person Erin's father was, what might have happened that night to Jocelyne. But without a visual on the house, I had the same as I had come here with. Nothing.

Determined to see the house, I got back into my car and drove around until I was perched on a hairpin bend across the valley. Through the treetops, I could see the sprawling mansion. It had big windows, an assortment of patios and decks coming off its sides like wings to a jet airliner. It was an imposing structure and looked completely out of place. It screamed of money and power, that directly clashed with the community of hippies, artists, and musicians who lived below it.

How did a young woman find herself in the house owned by a millionaire? Did she come here looking to party? Was there even a party? Who else was with her? Nora? Anybody else? And did Barry have the driveway gate when he lived here?

Everything I knew about Barry suggested he was a recluse in a town that hated him. But what was the reason for the hatred? There had to be something more to it than what I knew, but perhaps him having something most of the town didn't, was enough to spark the divide.

I continued to stare at the house. Its dark siding and steep, pitched roof had everything a person could possibly need. It also made sense of Erin's ability to work without pay, but it didn't tell me anything that I didn't already know.

Was Barry a predator who brought his victims home? Did his wealth protect him from getting caught? My mind was scrambling with possibility and I kept reminding myself that there was nothing to suggest any of the rumors were actually true.

I was wondering who lived there now, what kind of people they were, when Edgar Diaz called my cell.

"My deadline isn't for a few more hours," I said by way of greeting.

"Forget your deadline. A confession to the Hemet Lake murder just came through and I need you back in the city pronto."

CHAPTER FORTY-ONE

I UNDERESTIMATED TRAFFIC HEADING INTO LOS ANGELES and arrived at the newsroom just as the editorial meeting was finishing up. As soon I stepped off the elevator, I caught sight of Hineman and jogged to catch up to him.

It didn't get past me that Diaz said murder, as in singular. Carson and I knew for a fact there were two victims. What I didn't know was if it was a mistake in communication by Diaz, or something else entirely. Either way, I'd play my hand when the time came, making sure we were all on the same page. Until then, it was a secret I was closely guarding to keep an edge on the story.

I turned the corner and boomeranged around the cubicles just as a woman hurried to catch up to Hineman. She handed him something of interest and then quickly jetted off. Hineman stopped and read what she had handed him and then caught sight of me approaching.

"Oh, good. You're here. I wasn't sure you'd make it in time," he said to me.

"Underestimated traffic," I said. "What did I miss?"

Hineman backed into the wall and let his gaze travel over

my right shoulder. I turned to see what he was looking at and saw Diaz approach from behind. "What took you so long?" Diaz said into my ear as he joined the circle.

I ignored him and said to Hineman, "I got a lead on the Hemet Lake victim."

"And we have a confession to question," Diaz said, as if my words didn't matter.

"That's great, Samantha," Hineman said, handing Diaz and me each roundtrip plane tickets to San Francisco. "You two can swap notes in the air."

"Looking forward to it," Diaz said with a sly grin.

They both seemed energized by the development, but I was caught off guard. Did they like surprising me with planned misdirection? Or was this just how they were?

Hineman said, "You up for it, Samantha?"

I lifted my chin and nodded.

"Excellent." Hineman looked me in the eye. "This is a breadth and depth story. No allegedly, no police said, I want to hear it straight from the horse's mouth. Got it?" Hineman turned his focus to Diaz. "This racehorse we're betting on can't lose."

"Breadth and depth," Diaz reiterated.

"San Francisco?" I held up the plane ticket as if asking if they were sure they wanted to send me along for the ride. It was a huge expense for someone working freelance.

"Don't worry, Samantha," Hineman said, as if reading my mind. "We'll compensate fairly for your time and expertise."

"But my name goes on the byline," Diaz said to me.

"Fill Samantha in on the details on your way to the airport." Hineman raised his wrist, pulled up his cuff, and checked the time. "Now go before you miss your flight."

CHAPTER FORTY-TWO

WE SHARED AN UBER TO THE AIRPORT AND, WITH NO BAGS to check, were through the TSA security line and at our gate in record setting speed. We were seated at the gate when I shot off a quick message to both my sister and King to alert them of my travels and whereabouts.

Diaz was next to me working his phone, and I eavesdropped on his conversation. He was talking to an attorney I assumed represented the man we were on our way to meet. He kept finding an excuse to keep me in the dark, and I couldn't help but feel like he was doing it on purpose. When he got off the phone, he said, "We should be all set by the time we land."

"That's great," I said. "But you still haven't told me who we're going to see, and if they confessed to murder."

A woman sitting across from me lifted her gaze over the rim of her reading glasses and stared. Her eyes were round with obvious fear, wondering who we were and what we were up to. I ignored her gaze and continued to press Diaz for information.

Diaz said, "His name is Dale Tanner, currently sitting on

death row at San Quentin State Prison. Convicted of killing half a dozen strippers he buried in the trunks of his cars; his first known victim dates back to 2001."

"And his last?"

"Twenty-twelve." Diaz raised both eyebrows. "Got away with his crimes for eleven years before finally slipping up. Left a print in one of the cars he dumped his victim in." Diaz spoke loudly and drew the attention of people around us. He didn't seem to care. He kept at it, telling me, "We're lucky he hasn't been killed by the state. Through a recent executive order, the governor put a moratorium on the death penalty so he's just sitting there, locked up and bored. Probably why he confessed to this murder in Hemet Lake. Wants some company."

The woman across from me was once again staring at Diaz. When I met her gaze, she lowered her eyes and went back to her device. Diaz's loud talk wasn't surprising. It fit the character he first introduced me to in the hotel room. Reckless and ignorant, all wound into one. I supposed it was also a reflection of the current state of journalism and the fact that most of the *LA Times* competitors had gone out of business. There was no one in print to compete against and, though it gave us time to work stories without fear of a competing paper getting to it first, it also made it easy to make mistakes.

"Who told you he confessed?" I asked, thinking about Jocelyne and if it was possible she was a stripper. And that Diaz kept saying *murder*. The only thing I didn't know was how long the two victims I was aware of had been buried in the lake. Could they have been victims of Dale Tanner, too?

Diaz gave me a look, like he suspected I didn't believe him. "His attorney," he said. "The same person who is getting us the interview to crack this story wide open."

A bit of Diaz's ego was beginning to show. I wasn't one for cocky, but it was nice to finally see Diaz show some passion for reporting. I asked, "How was he able to arrange this on such short notice? We aren't part of Tanner's council."

"Tanner's attorney will be faxing a letter to the prison stating we're investigators working for him." Diaz pointed to his leather satchel and said, "He also faxed the same letter to me earlier, stating the same in case anyone asks."

Diaz seemed sure of his plan, and I suspected it would work, at least for him. He had the connections. But I didn't think Hineman would send me along if he didn't also believe Diaz's plan would get both of us inside. So I went along with it, and asked one final question.

"And if anyone asks me for a state investigator license?"

"You don't need one if you're working for an attorney."

The plane was beginning to board. We got in the front of the line and found ourselves sitting near the back, tucked against a window. I was thinking about how I should be flying home instead of heading to a maximum-security prison to speak with a death row inmate, when Diaz handed me Dale Tanner's file to review on our hour-and-twenty-five-minute flight up the Pacific Coast.

"Stay close to me," Diaz said. "Don't ask too many questions, and we'll be back in the City of Angels before you know it."

CHAPTER FORTY-THREE

BY THE TIME WE TOUCHED DOWN AT SFO, I HAD A GOOD understanding of the man we were about to meet. Dale Tanner was a forty-three year old psychopath with a hunger for teenage women who put themselves in compromising positions.

His murders, as well as his victims, all shared a similar pattern. What was most striking was how Jocelyne also fit inside Tanner's preferences. Though I still had my doubts Tanner was responsible for the Hemet Lake murders, I remained open to the idea it was possible.

We got into another Uber at the airport, and after a short drive, we were going through security at San Quentin, when Diaz made sure I knew I was only here to watch, as he took the lead.

He said, "Remember whose byline goes on this story."

I held my hands up in surrender, allowing him to set the ground rules. I assumed he knew the details to the job I was offered and how the pecking order would change if I accepted. Though I still didn't know what the future held for me, I graciously accepted to co-pilot on this one story.

It was the first time I'd seen Diaz fully tuned into his work and it was interesting to watch. I almost respected him for how much preparation he had already put into this interview. I just hoped he'd sustain his energy and see it through to completion.

When we arrived at the prison, Diaz produced his attorney papers and presented them when necessary. We went through security, checked our names in at the front, and no one questioned the paper's authenticity, just gave us a look that said, *Why would anyone want to speak with someone like Dale Tanner?*

It had been forever since my last visit to a maximum-security facility, and I was taking it all in as we walked the narrow, brightly lit, headache-inducing hallways. We were buzzed through several sets of heavy doors before finally completing the maze of corridors and arriving at a tiny, square room, where Tanner was already waiting with his hands and feet bound and restraints bolted to the floor.

Diaz faced the guard and said, "We'll take it from here."

Tanner wasn't physically intimidating, but had crazy, black eyes that pierced my soul. He wore the blazing orange jumpsuit and seemed to like the idea of having only us inside this small room with him.

As soon as the door shut behind us, I thought about the split second advantage Tanner had to attack us, if he managed to free his limbs. Though it seemed impossible, it was all I could think about as I followed Diaz to the table where we both took our seats. I sat in the chair next to him and kept my gaze forward. It seemed Tanner only cared about me, which I could see aggravated Diaz. To Tanner, Diaz was a ghost who didn't exist, while I was the pretty cherry on top of his ice cream.

"Dale, my name is Edgar Diaz, a reporter from the *Los Angeles Times*."

"Oh, forgive me for being rude. I'm so sorry I didn't greet you." Tanner's eyes clicked and shifted to Diaz, looking somewhat annoyed. "I know who you are, Edgar. No need to introduce yourself. You already did that with the article you wrote about me, STRIPPED TO CONFESSION. Clever headline by the way."

I noted how Tanner was quick to take control. He spoke intelligently, and I found his behavior entirely fascinating. But Tanner surprised us both when he shifted his focus back to me, saying, "But what a pleasure it is to meet you, Samantha."

I could feel Diaz staring with mild surprise. I locked eyes with Tanner and watched as they flashed with amusement. How did he know who I was? What kind of game was he playing? I cut through Diaz's rank and asked, "What can you tell us about the Hemet Lake murder?"

Diaz's jaw locked and I knew he was irritated with me. But I couldn't let Tanner think I was someone he could manipulate and walk all over. Like Diaz did to me, I needed to do to Tanner. It was all about establishing dominance, and I was accustomed to taking charge.

Tanner grinned. He seemed to like a no-nonsense woman. Then he said, "You remind me of my mother."

I took out my notepad and began taking notes. "How so?" I asked.

"Stop writing," he said. "I don't want my name in the news. I've had enough notoriety and it didn't bring me the expected joy I thought it would."

Tanner was looking directly at Diaz when he said this, as if he blamed the storyteller for not thrilling the audience. I assumed it was only Diaz's headline he liked, or perhaps he didn't. I couldn't decide.

Tanner continued, "People will never understand why I

did what I did, but I had a vision and was told by God to kill those women."

"Did God tell you to murder those people when you prayed? In your sleep? What?"

"The thing is, I can't recall if it actually happened or if I only imagined it."

"You can't recall God speaking to you? Or you can't recall if you actually killed those people?"

"No. The murders." Tanner glanced at Diaz, then brought his narrow eyes back to me. "It was a long time ago."

Diaz said, "The jury convicted you on eleven counts, and the judge agreed. I think we can all agree you murdered at least eleven women."

"You're the writer. Tell whatever story you want."

I said, "Why don't you tell us the story you would tell?"

Over the next sixty minutes, Tanner relived each of his murders, but never once did he touch on Hemet Lake. He was a great storyteller, providing very detailed descriptions of both the scene and victims. He was either telling the truth, or he had a great imagination. I couldn't decide what was real and what wasn't. I imagined solitary confinement would do that to a person, but Diaz ate up every word Tanner said, and I went along for the ride, silently promising to fact check later.

After a while, I dropped my pen and leaned back in my chair, thinking about how Tanner was giving Diaz the exact clickbait headline he was after. But if Tanner was telling the truth, I needed to know.

"This is all very interesting," I said, "But I want to know why you decided to plunge your own car into Hemet Lake."

It was a trick question, designed to feel out if we were wasting our time or not. Tanner gave a toothy smile and said, "It wasn't mine. I stole it from a man named Barry Tate."

CHAPTER FORTY-FOUR

DALE TANNER HAD MY FULL ATTENTION. WHEN OUR EYES met, neither of us blinked. Locked in a staring contest, I questioned how he knew about Barry Tate and if it was possible he was bluffing. Time passed and neither of us flinched.

Having just come onto this story, I wondered what had already been published and if it was possible Barry Tate's name had been mentioned in previous articles I hadn't read. I didn't recall seeing it in my original search, but from Tanner's story, there seemed to be another out there that I'd missed. I figured Barry's name had to have been printed somewhere when he went missing, and I suspected Tanner had access to a computer and had done his research before our meeting. But if he knew about Barry, did he also know about Jocelyne?

Diaz held still and waited to see what would happen next. I appreciated his patience. After another minute of stalemate, Diaz slowly turned his head and gave me a look that suggested I was now in command.

I said to Tanner, "You stole the car?"

"Yes."

"Do you remember where you picked it up?"

"At a party. In Idyllwild. Are you familiar with Idyllwild, Samantha?"

"I've visited."

Tanner gave me a knowing look that made my stomach turn. It seemed like he knew my whereabouts. I didn't know how, but something told me it had to have passed through Diaz, perhaps in conversation with Tanner's attorney.

"Tell me more about this party," I said.

"What's there to tell? It was a party at a mansion on the hill. Not too many people, but enough. Some real hotties. I get bored easily, so when I discovered a nice-looking car, I found the keys and took it."

I was taking notes when I thought about the story Carson had shared with me about Jocelyne finding herself at a party at Barry Tate's house. Could this have been the same party? I asked Tanner if he remembered the date. He didn't, but knew the season and it matched Carson's version. I wondered if Tanner knew Jocelyne.

I asked, "Do you remember what kind of car it was?"

"No. But I do remember it was fast."

"What else happened that night?"

"You mean, who did I take along with me?"

"Sure."

"A tipsy, slender-legged girl with fine golden hair."

I stopped writing and lifted my gaze. Tanner had his eyes closed as if dreaming about his days of freedom—perhaps the girl he took that night. But one thing was certain, he wasn't with Jocelyne. Jocelyne was black. I asked, "Does this girl have a name?"

His eyes were slow to open. "I never made it a priority to remember my victims' names. It's easier to kill the nameless."

"What happened to this girl?"

"She was reluctant to leave the party at first, but I promised she'd have a good time. We took the joyride of her life and it ended with a bang at Lake Hemet."

His smile hit his eyes. Pride swelled his chest and I imagined he was having a jolly time reliving his golden years. Diaz was furiously taking notes, but I had stopped. There were too many holes in Tanner's story for it to be true.

"When you say it ended with a bang, do you mean you shot her?"

"It means we fucked."

Diaz chuckled.

Tanner gave me a cockeyed grin when he proudly said, "I strangled her afterwards and then put her in the trunk before sending the car careening into the water, never to be seen again."

If I didn't know Jocelyne was black, and that two sets of bones had been recovered, I would have believed Tanner's story. He was a very convincing talker, and putting his victims in the trunk was his signature move. But this wasn't his murder.

I turned to face Diaz. "This guy is blowing smoke up our ass."

"Excuse me?" Tanner said, sounding offended.

I closed my notebook and pushed away from the table. Diaz remained seated, looking at me like I had lost my mind. "I'm telling you," I said. "He's lying."

Tanner asked Diaz, "Do you believe me?"

Before Diaz could answer, I told Tanner, "Your story doesn't make sense."

"Maybe not now it doesn't," he said to me. "But it's only the beginning of what's to come. Give it time and you'll understand what I'm saying."

I turned to the door, planning my exit. I was done with him. But he wasn't done with me.

Tanner said in a voice that sang, "Bye, Samantha. I hope you visit again soon."

CHAPTER FORTY-FIVE

I COULDN'T HELP BUT FEEL LIKE WE HAD WASTED OUR TIME by coming here. Tanner might be guilty of eleven murders, but he wasn't responsible for the two at Hemet Lake.

I waited in the hall for Diaz to finish, the guard standing nearby. My cellphone didn't have any bars to call Carson and give him a heads up to where I was and what had happened since we last talked, leaving me to wrestle my thoughts alone.

Twenty minutes after I had left the room, the door opened and Diaz came out. I pushed off the wall and let him come to me. He walked over to where I was standing and I said in a low voice, "It wasn't him. He didn't kill anybody at Hemet Lake."

Diaz turned his head and seemed to be piecing together everything that had happened. He turned back to face me, saying, "You let yourself go in there."

"Trust me on this."

"No," Diaz snapped, pointing his finger toward the floor. "He had total control over you and you nearly lost the story because of it."

Nearly lost the story? What was said after I left?

Diaz's eyes were full of fire but I wasn't going to just roll over and let him get away with this. I said, "The police found two victims inside the car registered to Barry Tate. Not one."

Diaz stared. "Where did you hear that?"

I motioned with my hand to begin making our way to the exit. We talked as we walked. The guard escorted us to the front of the prison. I said, "Tanner had a fraction of the story right, but only because burying his victims in the trunk was his signature move. Somehow he was tipped off to at least that much, but there are too many glaring holes in his story for it to be him."

Diaz stopped at one of the metal doors between corridors and looked me in the eye.

When he didn't say anything, I said, "Is it possible Tanner read between the lines of your mobile reporting and filled the rest in himself?"

"You heard him," Diaz said. "He name-dropped Barry Tate. I never mentioned Barry's name and, as far as I'm aware, no one else has either. Maybe you're right. Maybe Tanner didn't do it, but isn't it possible he's telling half the truth?"

"What are you thinking?" I asked.

"Maybe he was at the party that night."

I was about to mention the second glaring hole in Tanner's story about Jocelyne being black, but then I realized it was possible Tanner wasn't describing her. Maybe he had described Nora. Instead of giving away my source, I asked, "What did he say after I left?"

We exited the building and were standing beneath the clouds, when Diaz worked to get us a ride back to the airport. He finished what he was doing on his phone and said, "I'm paraphrasing here, but Tanner said there are still predators lurking in those mountains, preying on the vulnerable."

"Did he mention any names?"

"He wouldn't say, but he hinted at how he didn't work alone."

Was it possible Tanner had gotten his victims mixed up and forgotten the whole story? Or was he toying with us, hoping he could manipulate the narrative of how his legacy would be written? My few minutes with Tanner made me believe both were possible.

Diaz knew he had me when I shut up. I felt foolish for not realizing Tanner couldn't have worked alone, and Diaz knew it. But I was still skeptical of Tanner's involvement.

"You can't write about this," I said. "At least not until we know if Tanner was involved or not."

"But what if my story inspires him to talk?"

A Pulitzer shined in his eyes, but I could already see his clickbait headlines keeping our industry afloat through the exact type of journalism I wanted no part in.

"Remember, breadth and depth," I said.

Diaz nearly rolled his eyes before saying, "By the way, who is your source?"

"I caught a glimpse of the coroner's report."

"You're kidding."

I shoved my hands in my pocket to fight off the chill. "Do I look like I'm kidding?"

I knew he was angry enough to report back to Hineman, telling him how I didn't play well with others. But the deeper I got in this investigation, the less concerned I was about getting the job. I just wanted to know if Erin's father had killed Jocelyne or not.

Diaz said, "I'll need to see the report."

"I don't have it." It wasn't the complete truth. I still had the photos on my phone, but I couldn't risk having him run with it and tip off any unsuspected perps before we really knew what had happened.

"Tell me, Samantha. Why did you agree to stay in California? It's clear you don't like working with anybody but yourself."

I was feeling as frustrated as he was. I didn't expect to be running across California, but mostly I didn't expect to be away from my family for as long as I already had been. I turned to face Diaz when I said, "I'm not exactly sure. I guess I'm still trying to answer that for myself."

CHAPTER FORTY-SIX

I HAD NOTHING ELSE TO ADD TO DIAZ'S COMMENT. Apparently, he didn't either. We kept mostly to ourselves on the flight back to LA and not until we were outside the terminal waiting for each of our ride's to arrive did Diaz ask me, "Where do you go from here?"

It wasn't exactly clear what Diaz was asking me, but I said, "Back to Idyllwild to figure out who the victims are and who might have killed them."

Diaz nodded like he knew that's what I would do. When his Uber arrived, I asked, "And you?"

"Close out Tanner's story, see if what he said was true." He opened the back door and tossed his bag onto the backseat. Then he turned to me and said, "If you leave California, let me know. I'll need your notes before you go."

I watched Diaz climb inside the vehicle and ride away. I wondered if I'd see him again, and if he expected me to pitch my story idea to him once I had learned more. Today was a disaster and, for some reason, I was taking it personally, like it was somehow my fault all this had happened. Why send me to San Quentin in the first place? Was it because Hineman knew Erin's father had been found? Maybe. It gave them reason for me to stay and tell the story no one else could.

After I retrieved my rental car from the newsroom parking lot, I sat with the engine off, staring at the building for a long while. I thought a lot about my future, what I wanted to accomplish for, not only me, but for Mason as well.

Could I see myself living in Los Angeles? I wasn't sure I could. It was a big, dirty city with an ego unlike Denver. I only had a couple more years with my son before he went off to college and began figuring out his own career. I wasn't sure moving would be fair to him, even if he said he didn't mind. I knew he did.

I turned my head and glanced at my notepad resting in the passenger seat, debating if I should continue another two hours to the cabin or get myself a room for the night in the city, when Carson called me on my cell.

After a short greeting, he asked, "Have you heard?"

"Heard what?" I responded.

"Jesus, you're not in town, are you?" I told him I was in LA but said nothing about my journey to San Quentin. He said, "It's Nora. She's missing. How quickly can you get here?"

CHAPTER FORTY-SEVEN

I LEFT THE NEWSROOM PARKING LOT AND NEEDLED MY WAY through city traffic before opening up the throttle when the highway cleared. I drove as fast as I could, wanting to be in Idyllwild as soon as the investigation got started. The clock was ticking and it was going to be a long two hours.

Carson sounded as surprised by the news as I was, but I questioned if this was coincidence or something else. Did it relate to the Hemet Lake murders? Was that even possible? Life was full of coincidences and I wasn't about to try to understand something I knew nothing about.

Soon, the sun faded behind me and my headlights lit the road in front of me. I kept the radio off, and both hands on the wheel as I wrestled with my thoughts.

I couldn't stop thinking about how Tanner chose to describe the party he was supposedly at, and the victim he supposedly killed.

A tipsy, slender-legged girl with fine golden hair.

I was convinced it was Nora Barnes he was describing, but that was only because Nora fit the description and was one of the few people in Idyllwild I had actually met. If I was right, how did Tanner know she was going to go missing? It had only been a few hours since our talk and Carson's call. The likelihood of Tanner pulling it off seemed impossible.

But it's only the beginning of what's to come.

According to Diaz's statement, Tanner didn't work alone. It was possible he had a partner on the outside. If that was true, we had a bigger problem on our hands than a simple cold case resurfacing.

I followed the bend in the road and accelerated around it. The mountains glowed in the moonlight, and my engine hummed, as I remained on the lookout for traffic cops. I couldn't figure out how someone sitting on death row could still be planning hits on the outside. Was that what was even happening here?

Both Jocelyne and Nora's faces kept visiting me in my mind. I thought how one of them had likely been buried in the trunk of Barry Tate's Aston Martin and the other was harboring information that might lead us to the answers we were looking for. Was that the reason Nora disappeared?

I wondered when Nora had last thought about Jocelyne, and if Carson was right in assuming Nora was with his daughter the night Barry demanded she stay.

All these thoughts circled my head and I kept coming back to Nora's anxious energy when she made it a point to tell me to let this investigation go. What was she worried about? What did she know that she didn't want me to find out? I was hoping my intuition about her being the next victim was wrong, but something inside of me told me I was probably right.

It was well after dark by the time I arrived at Idyllwild and the streets were packed with motorists. There was a clear urgency in the people that I hadn't felt before. They all seemed to be in a hurry to go nowhere fast.

I pulled to the side of the road and called Carson. When he answered, I said, "I'm here."

"Good. Remember where Nora worked?" I said I did. "Excellent. Meet me there. And, Samantha?"

"Yeah?"

"Come prepared. It's going to be a long night."

CHAPTER FORTY-EIGHT

THE PARKING LOT WAS NEARLY FULL WHEN I ARRIVED AT the small green-sided restaurant on the north side of town. I squeezed my comparatively small sedan between two large SUVs and found Carson on the phone near the entrance. He paced in front of the porch. I could see that the inside was full of people, all coated up and full of energy. It looked more like a passionate town meeting, than it did the breakfast and lunch restaurant, I remembered from the day before.

I kept thinking I would see Nora somewhere in the crowd serving drinks, hustling for the tips she lived off of. Of course I never did, and I hated to think this might have been a kidnapping, but that's where my mind kept going.

When Carson ended his call, I turned to him and asked, "What happened? Are you sure Nora's missing?"

His shoulders were set back, his neck visibly tense. In a gravelly voice, he said, "I'm sure, Samantha."

Everything inside me froze. That's why everyone was here —at the restaurant she worked at. I knew this was coming but somehow I still couldn't believe it could be true.

Carson continued, "She didn't come in for work, and no one has seen her since last night."

I covered my mouth with my hand and turned back to the restaurant windows. Carson placed his hand on my shoulder and squeezed. Our eyes met, and I closed the lid on the emotions threatening to surface. It was nice to be working alongside Carson again. Nice to be next to a person who respected me for my intelligence, and didn't view me as a threat. The contrast between him and Diaz was enormous. When I pressed for more information, Carson continued to fill me in on the details, hiding nothing.

"Apparently, Nora sometimes disappears into the mountains alone. But she always comes back. It's possible she got lost on a hike."

I hoped that was all it was, but by judging the town's reaction, it was unlikely we were going to be that fortunate. I asked, "Does anyone know where she likes to hike?"

"There are dozens of trails in these mountains. Last I heard, a search and rescue team was scouring Suicide Rock."

"Suicide Rock?"

Carson gave me a look that said *it's not what you think*. He explained, "A granite outcrop popular with rock climbers. I volunteered us to hit a trail nearby to see if we can find her ourselves."

As awful as the name was, I thought I might know the area he was referring to, but there were many outcroppings in Riverside County, and all of them looked potentially deadly.

A group of five came spilling out of the restaurant. We watched them pile into a four-door Toyota Tacoma and drive off, probably to begin their search for Nora.

When it was quiet again, Carson asked, "What happened to you today?"

"It's a long story," I said. "And it's not what you're thinking."

"What am I thinking?"

When an Escalade backed out of its space, I caught sight of Sheriff Graves and a couple of his deputies meeting on the other side of the parking lot near a large ponderosa pine. The sheriff looked in my direction and we locked eyes. My first thought was what the dog walker had said to me that second day at the lake, how people often go missing here. If that was true, I suspected the response I was seeing tonight was the exception. Why now? Was it because Nora didn't actually go hiking and something else happened to her? Was the public being told the complete story, and did the sheriff know Nora was a potential witness to the deaths of Barry Tate and Jocelyne Reynolds? My guess was he did, but wasn't willing to say. And if the sheriff knew what we were piecing together ourselves, who else might know, and where were they now?

I asked Carson, "When was the last time you spoke to Nora?"

Carson looked at me funny and said he couldn't recall. I suspected he was hiding something from me and I couldn't figure out what that might be. Did it have something to do with his daughter? Or had he gone after Nora today while I was away, hoping to get answers himself? If so, was that the reason she disappeared? Both were possible, but he had made me believe I was his only chance at getting Nora to talk.

"What happened today, Samantha? Is there something I should know about?"

Carson tried to shift the conversation back to me, which only made me more suspicious. He made sure to look me in the eye when he talked. They were steady in their pursuit of answers, but all I could think about was how he was late arriving at the cabin last night and what, if anything, that meant.

"Who reported Nora missing?" I asked.

Carson flicked his gaze to the restaurant and said, "A woman Nora works with here at the restaurant. I don't think she's making this up."

CHAPTER FORTY-NINE

HER NAME WAS RACHEL SWEENEY AND, THOUGH THIS WAS the first I was hearing of her, I thought it might be time to introduce myself. I pushed past Carson and made for the restaurant's front door, assuming Rachel would be inside. Before I could get too far, Carson caught me at the elbow and said, "She's not here."

I twisted around and looked at Carson. "How do you know?"

"Because I saw a deputy take her away just before I called you. It's how I learned Nora was missing."

Naturally, I flicked my gaze to where I last saw Sheriff Graves standing. He was still there fielding questions from the public. I thought about lobbing him a couple questions of my own, but I didn't think it was worth our effort. Two hours since Carson's call and it seemed not much had happened. What was everyone waiting on? What were we waiting on?

I asked Carson, "They didn't arrest her, did they?"

"No. Nothing like that. I'm sure it was only to take her statement with hopes of learning where to concentrate their search efforts." Carson continued, "I don't know anything about Rachel, but the fact the sheriff has the entire town looking for Nora has me believing Rachel is a reliable source."

I watched the people inside and wondered where Nora lived, what her home was like, and what kind of people her close friends were. This story was unfolding fast. New developments were happening by the minute.

I met Carson's gaze and asked, "Did you go after Nora today?"

"You think I had something to do with this?"

Carson pointed at his chest with a look of disbelief filling his eyes. I stared back and asked myself if I might have been one of the last people Nora spoke to outside of work, and if Carson had set me up. I said, "I'm only asking because it might explain why she went off into the woods alone."

"I didn't," he said, sounding offended. "But I'm worried someone got to her before she could tell the truth of what happened at Barry Tate's house that night my daughter disappeared."

Though I didn't believe Carson had anything to do with Nora's disappearance, I could still understand his motive for wanting to get revenge. I said, "You warned me strange things might start happening to us."

Carson nodded and asked, "Why? Did something else happen to you?"

Carson needed to hear about my adventure today. Without having to say it, we both knew Nora's disappearance might be the beginning of more to come. "The reason I was gone today was because I was at San Quentin checking out a confession to the Hemet Lake murders."

Carson took a step back, as I looked for any signs of guilt that might indicate, he was the one on the outside working with Tanner. I didn't think he was, but I had to be sure. He continued staring with a quizzical look while I told him my story.

Listening to myself speak made me realize just how strange my day had been. I still couldn't believe it myself. It sounded too bizarre to be true. It had been a brutally long day that didn't produce anything useful—maybe even allowed Nora to go missing during my absence.

When I was finished, Carson asked, "Are you saying someone confessed to killing my baby girl?"

"That's exactly what I'm saying."

"Who?"

"Serial murderer Dale Tanner."

Carson didn't react to the name, but said he was aware of his story.

"But it doesn't matter," I said.

"Like hell it doesn't matter."

Carson was growing angry, and I quickly corrected course as I paraphrased the conversation I had with Tanner, ensuring Carson that Tanner had it all wrong. Carson listened carefully as I told him what Tanner said about the night of the party.

"Dale was very convincing," I said. "He made me believe he might have actually been there. "But he got the trunk victim wrong. Instead of describing Jocelyne, he described features that resemble Nora."

Carson took a deep breath, was slow with his words. It was a lot to take in. "Is it possible he might not have remembered things as clearly as he thought?"

"It crossed my mind," I said. Then I told Carson how Tanner seemed to have predicted Nora's disappearance. "Do you think it's possible?"

"Stranger things have happened, but only an insider could gain access to someone like Tanner." Carson was quiet for a beat, as he took his time processing everything I had just told him. "Let's say Tanner does have a partner, why take Nora now? It doesn't make sense, when we're the only people outside the sheriff's office who know who was inside that car."

Again, it felt like we were on the heels of someone running scared, and we couldn't figure out who it might be. I said, "Unless someone knew I had spoken to Nora about what happened that night and was worried she might talk."

"If that's the case, we better find her before someone gets to her first."

CHAPTER FIFTY

RIP PULLED HIS WRECKER UP NEXT TO LEFTY'S TRUCK AND powered down his window. Lefty had a stern look on his face as he stared ahead. Rip knew what he was looking at without having to see it for himself. They were parked in one of the dark corners of the school and away from the crowds assembling at the restaurant across the street.

"This shit is crazy," Rip said about the large-sized crowd in town. "Did you do this?"

Lefty turned his head and glared at Rip. He didn't like what Rip was insinuating. Lefty said, "Did I do what?"

Rip turned away as he murmured, "Nothing. Forget about it."

Lefty checked his mirrors just to be safe. Through his truck's exhaust, he could see traffic driving up and down the street behind him. It was heavier than usual, as was the foot traffic at the restaurant adjacent to where he was parked.

The restaurant was bustling with people, many of whom he knew. But Lefty didn't expect to see this kind of reaction from his town. This time was different and, though he'd never admit it to Rip, he was suspecting the police had figured out who was inside the Aston Martin, and had connected Nora to the victims.

Lefty said, "This is your fault Nora's missing. You know that, right?"

"My fault?" Rip said, sounding surprised.

"Need I remind you about the threatening visit you made?"

"It was nothing."

"You don't know what she said, who she told." Lefty paused for effect, thinking Rip probably didn't remember what he had said to Nora either. Lefty needed to make Rip paranoid, make him believe Nora might have gone to the cops and was with them now.

"You're the one who said we didn't need to worry."

"When the cops come knocking on your door—"

"Wait. What? Why would they do that?"

Lefty raised both his eyebrows. "The incident at the restaurant. People saw you harassing her. Either Nora has already mentioned it to them, or you were one of the last people she spoke with before she disappeared."

"But I didn't do anything."

Lefty squinted his eyes and nodded like he'd heard it all before. "I'm sure you didn't. But if you did, I suggest you keep your yap shut when they come, which they will, I can promise you that."

Rip frowned with obvious concern. His cheeks paled and it looked like he might be sick as realization sank in. Lefty stared at Rip's reaction and loathed his friendship. It was then and there, Lefty understood he needed to sever his ties before he, too, had a knock on the door from the police.

"I heard it was Rachel Sweeney who reported her missing," Rip said. "Maybe she can tell us where Nora is, and if she's spoken to the cops?"

"Leave Rachel out of this," Lefty instructed, already

coming up with a plan to take care of Rachel. "There's no need to draw more attention to ourselves than you've already done."

A thick knot of people cleared at the restaurant and, when the view opened up, Lefty caught sight of Carson Reynolds. Of course he would be here, he thought. And of course Carson would want to be the first to find Nora. Noticing Carson wasn't alone, but with that reporter Samantha Bell, Lefty had an idea. He pointed through his windshield and said, "Look there."

Rip saw what Lefty pointed at and added, "I haven't seen her all day. Thought she might have gone home."

"I guess she's back," Lefty said, as he watched both Carson and Samantha open the doors to a Toyota FJ Cruiser. "Keep an eye on them. And this time, don't let them get out of your sight."

Rip started his engine and backed out onto the street as Lefty reached across his seat and grabbed a plastic bag from the passenger side. He brought it to his lap and opened it up. Inside were the clothes and sneakers he had taken from Nora's closet during his visit last night—the clothes he planned to use in his master plot to keep the authorities from sniffing him out.

Lefty murmured, "Now it's time I poison the well."

CHAPTER FIFTY-ONE

WE CLIMBED INTO CARSON'S SUV AND I MENTALLY prepared myself for a long night ahead. When Carson turned the wheels toward the road, I caught the sheriff glaring from his post near the tree. I held his eyes as we drove past. He looked surprised to see I was still around, like he'd expected me to have moved on by now.

"How far until the trailhead?" I asked Carson.

He assured me it was only a couple of miles up the road. I checked my side mirror and saw a tow truck pull in behind us as Carson handed me the flier the sheriff provided to the volunteers about Nora.

I took the flier without taking my eyes off the mirror and Carson asked if something was wrong. The tow truck turned right onto a side street and I said, "It's nothing. I'm fine."

The flier had a colored photograph of Nora Barnes. It appeared to be a recent picture and it also provided details to help in locating her whereabouts. Name, age, hair and eye color, height and weight. It was all there, as well as what she was last seen wearing. Blue jeans, white V-neck t-shirt and a navy blue hooded sweatshirt with the Dodgers logo on the right breast. I wondered if she was still wearing those same clothes, when I asked Carson how he would describe Nora.

He drove with his left hand and gave his answer some thought before saying, "Slim. Golden hair. Youthful eyes."

Carson's description was nearly identical to Tanner's. Rather than making it a big deal, I made a mental note of the coincidence. I kept track of where Carson was taking me, drawing a map inside my head in case I needed to find my way back alone. He drove about a mile north before veering off onto a dirt road. It wound its way deeper into the thick pines and soon opened up to a trailhead parking area.

Carson parked near the sign, killed the engine, and tossed me a dark knitted ski cap and flashlight. As soon as I stepped out, I could hear Strawberry Creek gurgling against the boulders. This was the place Carson had volunteered us to search, and it appeared we were one of only two cars at this trailhead.

I wondered why he had chosen this area in particular. Was it because it was close to Suicide Rock? Or some other undisclosed reason he hadn't yet shared with me?

The temperature was chilly and had an early winter nip to it. I zipped up my jacket and met Carson at the back of his car.

"I'll follow you," I said.

Carson walked fast up the trail. We kept our lights to the ground, looking for clues. The terrain was rugged and thickly wooded. The gurgling of the water filled the air between breaths, and the harder we climbed, the thicker the clouds of condensation became.

It was a little eerie to be out in the woods knowing someone might have done something horrible to Nora. I couldn't help but feel like we were being played like a fiddle by a conductor sitting in prison half a state away. But, even worse than that, something told me the person behind this puzzle we were hoping to solve was here tonight, keeping a close eye on Carson and me.

Carson stopped and crouched. I followed his lead and, when he pointed to the ground, he said, "A footprint."

"A woman's size."

I twisted around and looked over my shoulder, flicking my beam of light into the deep, dark woods. The faint sound of an engine rumbled in the direction of where we parked. I thought how scary it must be to be lost in the woods alone and was thinking what it might be like for Nora. Was she out here? If she was, could she survive the night if we didn't find her? Though the trails were clearly marked, I figured Nora must also have known them well. Did she have experience on this one? Were we close to her whereabouts? How experienced an outdoorsman was she? It was like looking for a needle in a haystack and, though the odds were against us, I remained optimistic we'd find her.

The name Suicide Rock popped up in my mind and it gave me the shivers. As much as my gut told me that wasn't what happened to Nora, I didn't know. But maybe Rachel did? How well did she know Nora? Did Nora ever speak about the past to anyone she was close with?

Carson tapped my leg and told me to be quiet. A weak beam of light flickered between the trees not more than one hundred yards to the west. We stood still with our lights off. I whispered, "This must be their footprint."

Carson agreed. I was thinking how they were probably part of the search efforts, when their voices cut through the silence. I heard a woman say, "My guess is Nora made this up for attention and she'll miraculously show up come morning."

That was all I needed to hear, and it was enough for Carson to want to change direction. The comment was certainly interesting and had me thinking how much I didn't know about Nora. Why assume Nora made it all up? What did they know that we didn't?

We switched on our lights and, at the sight of their brightness, the women called out to us. Carson responded, "We're helping to look for Nora. Have you seen her?"

"Wish we had, but I'm afraid not."

They approached on the trail and we exchanged notes. They claimed to have been on the trail for the last hour and hadn't seen or heard anything. I said, "I overheard you say maybe Nora made this all up?"

"I'm sorry you heard that. I didn't mean anything by it," the woman with the brunette ponytail said.

"You sounded rather convincing."

Carson added, "Could have fooled me, too."

The woman shied and looked embarrassed. Defending her comment, she said, "It's just that Nora has never been the most honest person. She tends to make outrageous claims that never pan out. After crying wolf so many times, how many more are we supposed to believe?"

"Yet you came out tonight to look for her."

The woman said, "Let's just say, I hope Nora is found, but she better not have made this up."

CHAPTER FIFTY-TWO

AFTER WISHING EACH OTHER LUCK WITH FINDING NORA, I watched the two women head down the hill toward the trailhead parking lot, thinking about what they had said. I didn't like what they insinuated and hoped they were wrong, and this search for Nora wasn't a hoax.

When they were out of earshot, I turned to Carson and asked, "Any idea if what they said about Nora is true?"

Carson said, "It's possible they're basing their claim on Nora's involvement in Barry's disappearance."

When I asked him to explain, Carson told me the story of how Nora initially claimed she was at the party the night Barry disappeared, and then the next time she was asked, she wasn't. "It went back and forth like that for a while, to the point no one knew what to believe, and people stopped caring."

"If that's true, why did Nora retract her statement?" I asked.

"If I knew the answer to that, something tells me I wouldn't be here tonight."

Was this the reason Carson had me go after Nora? Send in

a harmless stranger, with the hopes of getting Nora to tell an honest account of what happened, without fear of judgment? If it was, I had failed miserably, and was still regretting my decision not to go after Nora harder, when I had the chance.

Carson flicked his light to the left and veered off the trail, wanting to check out a new area. I followed close behind, keeping my focus on the task at hand. Carson seemed convinced this wasn't a hoax and I chose to believe him. Besides, it was too cold to stop moving.

We hugged the creek shore and moved further up the valley looking for any signs Nora might have come through here. It was slippery and slow moving, but maybe that was the cause behind this search. Maybe Nora was injured and her cries for help were drowned out by the sounds of the running water.

We pushed forward and every once in a while we stopped to call out Nora's name. No matter how loudly we yelled, no one ever responded. A few cars passed on the road above and I was beginning to lose hope. After several weary hours with nothing to show for it, we found our way back to Carson's Cruiser.

Carson's vehicle was alone in the lot. Once I climbed inside, I allowed my head to loll back into the seat. I was exhausted from my busy day of travel and all I wanted was to call it quits and get some sleep. But when we pulled into the restaurant parking lot to retrieve my car, Carson asked, "Expecting company?"

I wasn't, but there was a familiar-looking woman who seemed to be waiting for me. She was leaning against my car, and pushed off when she saw me driving toward her with Carson. Few cars were still around; it appeared most of the town had gone home for the night. I hoped that whoever this was would tell us Nora had been found.

"Any idea who she is?" I asked Carson, trying to recall where I had last seen her.

Carson said, "I do. Rachel Sweeney."

We shared a curious look and I asked myself if she was waiting for me or Carson. The last time I saw her, Carson had charmed Rachel into getting free tater tots at the bar.

Carson parked next to my car and, as soon as the wheels stopped, I jumped out, suggesting Carson stay back—at least for the time being—so that we could have a girl talk alone.

Rachel came at me fast when she asked, "Are you Samantha Bell?"

I said I was, then added, "I'm so sorry—"

Rachel's hand came out of nowhere and I didn't have time to react before getting smacked. Her palm landed a hard slap against my cheekbone and sent me twirling around. The sting was wasp sharp but didn't knock me down. I turned back to face her, wondering what I'd done to deserve this.

Rachel said, "It's your fault Nora is gone. If not for you asking too many questions and getting rumors to surface, she'd still be here. Now go back to where you came from and quit sticking your nose where it doesn't belong."

CHAPTER FIFTY-THREE

I FELL ASLEEP WITH MY FACE PLANTED IN MY NOTES AND woke the same way. It was nearly ten o'clock the next morning by the time I got out of bed to check my phone.

According to the Riverside Facebook community page, Nora still hadn't been found. As disappointing as it was, I expected this to be the case. The longer she went missing, the more I believed someone had gotten to her. But who was it, and why?

I kept scrolling and reading the comments. The page was incredibly active. Though most of the search efforts had been relocated, the community wasn't giving up. That gave me hope that what those two women on the trail said was only their opinion of Nora, and didn't give a complete, nor accurate, picture. Then I stopped on a comment made by Julie Green that gave me pause.

Suicide Rock is named that for a reason. I'm not saying she killed herself, but we all know Nora is a known liar. Why dedicate so many of the county's resources toward her when the police just ignore the many other missing persons who still haven't been accounted for?

I sat back and stared out the window, thinking about

Nora and her blonde hair. I had asked myself the same question last night. It was a question that deserved a response, but I doubted we'd get one anytime soon.

Did someone, who also attended Barry Tate's party, threaten Nora to stay silent after she first admitted to being there? If what Carson said was true, it seemed likely, and made plenty of sense. Again, who was that person and how could we find them?

Then my thoughts shifted to Dale Tanner and his claim to have a partner on the outside. With Nora having gone missing within hours of Tanner telling me this, I was starting to believe it was not only possible, but likely. I still didn't know how he could pull it off from behind bars, but these events had to be connected. I just didn't know how I could prove my hypothesis, to get us on the right path.

I stood up from the couch and walked into the kitchen. On my way, I stopped at the front of the house and glanced at the front yard. The dry grass swayed in the breeze. My car was parked near the porch steps and was the only vehicle in sight.

I yawned and when my jaw stretched, I was reminded of Rachel Sweeney. There was a lingering pain and I expected to see a bruise when I looked in the mirror, but there wasn't one. I was thankful for that, but it still hurt like hell. If I hadn't felt like an outsider already, Rachel made sure I did.

I made a pot of coffee, thinking how long Rachel had been waiting for me, and how she knew what car I drove. Did she figure it out herself, or had someone told her it was mine? Either way, I didn't like the feeling I was being watched. Even worse, she refused to answer any of my questions, instead determined to blame me for everything that had happened since the Aston Martin was pulled from the lake.

My cellphone rang and broke the silence in the house. I

rushed to pick it up and smiled when I saw who was calling me.

"Hey," I answered.

King said, "Please tell me you're at the airport on your way home."

"I wish I was."

"This must be a hell of a story they have you working."

"You wouldn't believe it," I said, not sure if I was still on the *Times's* radar or if I would be publishing this story myself. I had kind of let the interview go once I got sucked into this investigation, and I was determined to see it through.

"Care to tell me about it? I've got time."

I could hear the loneliness in his voice and I liked knowing he was missing me as much as I missed him. "Well, for starters, I took a day trip to San Quentin."

"I didn't know they opened it up for tourism."

King's humor was exactly what I needed. There was a part of him that seemed jealous of my adventures, but when it came time to tell him about Nora, I kept most of the juicy details to myself, in order to keep Erin safe. I still didn't know how I was going to break the news to her or how involved she might be.

When I was finished, King said, "So what you're saying is you don't know when you'll be home."

"I can't let this story go unfinished."

"At least tell me this—are you safe?"

I heard a car drive up to the cabin and, when I moved to the window to see who was there, I said, "Don't worry about me. I'll be just fine."

CHAPTER FIFTY-FOUR

I OPENED THE DOOR FOR CARSON BEFORE HE HAD A CHANCE to ring the bell and greeted him by saying, "Did you ever think to call first?"

He was holding two to-go coffees and offered to give me one as his way of saying sorry. Even with the lid on, I could smell it was a better cup of joe, than the cheap brand I had made myself. When I accepted his gift, Carson said, "I would have called, but I much prefer to speak in person."

I took a step back and motioned for Carson to come inside. Carson headed for the kitchen and I watched as he made himself at home. He shed his jacket and hung it over the back of the wooden chair, before taking a seat at the kitchen table. When our eyes met, he said, "Forget about what Rachel said to you last night."

"I already have."

"She shouldn't have slapped you."

I agreed, but didn't comment. We both knew Rachel was acting on pure emotion and, for whatever reason, decided to take it out on me. I assumed it was because I was a reporter and had made a name for myself as the one wanting to learn what happened, but it was certainly possible she attacked me for a different reason, too. A reason still unknown to me.

Carson said, "I did a little recon mission this morning; found out where Rachel lives. Nothing suspicious about her, but it seems people in town are keeping a close eye on us."

It was reassuring to hear Carson was feeling the same as I was, and that he included the word *us* in his assessment. "We have to keep up the pressure, keep asking questions," I said. "Sooner or later someone will crack and we'll learn what maybe only Nora knew."

Carson took a sip of his coffee and shared a knowing look with me. His eyes said he had already come up with a plan—a plan to prove Barry had murdered his daughter.

Before asking what it was, I asked, "It's possible she might have overheard our conversation the other night."

"Nothing was said that night that the town didn't already know."

"There's something I didn't tell you about."

Carson set his cup back on the table and raised a single eyebrow.

"The other night, after our drinks at the bar, I came home to find fresh tire tracks in the driveway dirt."

Carson immediately stood and began checking the place for forced entry. He picked up the home phone and checked the breaker box. I wasn't exactly sure what he was looking for, but he seemed to know what he was doing. I told him I had locked the place up that night but I found the lights off when I got home.

I said, "I always leave a light on when I know I'll be out late."

Carson came back to the table and asked, "Have you found anything else out of the ordinary? Anything that would suggest someone comes to check in on you while you're away?"

Diaz pulling me away for the day crossed my mind, but it seemed like a stretch. I shook my head no, and said, "It was just that night, and the reason I even noticed it was because you mentioned this case might draw people's attention towards us."

Carson stared through the front window for a minute, appearing to be deep in thought. Then he turned to me and asked, "Were you with Edgar Diaz yesterday?"

I thought I told him I was, but I guess I hadn't. "Please don't tell me he's back," I said, hoping Carson wasn't about to tell me he discovered Diaz was somehow behind this.

The lines on Carson's forehead creased and I knew he was having his doubts too, but then he showed me something I couldn't believe.

I held his cellphone in the palm of my hand, reading something Diaz had tweeted about the same time I left LAX. I then scrolled down his feed and clicked on a link. It took me to an online *Times* article he had written about our interview with Dale Tanner. The publication date was marked for yesterday and I felt completely betrayed. Why hadn't I thought to check him last night? I wondered if this was what he was writing on the plane. How could Hineman sign off on something like this?

"I warned him not to publish this," I said to Carson, mentioning how Diaz even quoted Tanner as saying, *"Tipsy, slender-legged girl with fine golden hair."*

We both knew this was going to cause problems. Carson's look made me feel like my opinion didn't matter. And why should it? I was nobody to the *Times*. Just a freelance reporter they could pass the blame onto if, or when, the time came.

"I'm sorry for even asking," Carson said, "but have you published anything about this investigation yourself? Perhaps on your blog?"

I sat in a chair across from Carson and pushed my coffee

away. I was too shaken up by Diaz's article to need caffeine to wake me up further. "No. Nothing."

We sat quietly for a few minutes, staring at the wood grain in the table. Inside my head, I kept cursing myself for allowing something like this to happen. I wondered if Diaz had done this on purpose, placing this story where he knew I'd find it. Right on the homepage of the same digital arm of the paper Hineman had offered me to lead.

"This has to be the reason Nora disappeared," I said.

"If his quote is accurate, Tanner described Nora in exact detail."

"It's accurate," I said. "I was there. I heard it, too."

"Is it possible Tanner did it on purpose?"

"What, like speaking in code?"

Carson nodded. "That's exactly what I'm saying. You said he claimed to be working with someone on the outside. Maybe he chose to describe Nora as a way to send a message to his person?"

I didn't like what I was hearing, but it seemed plausible. I hadn't heard that part of the story myself. It was relayed through Diaz. Had I been manipulated by a serial killer? It certainly seemed that way. It didn't matter my name wasn't on the byline; I had been in the room with Diaz, and we discussed it, and broke it down afterward. This was on me as much as it was on him.

I said, "If that's true, that means the killer, or the killer's accomplice, is still here among us in Riverside County."

Carson gave a knowing look. "And if Rachel knows what we're up to, you can count on this person knowing, too."

But what was the big secret? If Tanner was communicating with someone in Riverside through code, was it not still Barry Tate who was responsible for the murder of Jocelyne? And was Nora the only other person who knew the truth of what happened that night? It didn't make sense. What were we missing?

Carson's phone buzzed with a message and I watched his look change when he read the text. He sprung to his feet and I asked what was going on.

"We have to go," he said. "It appears the police might have just found Nora."

CHAPTER FIFTY-FIVE

WE DIDN'T KNOW IF NORA HAD BEEN FOUND DEAD OR alive. Carson took the turns tight, fishtailing around a couple bends, hurrying to the same densely wooded area Carson and I had searched only hours before.

I kept glancing in Carson's direction. What were the chances? This couldn't be coincidence. There had to be a reason for us coming back. Were we getting set up? Or had we missed seeing the signs when we were out on the trail?

Carson's tires kicked up the dust and I tightened my grip on the grab handle. Suicide Rock hung over us on the horizon, subtly reminding me why it was I was here. When I brought up my concerns with Carson, he promised not to back us into a corner.

"Don't make any promises you can't keep," I said, pointing over the dash to the roadblock ahead.

Half a mile up the road, a single sheriff's vehicle was parked with its bar lights flashing. The deputy flagged us down and motioned for us to stop. Climbers trailhead—where we had parked last night—was just around the next bend. Carson slowed and eased to a stop. Then he powered down his window and greeted the deputy.

"Where is she?" Carson asked.

"I'll let the sheriff give you the details, as he's the one who requested you come." The deputy bent over and peeked inside the cab. He glared at me before straightening his neck. He was tall; when he stood upright I couldn't see his face. "We were hoping you would come alone," I heard him say.

"That wasn't made clear," Carson said.

"I'm sure the sheriff will tell you the same, but this has to be completely off-record."

I wasn't about to make any promises to keep anything I saw a secret, but Carson assured the deputy I could be trusted. He seemed satisfied enough with the answer to let us both through. Then we were told to continue on down the road to meet with Sheriff Graves.

As soon as Carson's window was up, I asked, "How did he get your number?"

Carson looked me in the eye when he said, "I've been on their list for a while now, but he's a point of contact with regards to information about Jocelyne."

I found that interesting and thought we might have been called here for something other than information about Nora. By the time I spotted the sheriff's truck parked on the side of the road, and a deputy's vehicle opposite that, I didn't have a good feeling about us being here. Something about it felt off but I couldn't explain why that was. Maybe it was because Carson was supposed to come alone.

I asked Carson, "Can you trust him?"

"Do I have a choice?"

There wasn't anybody else here. No coroner's van, no search and rescue. It was clear they wanted to keep things quiet, which also explained them not wanting any reporters to see what they had found—*if* they had found anything at all.

Carson parked behind the sheriff and we both stepped out at the same time. I stuffed my cellphone into my coat pocket and followed Carson to the embankment. Together we peered over the side, listening to the trickling sound of water, when male voices suddenly echoed off the rocks.

Carson raised a hand when the deputy spotted us and he motioned with his hand to Sheriff Graves, who didn't seem happy to see us. I ignored his sour look and continued looking for any signs pointing to Nora's whereabouts. Though I didn't see any specifics, the sheriff had flagged a couple areas of interest, and it was clear he was still treating this like an active investigation. Was it a missing persons case, or had it turned into a homicide?

The sheriff scrambled up the side of the hill and said, "Whoever decided to let you two through should get fired."

I couldn't tell if he was joking, or if Carson had somehow worked a deal with the previous deputy to get a seat at the table, but that's when I spotted a pair of shoes in the grass, flagged for evidence. If they were Nora's like I suspected, they were the only item not mentioned on the search flier.

Since I was here, I asked, "Are those Nora's shoes?"

Sheriff Graves didn't bother to look at what I was asking about, but I assumed he knew. Instead he said, "You two searched this area last night, isn't that right?"

"We started up the road at Climbers trailhead," Carson said. "We never saw anything, and we weren't alone, either. There were two women we didn't know, searching the area as well."

The sheriff listened but he didn't seem to care what we had to say. He turned his attention to me and said, "Since you got through the barricade, should I also be expecting to see Erin sometime in the near future, too?"

We all knew Nora's disappearance was related to the Hemet Lake incident, but no one wanted to come out and say it. Instead, the sheriff seemed as if he wanted to distract me by bringing up Erin. Needing to understand why, I asked, "Was Barry Tate in the car?"

Carson added, "Who was with him?"

The sheriff eyed me with a look that said I knew far too much, for someone in his office to have not said anything. He never mentioned what he was thinking, but a leak inside the department would surely spread like brush fire once the town got word of the story. I was pretty sure his office was sealed tight because of it.

The sheriff said, "Erin disappeared once she got her money."

Was that his way of confirming Barry was one of the victims found inside the Aston Martin? I assumed it was. I said, "Then why not extradite her if you have the evidence proving she murdered her father? I'll tell you why. Because you're not convinced she's responsible."

I could tell the sheriff wasn't used to being challenged, but I wondered what had changed.

He turned his attention to Carson and said, "Your daughter was in the car. The coroner confirmed it with my office this morning."

"Who was she with?" Carson pressed. "And don't bullshit me either, sheriff. I know she wasn't alone. Did Barry kill her?"

The sheriff frowned and said, "Barry's bones were in the trunk. I'm afraid it looks as if your daughter was the one who killed Barry."

CHAPTER FIFTY-SIX

CARSON DIDN'T TAKE THE NEWS WELL. HOW COULD HE? HE stood there staring ahead at nothing in particular, looking like he'd lost everything. The sheriff never offered any condolences, only looked at Carson as he would any other suspect in his own daughter's death.

"That's all for now," Sheriff Graves said, before he turned and walked away.

Anger coursed through my veins as I watched the sheriff head back down the hill. I disliked his bullish style, but also wondered if this was the reason he called us here—to break the news to Carson.

I couldn't believe the turn of events. It was the exact opposite of what we thought we were walking into. By the look on Carson's face, distant and pale, he couldn't believe it either. Neither of us could have predicted this.

"C'mon, let's get out of the cold," I murmured.

Carson was a shell of the person he was when we first arrived. I looped my arm around Carson's waist and tried to steer him to the car, but he wouldn't move. His muscles were tense, and I could feel his own anger threatening to explode.

I couldn't imagine what he was feeling, but then he said what I was already thinking.

"Someone wanted the sheriff to think we planted Nora's shoes there."

I turned to look over the edge of the hillside. The pair of black sneakers were the only flagged piece of evidence we could clearly see from our vantage point, but there were others that were hidden. I wondered if that was by design. I kept flitting my eyes across the ground, asking how Nora's shoes got here in the first place. Was it possible she was nearby? Though I couldn't see it from where we were standing, I suspected other items of Nora's clothing rested at each of the yellow flagged markers, dotted across the pine needle covered ground. But what bothered me more was how the sheriff had said nothing about Nora. Where was she, and did the sheriff know if she was alive or not?

Carson breathed heavily through a clenched jaw. It was one thing to accept his daughter's death, but it was an entirely new perspective to have to accept she might also be a murderer.

Was that the secret Nora was hiding? Did she know Jocelyne killed Barry? If it was her secret, she must have known the truth was bound to get out eventually, now that Barry's car had been found. But why bring Carson all the way out here just to tell him this? Did the sheriff also want to see our faces when he asked about our search last night?

"C'mon," I said again, trying to get Carson to move. "There's nothing for us here."

I finally got Carson to move his feet. He turned to the car and, once at the Cruiser, I opened the passenger door for him. He climbed inside without saying a word. I went around the back of the vehicle and all I could think was how it seemed we'd suddenly become suspects in the same investigation we were working to solve. It was the greatest irony of all.

I was sure it was no mistake. I was meant to be here, even if I didn't understand why.

I got behind the wheel and Carson handed me the keys. I forced myself to stay strong, if only for him, but didn't know what I could say to make him feel better. There was nothing. We were each other's alibi up to a certain time, then I had no one to vouch for my whereabouts. I assumed he didn't either.

"I'm sorry," I whispered. "If there is anything I can do to help—"

My offer felt empty, but I was sincere in what I said. I hated knowing the Hemet Lake case would officially be closed for everyone but Carson. But if what the sheriff said was true, Jocelyne must have had good reason to kill Barry, and I planned to find out what that reason was.

When Carson finally turned his head to look at me, my heart broke. I could see he was working a plan to exonerate his daughter's name. Though he never asked, I planned to help him answer those questions I saw swirling in his watery brown eyes. We'd do whatever it took. Before that could happen, it was time I finally broke the news to Erin.

CHAPTER FIFTY-SEVEN

THE DRIVE TO TOWN WAS SLOW AND SILENT. CARSON KEPT his head turned toward the window but it was clear his attention was focused inward. I found an empty space in front on the Village Market and parked. Turning to Carson, I asked, "Are you going to be okay?"

He looked me in the eye and said, "Are you?"

It was a fair question and one that must have been written in the lines of my forehead. I was nervous to break the news to Erin, scared how she might react and worried she might blame me for keeping this from her for longer than I should have.

"I'll only be a moment," I said as I opened my door and stepped outside.

A steady stream of vehicles moved up and down the street and people were coming and going from the market. With phone in hand, I dialed Erin's number and pressed the device to my ear. I found a spot against the large pine tree ten feet from the car and listened. When the call connected, Erin answered.

"Have you made a decision?" she asked. "Are you leaving

me? After all our hard work to make our podcast into a reputable news source?"

"I haven't made a decision. And let's get something clear: I'd never leave you."

An awkward silence followed and, for once, I couldn't find the words to break the news to her. It was odd considering I'd done this task hundreds of times before when reporting crimes through the paper and our blog. But I had never done it to a friend, someone I cared deeply for and knew would be hurt by what I had to say.

"What are you still doing out there, Sam?"

"Why haven't you ever told me about your father?"

"Why are you asking?" Erin didn't sound happy by my inquiry.

I stared up into the mountaintops thinking about my visit to Barry Tate's old house and the image I conjured up about the party Jocelyne had supposedly found herself at. The story in my head was equally as dark as the one Carson had shared, and it killed me to think how that night supposedly ended.

I asked, "Did he own property in Idyllwild?"

Mildly suspicious, Erin said, "Why am I not surprised you found yourself there?"

"It just happened," I assured her, wanting her to believe I didn't set out to look for it. "I didn't come here looking to dig up your past."

There was another short pause before Erin said, "You found him, didn't you? You found Barry Tate."

She hesitated, but sounded relieved by the news. I could understand if she was, but I didn't want to make the assumption. Eighteen years of not knowing was a long time to deal with grief. I imagined there had been quite a few long nights along the way that left her wondering if she'd ever get an answer to what happened, or learn where her father went.

But that was also assuming they had a good relationship—which I didn't know.

I faced the vehicle and saw Carson sitting with his head leaned back and his eyes closed. I said to Erin, "I did."

"Is he alive?"

Her voice was soft and I felt my throat constrict as I imagined I would ask the same question if I were in her shoes. I told her what had happened, how I came on to the story, and ended it with what I just learned without mentioning Jocelyne's name.

Erin was quiet for a long while and I could hear her crying. Then she said, "In my heart, I knew he was dead."

"I'm sorry to be the one to tell you," I said, wishing I was with her to hug and hold her tight.

"I'd rather hear it from you. I'm glad you called."

"Is there anything I can do to make this easier for you?"

"The reason I didn't ever talk about him was because I always suspected he'd been murdered."

"Who would want to kill your father?" I asked, hoping she could do the hard work for me by naming Jocelyne. As I waited to hear her response, I found myself not breathing.

"I'm not sure, but I have a couple different ideas of who might be responsible. I'd rather not discuss it over the phone."

I knew what Erin was asking, knew that I had to invite her to California and join our investigation. But I was afraid of mixing parties, of what it might do once either she or Carson learned they were after different conclusions to the same story.

"He wasn't alone," I said, hoping to hook her into revealing the names on her list of possible suspects without revealing how Barry might have been with the same person who murdered him.

"Do they know who he was with?"

I mentioned Jocelyne and Erin recognized the name, but only because she was aware of who Carson was and what he had imagined happened to his daughter.

"Jesus, the rumors were true," Erin said, sounding the least bit suspicious.

"It's complicated."

"I should really come out there. Maybe there is something I can do to help?"

These were the words I needed to hear. "How soon can you get here?"

CHAPTER FIFTY-EIGHT

MY CONVERSATION WITH ERIN WENT BETTER THAN expected and I was rejuvenated by the prospect of having her join me in California. But I was still worried what Carson might think now that it appeared his daughter had murdered Barry.

As soon as I ended my call with Erin, I turned away from Carson and closed my eyes, swallowing back the tears. It was such a sad situation. Two people were dead—maybe Nora too—and it was looking as if at least one of them had been murdered. A moment passed before I turned to face the Cruiser.

Carson had his head bowed. It looked like he was staring at something in his right hand. Because of the window's glare, I couldn't tell what it was until I opened the door. Once I was inside, Carson said, "My daughter was many things, but she wasn't a killer."

I wanted to believe it too, but the evidence suggested otherwise. Of course I couldn't tell him that. Carson was smart; he knew how it looked.

He lifted his watery eyes and, when they met mine, I asked, "May I see it?"

It was a photo of Jocelyne. When Carson handed it over, I stared into the face of a happy, carefree young woman. Her skin was as vibrant as her brown eyes, and she had the most beautiful black hair. I could see Jocelyne's infectious energy, but it was who she was with that had me taking a second look.

"Where did you get this?" I asked.

"It was attached to the last email Jocelyne ever sent to me."

"And this picture is why you know Nora knows something?"

Carson nodded, but didn't add to the story. Why he waited to show this to me until now was anybody's guess, but I assumed he had his reasons.

Carson said, "Look at the table. They aren't alone. Someone took that photo and I think whoever did, is the one who killed my daughter."

His determination was back; he seemed set on proving his daughter's innocence. I admired his tenacity, but I didn't want him to forget to grieve, either.

Focusing on the photograph, I studied the table top: Red beer cups, a pack of cigarettes, an ash tray, empty beer cans, and three bottles of hard liquor. When I asked, Carson told me more about the details he'd gathered over the years while looking for Jocelyne. He knew everything. Where she stayed, the dates she came to Idyllwild, what she did, where she ate, all leading up to that night she suppos-edly went to Barry's mansion on the mountain. He had covered his bases but we both understood he was missing something that would help explain Jocelyne's last hours on earth.

I asked, "Was this picture taken at Barry's?"

"I don't think so. It looks like the house of a younger person."

I agreed. It had the appearance of a college party, not somebody worth millions. But was this picture taken before the party at Barry's? It appeared these girls were pregaming pretty hard with the booze and, if so, would certainly explain why Carson believed Jocelyne might have been left at Barry's house—too drunk to leave on her own volition. But if that was the case, how did Jocelyne send it to Carson before she disappeared?

The one detail Carson didn't have was the names of the people Jocelyne had met along the way. Who were they, and how could we find out? How could we discover the details to something that happened eighteen summers ago? Was it possible these same people were still living in the area?

My thoughts jumped to Dale Tanner and who he might have told through code to kidnap Nora—if what we thought had happened, actually did. We needed that one piece of information to solve this mystery. A name, perhaps two. Whoever it was, I was certain they wouldn't be happy to see the sheriff finally close the case for good.

I said, "Erin is on her way here."

Carson's reaction was neutral. He didn't seem to care either way. Or maybe, he was still in shock.

"She wants to help out with the investigation."

Carson gave it some thought before saying, "As long as it's understood that my daughter didn't kill her father, I'm fine with her coming."

I wasn't going to speak for Erin, but I agreed to go along with it so we could concentrate our energies on finding Nora. I was losing hope she might still be alive, but I fooled myself into believing she was, so that we could keep our heads on straight.

As if reading my mind, Carson took the photo back into

his hand and said, "We have to find Nora. She's the only person who can tell us who took this picture of the two of them."

I asked, "Why won't Nora speak to you?"

Carson stared at the photograph as he told his story. It was a depressing tale, but an honest account of what had happened. He said, "I lost my temper with her and blamed her for Jocelyne's disappearance. I knew Nora was with Jocelyne, was certain she knew what happened that night. I scared her pretty good, trying to get her to open up and confess, but she never would. She kept her mouth shut. Shortly after that visit, I was notified by the police that Nora had put a restraining order on me."

I was thinking of the sneakers the sheriff flagged for evidence and how it seemed he wanted us to know what he had found. "You said something in Barry snapped that night and he kicked everyone out but Jocelyne." Carson nodded and I asked, "Where did you hear that?"

"Through the grapevine, I was told Nora had said it."

I was thinking about Nora's credibility and how her own community couldn't even believe what she said. If they couldn't trust her, how could we?

Carson said, "I'm certain whoever Nora's protecting is either someone close to her, like a family relative, or has done a better job of making her fear for her life, than what I could do myself. She wouldn't talk no matter how many nasty threats I lobbed at her feet."

I thought about how the sheriff must have known this about Carson, and how it made Carson appear to be guilty of the sudden disappearance of Nora. Did Carson ever have a chance to learn what happened? I wasn't convinced he did. From an outside perspective, Carson had every reason to kill Nora, if what he said about her leaving Jocelyne behind was true. But did he? Was that the reason the sheriff invited us to the scene today? To see how Carson would react? If Jocelyne could kill, why couldn't he?

Carson turned his head and looked me directly in the eye, when he said, "It was a mistake I've regretted every day since it happened, and I'd do anything to make it right."

CHAPTER FIFTY-NINE

LEFTY WAS LOST IN HIS THOUGHTS WHEN HE FELT HIS cellphone buzz in his pocket. Instead of seeing who was demanding his attention, he chose to ignore the call. He was too concerned with how the sheriff's department would interpret the items of clothing he had left behind in the woods. Would it be too difficult to identify them as Nora's? It seemed easy enough, at least to him. But perhaps he was too close to the crime to see it for what it truly was.

He suddenly worried he might have to go back to the woods. He heard the bedroom door open in the rear of the small house. Lefty lifted his head and when Rachel Sweeney stepped into the light, their eyes met. Lefty smiled.

He was sitting on the couch, his left arm slung over the back, his right knee crossed over his left. Lefty said, "Tell me, sweetheart, what's it like to never age?"

Rachel cracked a smile, the first one today, though Lefty could see she was still struggling with Nora's disappearance. Rachel said, "Are you hungry? I can make you a sandwich."

Lefty said, "Shouldn't I be the one to offer to take you out?"

"And go where? To another restaurant? No thanks. I spend my life serving meals inside restaurants. When I'm home, I want to *stay* home."

"I'm not hungry," Lefty said. "But thanks, anyway."

He extended his arm and offered his hand to Rachel. She stepped forward and put her small hand into his. Lefty closed his fingers around her wrists and yanked her to the couch, where he wrapped her up in his arms. He said, "However, I would like to take a vacation with you."

Rachel angled her head and turned to face Lefty. She gave him a curious look and said, "A vacation?"

Lefty said, "What do you say? Let's leave this county and go somewhere neither of us has ever been. It would be fun. I'll pay. You don't have to worry about anything, other than packing your own bags."

"You're serious?"

Lefty grinned. "I could use a vacation, and I know you could too. Besides, it would be good for us to take our minds off of things."

Rachel leaned back and snuggled deeper into Lefty's arms. She stroked his forearm with her painted nails and, without thinking, Lefty kissed the top of her head as he gently played with her soft hair.

"Before you let yourself get too far," Rachel said, "you should think about your wife and family."

Lefty kissed her head again and said, "This has nothing to do with them."

Rachel unwrapped herself and got up off the couch. Lefty remained seated and watched a noticeably tense Rachel begin to pace the floor. What was she thinking? Whatever it was, he was certain she was overthinking it.

Lefty said, "I heard the sheriff was out near Climbers trailhead this morning."

Rachel stopped and asked, "Did they find her?"

Lefty shook his head no. "We would have heard if they did."

"I'm worried something happened to her. It isn't like Nora to not show up for work."

"Have you called to see if she's there today? Maybe she took a vacation herself?"

Rachel shook her head, said the restaurant was closed. "Nora can't afford a vacation. You know that." Rachel paused and lowered her voice to a whisper when she said, "I wish there was something I could do."

"She'll turn up soon."

"How can you say that with such conviction?"

Lefty shrugged. "I'm an optimist, I guess."

"Not me. I have a feeling something bad happened to her."

Lefty stood and made his way to Rachel. With his hand on the small of her back, he looked her in the eye and said, "I'm sure it's nothing, but I did hear Nora has been seen hanging out with Brenden Donaldson."

"You don't think—"

"I don't know what to think," Lefty said, turning his back.

"I'm losing my mind thinking about her," Rachel said, telling him how she had slapped the reporter Samantha Bell last night.

Lefty turned on a heel, raised both his eyebrows, and had to stifle his laugh. "I didn't know you had it in you?"

Rachel tilted her head and said, "Did you know Samantha went to speak to Nora at the restaurant?" Lefty said he didn't. "I don't know what exactly was said, but I do know that after that conversation, Nora wasn't the same."

"You can't trust reporters. Wait, she's not harassing you, too, is she?" Lefty gripped Rachel's shoulders, turned her to face him. He tucked a loose strand of hair behind her ear and said, "If so, we can put a restraining order on her."

Her eyes flitted back and forth between his. There was something else on her mind but Lefty couldn't figure out what that was. Rachel said, "I really need to apologize to her. It wasn't fair of me. She's only doing her job."

"Want me to take care of it for you?"

Rachel gave him a skeptical look when asking, "What are you going to do that I can't?"

"Lots of things," Lefty said. "I'm the man of action. Remember?" He grabbed her ass and this time Rachel didn't push him away.

After a sensual kiss, Rachel asked, "Will we find her?"

Lefty tipped his head back and answered with a single look—a look that said he couldn't lie to the sweet little darling, whose friend he was planning to kill in the next couple of hours.

"Yeah," he said. "I'm sure we'll find her."

CHAPTER SIXTY

I ASKED TO SEE NORA'S HOME AND CARSON SAID HE COULD take me there. I needed to get a feel for where she lived, what kind of neighbors she had. Despite what we thought the sheriff wanted us to believe, Carson and I both agreed to assume Nora was still alive.

Soon, I was driving through a quaint neighborhood on the southern end of Idyllwild, home to small houses in the woods. It wasn't the nicest place I'd seen, but the area looked safe—at least on the surface.

"It's that one there," Carson said, pointing to a white-sided trailer with a slanted roof.

I eased on the brakes, pulled to the front of the house, and parked. It was nondescript—ordinary and well-kept. The gutters were clean and the roof looked new. Though there were no signs of life inside or out; only Nora's little, silver car sitting cold and empty, gave the appearance that Nora had never left. If she went hiking, how did she get there?

Carson said, "She's been renting this place for the last five years."

"Where did she live before?"

"She bounced around between friends before landing herself a place of her own. Nora is from here. Grew up and went to school in the county. Her parents are both dead and she doesn't have any relatives in the state."

A true loner, I thought as I continued staring at the house. I wanted to get out, have a look inside, but I didn't have a way in and didn't know how to make that happen. Nora was our only hope at learning why Jocelyne might have wanted Barry dead. If we couldn't speak to Nora directly, searching her things was the next best option. But how could we do that legally?

Carson said, "I shouldn't be here. Not with the restraining order against me."

As difficult as it was for me to leave, I agreed, but vowed to come back. I needed Carson and couldn't afford to lose him on a stupid technicality. We left the neighborhood and drove back to town. I parked at the restaurant Nora worked at and, though it was still closed, I stepped out of the car and made my way inside, hoping to speak with a colleague who could possibly give me a clearer picture of who she was.

"Sorry, we're closed for the day," a male voice said from the back of the building.

"I'm not here for food."

A man of about fifty with gray hair met me in the front and introduced himself as the owner. His name was Daniel Mahoney and he was wiping his hands dry on a white towel as he gave me a questioning look. "Is there something I can help you with?"

"Have you heard anything new about Nora?"

"You were part of the search efforts last night?" Daniel was guessing and I said I was. He said, "I was told the search has been called off."

"Did they find Nora?"

"Not that I'm aware of."

"Then why call off the search?"

"I'm not sure why, but I assume it's because resources and money were already stretched thin. The sad reality about this beautiful place is that if we go looking for every person who goes missing in these woods, we'd never get any actual work done."

"Forgive my ignorance," I said. "But why was Nora's case different from the others?"

Daniel shrugged. "Beats me. But I'm not complaining. I need her working. She's one of my best."

Made curious by his words of encouragement, I took a step forward and asked, "Did you notice anything strange before she went missing? Perhaps any secret admirers or old boyfriends who wouldn't leave her alone?"

"I work mostly in the back but I didn't hear of anything odd happening. Nora is a kind woman, and a loyal employee who works hard. She keeps her head down and the drama low. It's what I like most about her."

I held his eye and thought it interesting how everyone kept telling us the same story of Nora being a loner who stuck to herself. I could see how that might give the wrong impression to some people—be misconstrued as being better than others or not playing nice—but was it accurate? Was that what I overheard last night from those two women talking? Possibly. But, ironically, it was also the story of what was said about Barry. I wondered if that was coincidence.

"Did she ever talk about Barry Tate?"

The man laughed and wagged his finger at me. "I'm not about to begin discussing the conspiracy theories with you, but no. Nora never mentioned his name. At least not to me. Once Barry was gone, his name was rarely mentioned in town."

As I looked around the restaurant, I imagined what it was like working here, the hours Nora had put in to make a life for herself. Few wanted to comment on Barry Tate and it seemed people were afraid to even mention his name. Why was that? What else wasn't I being told?

I asked Daniel, "Do you think Nora made this up? Do you think she did this for attention?"

"That isn't the Nora I know. But, if she did, she can expect to repay me for the lost business. That, I can assure you."

CHAPTER SIXTY-ONE

I WALKED BACK TO THE CAR WITH MY EYES POINTED TO THE ground, asking myself why it seemed everyone in town tip-toed around the situation with Barry Tate. I had a feeling this was the same runaround Carson had received early in the investigation and now I understood why he didn't get anywhere fast. This town had a secret—one everyone was sworn to protect.

Carson was back behind the wheel and I climbed into the passenger seat. As soon as the door shut, he asked, "Well?"

I briefed him on the short conversation I had with Daniel, and concluded, "I don't think he wants to know what his employees do off the clock."

With his left hand on the steering wheel, Carson stared straight ahead. "If the sheriff is calling off the search, he must know whether Nora's alive or not."

As much as I didn't want to admit it, I was beginning to think Nora was dead. There were too many clues to convince me otherwise, but I couldn't come out and say it for fear of making it real. Instead, I said, "Then why not tell the town? Calm their worries? Settle their fears?"

"If there is anything I've come to learn about Sheriff Graves, it's that he will do anything to keep control, including keeping valuable information to himself for as long as he sees fit."

"What are you saying? It's a power thing?"

Carson turned his head and met my eyes. "That's exactly what I'm saying. This is his town and he controls the message. People are disappearing and his office doesn't seem to be doing anything about it. Why is that?"

I was asking myself why the sheriff would purposely choose to keep his constituents living in fear, when my cell-phone rang. I freed it from my pocket, saw who was calling, and told Carson to brace for impact.

"What can I do for you, Edgar?"

Diaz said, "Where are you?"

"You know where I am. And you should know your mojo reporting caused someone to disappear."

"Please. Spare me. If I had that kind of power, I wouldn't be stuck writing for the *Times.*"

He had no idea the chaos he had stirred. No matter what he claimed, Diaz knew the power he held in the tip of his pen. We all did. Diaz wasn't an exception.

Diaz said, "Do you even want this job?"

"I *am* on the job." *Do you want to keep your job?* I wanted to say back, but didn't.

"Seems like Hineman may have made a mistake by letting you do as you please."

"What does that mean?" I heard my voice tense and felt the heat rise beneath my collar.

"This is why the freelancer model will never work." Diaz paused and the line went silent. Then he continued, "I'd like to have your notes, and not just what you discovered since our trip to San Quentin. *Everything.*"

"Not until we get something straight," I said.

"Then straighten me out, Mile High."

Had he given me a nickname? Apparently so. It wasn't a bad one; I'd had much worse over the course of my life. Instead of taking it as an insult, I thought maybe this was my chance to get inside the wall he had built up to keep me out.

"Tell me again," I said. "What was said after I left you to talk to Dale Tanner alone?"

"I've already told you everything. There's nothing else to tell."

"Are you sure he never mentioned who he was working with on the outside?"

"Does this have something to do with the disappearance you mentioned?"

Now we were getting somewhere, I thought. "I believe Tanner used us to speak in code to whoever he's working with on the outside. If what he said is true, your article may have tipped this person off, which resulted in the kidnapping of a key witness to the murder we're trying to solve."

Carson gave me a look like he was worried I would reveal too much and it would backfire on us. He might be right, but I had to work all angles knowing I couldn't afford to let another opportunity slip by me. I took a deep breath to calm down, reminding myself to believe Nora was still alive; the clock was ticking and the pressure was on.

I asked Diaz, "How did you learn about Tanner's confession?"

"I'm not at liberty to reveal my sources. Sorry, but I'm sure you understand why."

I balled my hand into a fist and said, "Fine. But you may have spooked whoever is responsible for the Hemet Lake murders and now we might not be able to catch up to them before they get away."

"Was it murder? And did you say, *murders?*"

"Yes. Plural. As in two. Now tell me what you know."

"Is that what the sheriff's department has said? Christ, if Barry Tate was in that car, I need your notes. We need to get this story out before someone else gets to it first."

I had a feeling he was referring to Erin, but maybe that was my own paranoid thoughts seeping in to the conversation. What other competitors were there?

I knew from the beginning that Diaz had an ego, but this was getting ridiculous. I couldn't stand the thought of the killer going underground for another eighteen years. Feeling like I was close to cracking Diaz wide open, I kept the pressure on.

"Quit playing games, Edgar. Didn't you hear a word I said? Someone may have been kidnapped or killed because of your quick, half-assed reporting."

"Is that your professional opinion?"

"Forget it. Call me back when you have something of value to exchange."

"Here's something for you, Mile High. I just spoke to someone who blamed *you* for Nora's disappearance. Care to explain that to me?"

I clenched my teeth. How could he? Diaz had led me on when he knew about Nora Barnes this whole time. How was that possible? Did he not have an empathetic bone in his body?

Then it hit me: Diaz was here in Idyllwild after following up on Tanner's prediction. How could I have not predicted that? Of course he wanted to take the lead, get the credit, go behind my back. I thought I knew where he was and who he was with.

"Maybe if you were here with me, you'd understand," I said.

I hoped I was right. It had to be the reason he was fighting me for inside information. I waited for him to respond. It was a long, anxious minute. Then Diaz said, "Thanks, but I prefer to work alone."

The line clicked off. Diaz didn't take my bait by revealing his location, but I knew he had to be referring to Rachel Sweeney. I glanced at the clock and hoped we could get to her house before it was too late.

CHAPTER SIXTY-TWO

CARSON SAID, "DON'T WORRY. I KNOW WHERE RACHEL lives."

He backed out, turned the wheel west, and stomped on the gas.

I buckled up and hung on as we sped across town. I had to assume Diaz hadn't told me everything. Why would he? He had no incentive to do so. I should have never walked out of that meeting at San Quentin. Now I was regretting what I had missed out on, thinking it could be the key to solving this case—finding Nora and determining if Jocelyne had killed Barry or not. If she did, could she have been strong enough to put him in the trunk herself? I shared my thoughts with Carson and he listened with an attentive ear.

"It was my only chance and I blew it," I said.

"You thought Tanner was only looking for publicity. You could still be right."

Was it possible Tanner was speaking in code, or was I reaching? It wasn't just the words he chose to describe Nora, but also the timing of her disappearance. That couldn't have been coincidence, but who was Tanner communicating with if we were right? Did Diaz know but wasn't willing to tell me?

Diaz was up to something but I didn't know what. He'd been chosen by Tanner for a reason. I had to assume he wouldn't have just called me if he did know the name of Tanner's guy. What was Diaz up to? Where was he going next? How could I get him on the same page?

As if reading my internal struggles, Carson asked, "You think Diaz is still in Riverside?"

"I don't know if he ever was here. It's not his style to work hard. I bet he worked the phones until he found Rachel's number," I said, thinking about what we were missing by choosing not to work together on this story.

Carson drove with a steady hand and I was thankful for his ability to bounce back. I couldn't shake my mistake and speculated that this was probably the end of my work with the *LA Times*, and certainly Diaz.

When we arrived at Rachel's neighborhood, Carson parked across the street and we both stared at the front door, deciding on a strategy to get her to talk. I couldn't afford to take another loss. That was in the back of my mind as I came up with a plan.

It was an older cabin painted brown with white trim. The door was yellow and everything appeared to be in decent shape. A homey place with gnomes in the flower garden. It contradicted the darker side of Rachel I had experienced last night. The warm sight gave me the hope I needed to confront her on my own terms.

"Want me to come with you?" Carson asked kindly. Not because I couldn't handle it myself, but because we both assumed Rachel was still unpredictable.

Just thinking about her attack on me last night had my cheek throbbing with pain. I recalled the surprise, the sudden sting and strength behind her slap. It was all in the back of my mind when I told Carson I needed to have a few minutes with Rachel alone.

We opened our doors at the same time and I said, "I'll keep my distance."

Carson looked me in the eye and responded, "I'll stay at the car, but I'm going to be watching closely in case she decides to attack you again."

I appreciated his concern, and certainly wasn't going to argue with him choosing to be on standby. I crossed the street and moved beneath a gray sky that resembled the town's mood, as well as maybe my own. There was a slight drizzle coming down and it made me think about Jocelyne and Barry and the others who disappeared without reason.

I walked by a mid-sized SUV parked in the driveway and glanced through the windows, assuming it was Rachel's. It was clean and not much was inside. I continued up the front steps and rang the bell at the door before taking a step back. My heart was pounding in anticipation of facing off with the woman who nearly put me on the ground. I felt it stop the moment she opened the door.

CHAPTER SIXTY-THREE

RACHEL OPENED THE DOOR, SQUINTED HER EYES, AND didn't look happy to see me. I was hit with a musky scent that had me thinking of Diaz. I knew it wasn't his. Diaz was more spice than musk, but Rachel definitely smelled like she'd recently been wrapped up in a man's arms.

I asked, "Am I interrupting anything?"

Rachel wedged herself between the door and the house and said, "Look, about last night... I let my emotions get the best of me."

I had to admit, the last thing I expected was to receive an apology from Rachel. Was it genuine? Or was there someone inside the house who she didn't want me to know about?

"Water under the bridge," I said, and watched her gaze flick over my shoulder to Carson. "But you should know I'm only trying to help."

She brought her eyes back to mine. "Just so we're clear, I was warned about what your intentions might be."

"Warned about me? By who?" I nudged her in the direction I thought she was heading to see if she would bite. "Edgar Diaz?"

Rachel's brow furrowed enough to let me know she didn't know who Diaz was. What happened to the nice woman who freely served Carson tater tots my first night in town? Or the woman who had just apologized to me? I kept my distance as Rachel made it clear she walked a fine line between being apologetic and a cat ready to pounce.

"It doesn't matter," she said. "Not as long as Nora remains missing."

"I'm not the enemy here. I want what you want."

"Which is?"

"To find Nora. Bring her home safe and sound."

Rachel's eyes moved back to Carson and asked, "Is he with you?"

I turned toward Carson. He pushed off the hood of his car and I watched him approach the house with a swagger in his step. He retrieved the photograph of Jocelyne from his coat pocket and, once standing next to me, he asked Rachel, "Do you remember me, Rachel?"

"Of course I do." Her eyes relaxed, along with her shoulders. "Mr. Potato Head," Rachel said lightly as if there was an unspoken attraction between them.

Carson chuckled and put on his charm while showing Rachel the photograph of his daughter. "I'm that young woman's father."

Rachel eyed Carson and eventually took the photo into her hand. She was quick to recognize Nora and I watched her eyes begin to water.

Knowing this was our chance, Carson said, "My daughter's name is Jocelyne. She was found in the car they pulled from Hemet Lake; a car owned by Barry Tate. His remains were also inside the car and the sheriff just told me an hour ago that my baby killed Mr. Tate."

"Oh my god."

"The thing is, I don't believe it. I know my daughter and

she didn't do what the sheriff thinks she did. It's why we're here. Nora might know who did kill Barry. It's also why we believe Nora's missing. We believe whoever took her is also behind these murders."

Rachel's voice caught in her throat when she asked, "Took Nora?"

"That's right," I said. "We don't believe she disappeared on her own."

Rachel held my eyes but she wasn't looking at me. She was deep inside herself. What was she thinking? Did she know what Nora knew? After a minute of staring at the photograph still pinched between her fingers, Rachel murmured, "Jesus. This town, I swear it's not what it appears." She lifted her eyes and asked Carson, "What about the other missing people? Were they also kidnapped?"

"We haven't identified a pattern," he said. "But we're not ruling it out either."

When we asked for names of the missing, Rachel couldn't provide us with specifics. She only heard a hiker here, a traveler there. They were all outsiders, just like Jocelyne, so no one really cared.

I thought that might explain the response we saw the town pull together for Nora. I retrieved my phone from my pocket and turned the screen towards Rachel.

"Do you recognize this man, Dale Tanner?" I asked.

"No. Who is he?"

I told her only that he was on death row and what he did to get there, worried that if I told her more I'd lose her completely. "We believe he might be secretly communicating with someone in the county to cover their crimes from eighteen years ago."

There was fear in her face. I had to assume this was the reason the sheriff was staying quiet. I asked, "Was Nora dating anyone? Did she have any family in town we can speak to?" I knew the answer to the second question but asked it to gauge how well Rachel actually knew Nora.

Rachel said, "Shouldn't the police be asking these questions? No offense to you two, but—"

"They are," Carson said. "But I'm asking because of my daughter. I'm sure you can understand."

Rachel gave the photograph back to Carson and wrapped herself inside her arms. Her hair was blowing in her eyes when she said, "Nora was a loner. When not at work, she stuck mostly to herself."

"Did Nora ever speak to you about a party she attended at Barry Tate's house?"

Rachel said, "Nora never spoke about it to me personally, but I heard about it through other people in town. Mostly whispers and jokes about it in passing. Nothing ever said seriously."

"Can you tell us what you have heard?"

Rachel gave us a few weak examples and added, "I haven't always lived in Riverside County. I came here ten years ago, eight years after this supposedly happened, but I assumed since Nora refused to talk about it, it couldn't be good."

"So you believed her?"

"I had no reason not to." Rachel's face twisted up again. "You're sure Barry is dead?"

I nodded and said, "We're sure." Her gaze softened with apparent relief. It seemed there was more she wanted to say but couldn't. I asked, "What is it, Rachel? If you know something, please tell us. It could save Nora's life."

Rachel swiped a hand over her head and cursed. "Christ, I don't know if I should be telling you this, but Nora mentioned in passing that now that the car had been pulled from the lake, she was going to go back to the police and remind them of what had happened to her that night."

Feeling like Rachel was about to open up and reveal everything she knew, I said, "You have an idea of who might have taken her?"

She pressed her hands on her stomach like she might be sick and nodded. She told us about a man by the name of Brenden Donaldson, a man she said Nora had secretly been seeing. It was the first solid lead we had and I felt a surge of excitement race through me.

Then Rachel said, "All Nora ever wanted was to get out. I suppose it's why I came here, too. To escape my past. Perhaps that's all this is? Maybe Nora finally had enough and decided to leave it all behind."

CHAPTER SIXTY-FOUR

NORA BARNES'S EYES WERE OPEN BUT SHE COULDN'T SEE A thing. The room was too dark and she was too weak to care about lying on the cold, damp dirt floor. She'd long given up on trying to escape. Her fingernails were chipped and cracked from clawing at the wooden door, and the concrete walls didn't give, no matter how hard she pounded or kicked. Worse, Nora had expected this day would come. The only surprise was in thinking it should have come sooner. Much sooner.

She flopped onto her back and spread her arms out wide. Each time she blinked, a flash of light lit up behind her eyelids and took her away to far-flung childhood memories of making snow angels in winter.

It was completely silent in the root cellar and Nora had just urinated on herself. As embarrassing as it was, her face didn't show it. She was still fully clothed—minus her black sneakers—and though she couldn't be sure, she assumed she'd been in captivity for at least twenty-four hours, maybe longer, without food or water.

Nora listened to her shallow breaths between wrestling

with her thoughts. She only had one regret in life, and this wasn't the one. No. She deserved this—punishment for what she had done. Though she did want to know who took her and where they had brought her.

You know who took you.

Was it that reporter who knew more than she should? Nora couldn't say. Or was it Brenden? Again, she had her doubts, but it did happen shortly after she'd visited him.

Did I trust the wrong man?

Nora closed her eyes and ignored her damp crotch as best she could, trying to recall what had happened. She arrived home. It was late. After midnight. It happened fast. Like the person was waiting for her. There weren't any distinguishing sounds, at least none she could remember, and then her world went dark. *What happened after that?*

"Oh, god, I don't know," she cried.

Now she worried that she shouldn't have told Brenden what she had. Had she made a mistake? She thought she had. But she hadn't lied. Not then, and certainly not now. Yes, her story had changed, but only because she was scared, knowing damn well her story might eventually get her killed.

It's him. He betrayed you.

"It couldn't be Brenden. Impossible," she whispered at the ceiling.

But if it wasn't Brenden, then it had to be Rip. Rip made the most sense. *Didn't it?* She knew what he was capable of doing. He was mean, aggressive, a total loose cannon. Especially when drunk. And it was Rip who had warned her to stay quiet. She'd gotten brave, and now her courage was what was going to kill her.

"Rip? Are you there? I know it was you, asshole!" Nora screamed at the top of her lungs.

Her voice echoed off the walls of the small room and made her sound larger than she actually was. But no one responded. She was completely alone. This was how she was going to die, and no one would miss her.

More tears fell and Nora had to remind herself that she wasn't making any of this up. She knew what had happened that night at Barry's. Whoever took her and put her here had to know that the community would also believe her now that the Aston Martin had been found.

"You're not going to get away with this, you freak!"

Nora dropped her head back to the cold, wet floor and started to cry. She knew why she was here, why she was going to die. But she was surprised it had taken this long for it to happen.

"Just do it already. Just kill me," she whispered.

A door creaked open somewhere inside the house and everything inside Nora froze as she listened to the sounds of heavy footsteps slowly approaching. Pushing herself up off the floor as quietly as she could, Nora didn't mean what she just said and prepared herself for the fight of her life.

CHAPTER SIXTY-FIVE

THE FRONT DOOR SLAMMED SHUT BEHIND LEFTY, THOUGH he barely noticed as he whistled a joyful tune while thinking about the last time he and Rachel had sex. She was a vixen in bed, rivaling his own appetite for hard and fast thrills and spills. But something about her tonight was different. He couldn't help but think she had changed her mind about him.

"Hello? Anyone home?" Lefty called out to an empty house.

When no one responded, he twirled the house key once around his finger and tossed it into the bowl by the door. He saw his wife's car keys were gone, but assumed she'd be back soon. She was *always* back soon and rarely strayed too far.

Making his way to the kitchen, Lefty stopped at the counter to take the phone off its docking station. He dialed Sheriff Graves's desk and, when the sheriff answered, Lefty introduced himself. "Sheriff, the reason I'm calling is to ask about the Nora Barnes situation."

Sheriff Graves didn't give too much detail away but said, "We've called off the search."

"Oh. Does that mean you found her?" Lefty tried to sound upbeat about it, even if he knew it was only an act.

"I'm afraid not. Why? Have you heard something? Is that the reason you're calling?"

"Well, you know me. I can't go anywhere without hearing something."

"Yes. Go on."

"I don't know if this will help, but I was just at Rachel Sweeney's house and she mentioned that a reporter from LA, or maybe it was Denver, hell I don't know. Anyway, a reporter by the name of Samantha Bell went to speak to Nora the morning before she disappeared."

"Samantha Bell, you said?"

"That's right. You can look her up. Her name is all over the internet. Her picture, too. Now, Rachel didn't go into what was said between Samantha and Nora—I don't think she really knows herself—but Rachel did say Nora seemed pretty upset by it."

"I'll look into it."

"I don't know if it's anything, but I thought maybe you should know."

"Any information is good information."

Lefty knew the sheriff was busy with the investigation and cut his call short after revealing only what he needed to, to take the pressure off his back. He hung the phone back in the cradle and made himself a stiff drink—a straight bourbon— and settled into his recliner in front of the TV.

"This one is for you, Rip." Lefty burst out laughing. He was feeling good about his plan and that he even got the sheriff to drink his Kool-Aid. "They're looking in every direction but at me."

With the bourbon warming his gut, Lefty pulled out his cellphone and checked on what Edgar Diaz was reporting on Twitter. He scanned the articles and looked for catchy headlines. Soon, he exhausted his interest and turned to his laptop computer where he continued his search into the life of Samantha Bell. How soon would the sheriff make contact? Would it be enough to drive her out of town? Or would he go to Rachel first?

"Interesting," Lefty said when reading about a recent case of corruption Samantha reported on in Denver. "The Denver Police Department, corrupt? Surprise. Surprise." Lefty couldn't believe Samantha had managed to get the chief of police arrested. Could that be why she was here? Had her life been threatened in her home state of Colorado? "You're smarter than you look," he said. "Should I be worried about you?"

Lefty's laugh was quick to fade as he began thinking of a way to compromise her position. He'd do anything short of killing her just to get her out of his hair, but even murder wasn't beyond his list of options.

"What are you doing here, Samantha?" he whispered as he scrolled, unable to find any articles related to Hemet Lake, or California for that matter. "Do you have a loved one? Someone important in your life? Please, reveal it to me if you do. I would love to know."

Then he clicked on the contact page on the Real Crime News website. A phone number was there, as well as an email. Lefty stared at the number for a minute before finally deciding to give it a call. Would it go to a news desk, home office, or be rerouted to a mobile number?

The line rang and Lefty wasn't sure who was going to answer. Would it be Erin or Samantha? Or perhaps someone else? Either way, he knew before deciding to make the call that his number would be blocked to protect his own identity. It was important to keep his anonymity in the age of data harvesting and manipulation, and something told him Samantha knew it just as well.

The ringing stopped and a woman's voice answered. "Hello, this is Erin Tate."

Lefty paused, listened, but couldn't find the words he needed to say. Then Erin gave him the clue he needed to confirm what he already assumed.

"King, is that you? Hello? Alex?"

Lefty quickly hung up. *King. Alex. Alex King.* Lefty recalled reading the name in the article about police corruption. Did Erin just reveal her source? Or was Alex King something more to her?

Back on his laptop, Lefty went to work to learn everything he could about Alex King. Alex was a homicide detective with the Denver Police Department and was close friends with Samantha Bell's late husband, Gavin. *Interesting.* Lefty knew Alex was obviously still in her life, but in what capacity? *You two aren't dating, are you?*

It took a little bit of work but, an hour later, Lefty had Samantha's home phone number written down. He gave it a call and a teenage boy answered.

"Hi. My name is John Travis," Lefty said as friendly as he could into the phone, giving a fake name to the boy. "I'm calling to speak with Samantha. Is she home?"

"Nah, she's not here right now. Can I take a message?"

"How about your father, can I speak with him?"

"Well, I don't have a father."

"I'm so sorry. What about the man of the house? Do you have one of those?"

"You mean Alex King?"

Lefty grinned. "Yes. Is he there?"

"No. He doesn't live here, but I can pass a message along if you like?"

"That's quite all right. I'll try again some other time."

Lefty set his phone down on the end table, with a plan taking root in his mind. It might be an awfully big assumption on Lefty's part, but he was willing to risk it if it meant sending Samantha's personal life into a downward spiral. Would it be enough to get Carson to leave town, too? As far as Lefty knew, Carson didn't have anyone special in his life—Jocelyne was it—and that might be a problem if his plan was to work.

It will work. He convinced himself. *What else do you have to lose?*

He was debating the answer to that question when his cellphone rang, taking him out of his thoughts. Thinking it might be Erin reverse calling, he wasn't quick to pick up. He turned his head and watched the screen, waiting for the number to reveal itself. When Rip's name flashed across the screen, Lefty reached for his phone and answered.

"Riverside Sheriff's Department." Rip was quiet and Lefty could imagine the scared look on his face. Lefty burst out laughing. "It's just me, asshole. You didn't really think you called the sheriff's department did you?"

"Jesus. You had me fooled for a second," Rip said. "I thought I might have dialed the wrong number."

"Why, Rip? You planning on talking to the sheriff?"

"No."

"Are you sure?" Lefty could hear Rip was nervous. He could use that to his advantage.

"Would you shut up and listen," Rip barked. "The sheriff was just seen combing the area where you told me to follow Carson and Samantha to last night. That's why your stupid joke isn't funny."

"I'm not funny?" Lefty grinned.

"Are you trying to set me up? Is that why you had me following them last night?"

Lefty knew Rip wasn't the sharpest knife in the drawer, but his fear was really making him lose what little wits he had. "I'm not setting you up, fool. But apparently you're the only one taking the bait."

"I don't know, Lefty. I don't like this. It's crazy, isn't it? What else did you do?"

"Nothing more than what had to be done."

It was quiet for a long minute and Lefty knew what Rip was thinking. Finally, Rip admitted, "I don't want to do this anymore. It needs to stop before we make a mistake and end up in jail."

Lefty thought this day would come and had already been planning for it. He had another idea—one he didn't particularly love—but he also wasn't going to allow his future to be decided for him. Lefty said to Rip, "The only way you'll end up in jail is if you stop listening to me. Now, go home, relax, and leave the heavy lifting to me."

CHAPTER SIXTY-SIX

As good as it felt to finally have a name to chase, I remained skeptical. It was possible Rachel was only telling us what we wanted to hear. If Nora did have a secret she wanted to keep from others, why did she tell anyone at all before going to the police? And why leave her car behind if she wanted to escape Idyllwild for a new beginning? We were making progress but there was still a lot we didn't know.

"You believe her?" I asked Carson.

Carson gave it some thought as he drove south to a town called Mountain Center—about a five mile drive. "I do."

Unfortunately, Nora's disappearance happened about the same time she was seeking retribution. I wanted to believe Rachel, too—believe she knew the real Nora and not the one we'd heard about in town—because in doing so we could learn how Jocelyne ended up in the driver's seat of Barry's Aston Martin. That was what we were after and it was critical we find Nora.

"Did you get a whiff of the cologne she was wearing?" I asked.

Carson shook his head no, said he was too far away. Then he asked, "Should we be worried about Edgar Diaz?"

Something told me Diaz wouldn't actually make the effort to drive to Riverside. He'd approach it differently. I said, "I think he's only working the phones, but I can't promise you he won't publish anything."

"What if Edgar is Tanner's contact?"

The thought hadn't crossed my mind, but now that Carson said it, it made sense. But only if Diaz was in Riverside. I felt a shiver move up my spine and asked if it was even possible? Is that why he couldn't reveal his source when I asked? I thought Diaz was only protecting his job because he saw me as a threat but now I was wondering if I was wrong. Could he be behind Nora's disappearance? Again, the math didn't add up.

Digging out my cellphone from my pocket, I got Jeffrey Hineman on the line. He picked up after the second ring.

"Samantha, how are things going? Have you touched base with Edgar?"

"That's why I'm calling. I'm trying to track him down. I thought he might have come to Idyllwild but can't confirm it. I was hoping you could tell me where he is?"

"That's a great question. I'm not sure I have an answer for you."

"Then maybe you can answer this. Was it you who approved the publication of our interview with Dale Tanner?"

"Is that a problem? I sense it might be."

Of course it was a problem, but I didn't let it become a bigger issue than it already was. I said, "There's just a lot we still don't know. But maybe you can tell me what other angles Diaz is working."

"If I'm being honest Samantha, I don't what I'm hearing. When is the last time you two talked?"

"He's keeping me in the dark," I admitted, after explaining our last conversation.

"I don't have exact details, but he's digging through the incident at Hemet Lake. That's all I know."

I held my breath and debated whether or not I should reveal my theory about how Diaz was used by Tanner to speak through code to a mysterious source who may have in turn kidnapped Nora. It seemed like a conspiracy meant for the tabloids—a statement that would discredit everything the *LA Times* loved about my résumé. It was clear from the beginning that Diaz and I had conflicting reporting styles, but this was getting absurd.

I said, "Diaz is going to need some encouragement if we're going to be working this story together. I have to admit, working with Diaz feels like I'm investigating two stories."

"Samantha, I think I know what you're saying. How about this? Forget Edgar. You let me worry about him and, in the meantime, how about you work an angle I know only you can get?"

I didn't know where he was going with this, but I asked, "What's that?"

"Interview your friend, Erin Tate. Get her on record telling her side of the story. See if you can get her to reveal information about her father that hasn't already been said. You think you could do that for me?"

Breadth and depth. It was the only thing I could hear inside my head as I thought about what exactly he was asking me to do. Hineman was asking for too much. Getting Erin involved was taking it too far, but I couldn't tell him Erin was already on her way to Los Angeles. Of course I could get Erin's thoughts on the subject, but did I want to? It wasn't going to be easy, but I had to keep her location a secret.

"What do you say?" Hineman put on the pressure. "You do that for me and I'll make sure Edgar plays nice."

Why did it suddenly feel like I was being asked to join the boys club? Were they using me for the contacts only I had? Two could play at this game.

I said, "Talk to Edgar. When I see he's ready to include me, I'll see what I can do about Erin."

I killed the call with a sour taste in my mouth. Hineman had made himself clear, and now I understood why he put me on this story. Luck happened to fall into the paper's lap and they planned to capitalize on my connections. Once again, I was reminded what I loved about Denver: My relationship with Ryan Dawson and how great it was working with an intelligent woman like Erin.

Carson tapped me on the knee and pointed to the side mirror. "It appears we're being followed."

CHAPTER SIXTY-SEVEN

MY SUSPICIONS ABOUT WHAT WAS HAPPENING IN RIVERSIDE only grew more wild when I saw the sheriff pull in behind us. This couldn't be coincidence. Was he after me or Carson? He trailed us for several miles and I kept thinking back to Nora's restraining order against Carson. With Nora's whereabouts still unknown, and assuming the sheriff didn't have any leads, Carson made for the perfect suspect.

I asked Carson, "What do you think this is about?"

"Maybe we should find out."

Carson locked eyes and put on his blinker. He made the next right-hand turn and pulled to the side of the road. I didn't argue. If the sheriff wanted to talk to Carson, he'd find a way.

Keeping my eyes on the mirror, I watched the sheriff follow Carson's lead. I hoped this was about Jocelyne, but something inside me knew it wasn't. Carson seemed on edge as well. He patted his chest down, looking for his wallet, and when I reached my hand across the cab and gripped his arm, I said, "Let me talk to him."

Carson met my gaze and I could see he was a little shaken

up. I figured he was afraid of learning more about what his daughter might have done, and I could understand if he was.

I said, "It might be about Nora."

Carson nodded like I might be right, but he surprised me with, "It's better if you stay in the vehicle. If this is about something else, I'd rather hear it directly from the horse's mouth."

I took a deep breath and reeled my hand back to my lap. Carson had a look in his eye that told me he had something he'd like to say. I watched him unbuckle his seatbelt and step out. After Carson shut his door, I cracked my window and kept my eyes on the mirror.

The sheriff met Carson at the rear of Carson's Cruiser and I heard Carson ask, "What can I do for you sheriff?"

"It occurred to me that you may have seen something you shouldn't have earlier when called out to Climbers trailhead."

"And what might that be?"

Carson was keeping his cool. I appreciated how easily he was able to hide his fears. I was thinking about the pair of black sneakers I saw and whether or not they were Nora's when the sheriff glanced through the back window and asked Carson, "Where are you coming from?"

"Why, Sheriff? Am I in some kind of trouble?"

"No. Nothing like that. I'm just trying to make sense of a few things."

"Is this about Nora?"

The sheriff was slow to respond as he studied Carson's every move. "After your search last night, did you go anywhere?"

I was starting to get a bad feeling about this, but Carson remained calm—even under a suspicious eye. Did Rachel say something after we left? Possibly, but I thought we had gotten past last night. With my hand to my lips I wondered how Carson was going to answer the sheriff's question.

Carson said to the sheriff, "Forgive me for asking, but why does it feel like I'm being put under the lights here?"

The sheriff turned his head and peered through the back window. "Is that Samantha Bell I see in the front seat?"

"That's right," Carson said. "She's with me. Same as before."

As soon as I heard my name, I opened my door and made my way to the back of the Cruiser. The sheriff locked eyes and he gave me a look like he knew I had been listening. Had this been his intention all along? To lure me out so he could shift the spotlight and make me sweat it out next.

"How are you doing, Ms. Bell?"

"Sheriff." I nodded and glanced at Carson as if looking for an explanation to what was happening. Neither of us could make sense of the situation but I asked the sheriff, "Everything all right?"

"Actually, no." His eyes were steady as he spoke. "I'm afraid my office has just received a harassment complaint."

I felt my blood pressure tick up a notch. I asked, "Against who?"

The sheriff was still staring at me when he said, "You."

Carson stepped in and immediately defended me. "This is wrong, Sheriff. I've been with Samantha the entire day. She's hasn't harassed anyone. I can attest to that."

"No offense, Mr. Reynolds. But you're not one to speak about harassment."

The sheriff's statement shocked us both as this turned personal. Though I appreciated Carson's defense, I was assuming the complaint had to have come from Rachel. Perhaps I was wrong and this was about my visit to Nora the other day. Either way, the sheriff was quick to make his point by indirectly warning me to step back and let off the gas.

I said, "At least tell me who made the complaint."

The sheriff's boots shifted on the dirt. He said, "You

know I'm not at liberty to say. But since we're here, let me ask you what you spoke to Nora about the morning before she disappeared."

Was she still missing? Or had she been found and mentioned my name in an interview?

"Don't answer that," Carson said before I had come up with a response.

Tensions were high. I suddenly felt like I was a suspect in her disappearance. I didn't like our odds. There was a lot of time between last night when we called quits on our search and this morning when we were called to the scene at Climbers trailhead, hours that were unaccounted for, an entire night I didn't even know where Carson was. Did the sheriff know that, too? I had to assume he did. What worried me more was what wasn't being said.

The sheriff squinted his eyes at me when he said, "It wasn't a friendly conversation, was it? You told her something she didn't want to hear. Isn't that right?" He paused and lowered his voice when he asked me, "At least tell me how Nora reacted to you confronting her outside her workplace."

Carson's hand landed on my shoulder and I flinched. The sheriff had me in his crosshairs and I stood there like a fool waiting for the kill shot to strike.

Carson said, "This conversation is over."

He turned me toward the car and pushed me toward the door. My knees were sticking and I kept waiting for the sheriff to find a reason to take me into custody. I knew I was innocent, but I felt guilty for Nora's sudden disappearance.

The sheriff called over my shoulder and slung a list of potential charges at my back—obstructing justice, harassment, and even trespassing—but none of them stuck. They were only meant to intimidate.

I stumbled on the dirt and my head started to spin as I asked myself who was feeding him my life and where I had been, who I had been speaking to. Inside my head, I filed through a list of names but nothing stuck out.

What the hell was happening and why did it feel like the sheriff was trying to drive me out of his county? There was something going on. And it felt like he was purposely blocking us from doing the job he refused to do himself.

Carson opened my door and I climbed into my seat as I heard the sheriff say to Carson, "You two behave yourselves, and stop harassing the peaceful citizens of Riverside County or I'll have to ask you to leave."

CHAPTER SIXTY-EIGHT

As soon as Carson climbed into the driver's seat he closed his eyes. He had the appearance he was praying and I wondered if he was. It had been quite a day for him already. First, the news that Jocelyne had murdered Barry; then being told to back off his daughter's case. Through it all, Carson's composure was pure confidence and I admired him for remaining as collected as he was.

I caught movement in the mirror and watched the sheriff turn around and head back the way he'd come. A gentle wave of relief swept over my shoulders now that he was gone. There was so much I wanted to say, so much I needed to ask Carson. What I couldn't get past, though, was that it seemed Rachel had accused me of harassment right after her apology.

When Carson opened his eyes, I asked, "Was Nora's restraining order against you meant to drive you out of town?"

Carson turned his head and gave my question some thought. "Of course it was. But I crossed a line with her and that's why the sheriff was here now."

"Are you sure? What was that about, us maybe seeing something we shouldn't have at Climbers trailhead?"

"It's just an excuse he's using to intimidate us into staying out of his investigation."

"Except the cases of Hemet Lake and Nora's disappearance are linked."

I could hear myself getting angry and felt embarrassed compared to Carson's calm demeanor. We had different backgrounds, different reasons for wanting to fight. Asking questions was what we did—what we would continue to do until an answer was found.

I said, "We can't stop just because of some unfounded claim of harassment."

Carson put the keys into the ignition and started the car. Checking his mirrors, he asked, "Is it obvious where we're headed?"

The thought had crossed my mind, too, and I wondered if the sheriff had somehow anticipated our next move. We had to assume he knew where we were going, especially if it was Rachel who made the harassment complaint, but we couldn't let it stop us. Not now. Not ever.

I said, "There's only one way to find out."

CHAPTER SIXTY-NINE

TWENTY MINUTES LATER WE ARRIVED AT BRENDEN Donaldson's secluded A-frame on a small, heavily wooded piece of land. Situated among large granite boulders, it had a magnificent view of the distant ridgeline.

"I didn't expect it to be so secluded," I said when Carson parked near the front of the house.

He said, "Neither did I."

We both looked around before exiting the vehicle. We met at the front of his car and I was quick to notice how quiet it was out here as the wind howled between the deep valleys. I always romanticized what it would be like to live alone in the woods. I wasn't sure I could do it myself, but apparently Brenden preferred the quiet life to a life filled with neighborhood barbeques.

The sheriff was on both of our minds when Carson said, "You check the house; I'll go around back."

I watched Carson disappear around the side as I climbed the creaking wooden staircase that led to the front door. I pulled open the screen door and knocked. A deep, wooden block sound echoed off the pines behind me. I waited a minute before knocking again. There was no answer when suddenly I heard Carson calling me to the back, telling me to hurry.

I jumped off the stairs and followed Carson's voice to the back of the house. He was standing in front of a ShelterLogic temporary garage. Inside was a dark blue Ford F-150 truck with an open bed on the back. I immediately started to study the deep treads on the tires.

Carson was curious to know what I thought. "Well?" he said. "Was this the truck who visited you the other night?"

I wished I knew. "I don't know," I said.

Carson entered the temporary garage and peeked inside the front cab of the truck.

"Anything?" I asked.

Carson shook his head no and turned his attention toward the back of the house. He stepped out and zipped up the door before making his way to the cabin. He peeked through some more windows and we both looked for any signs of Brenden.

"Maybe he has another car?" I suggested, thinking he was off at work or something.

"It's hard to see inside. If he is home, he would have heard us coming before we arrived."

I was certain Brenden wasn't home when suddenly I heard a dog bark. I stepped around the side of the house and saw a black lab sprinting down the driveway heading directly for us. Carson was steady on his feet and soon a man came jogging toward us, calling after his dog. When I got a good look at his face, I almost didn't believe it. He was the dog walker from Hemet Lake.

CHAPTER SEVENTY

BRENDEN CALLED HIS DOG, MOLLY, AND SHE WENT running back to him. He greeted us with a curious but friendly look. "I'm sorry if she jumped on you. She's still a puppy in training. I promise you she's not as mean as she sounds."

Carson introduced himself and said, "Nice place you have out here."

"I like it," Brenden flicked his gaze to the house, "but I can't say it gets too many visitors."

Brenden was friendly, if not a bit suspicious to who we were and what our intention was. He didn't seem nervous, which relaxed me about trusting Rachel for sending us here to speak to Brenden about his relationship with Nora.

I kept waiting for him to recognize me as my thoughts took me back to when I first saw him at Hemet Lake the day after Barry's car was pulled from the water. Brenden was the one who warned me Jocelyne and Barry were the lucky ones because they had been found, but how did he know who was inside the car that day?

After I gave him my business card and told him who we

were, Brenden tossed a stick to his dog and asked, "So, what brings you out to no man's land?"

"Rachel Sweeney sent us."

The friendly crinkle around Brenden's eyes vanished and his body language changed. "You spoke to Rachel?"

"Just a little while ago." Brenden said something about how he wished Rachel would have warned him we were coming, and I said, "Would you prefer us to leave?"

Molly was back with the stick and Brenden snatched it away and tossed it into the woods, this time a little further. "Only if you're here about something other than Nora."

"We're worried about her, too," I said.

Brenden shifted his eyes to Carson, then back to me. He said, "Nora just doesn't disappear for more than a few hours without letting someone know where she's going. And, contrary to what you might have heard, Nora isn't a liar."

"When was the last time you saw her?" I asked.

"I'm not a suspect, and I've already told the sheriff everything I know. I guess it hasn't been enough. Disappearances have become too normal around here."

Brenden's story hadn't changed from the first time we had met before Nora disappeared. What else did he know? What could he tell us that might lead us to Nora?

I wondered what his take was on the sheriff, if he believed they were serious about finding Nora. But I didn't know their relationship and didn't want to chance having another harassment claim come against us. Instead, I said, "The other day you said something to me at the lake."

"I remember," Brenden said, not missing a beat.

"How did you know the sheriff would find two victims inside the car?"

Brenden's eyes lit up. "Has it been confirmed?"

"Unofficially," I said. Brenden held my stare when I asked, "Did you know Barry Tate?"

Brenden assured me he knew where I was going with this and said, "I have only lived here for the past six years, but I've heard enough to know no one in Idyllwild misses Barry Tate. But it was Nora who told me she believed he was in the vehicle along with another young woman she had met who had also gone missing around the same time."

"That girl was my daughter," Carson said, stepping forward to show Brenden the photograph of his daughter with Nora.

"I'm sorry," Brenden said solemnly as he stared at the picture.

Carson asked, "Do you recognize the house they're at?"

I knew it was a stretch, but it was worth asking. Brenden said he didn't and I followed up with another question. "Did Nora ever tell you what happened that night?"

"I can't speak for Nora, but I do know she was at Barry's house." Brenden turned to Carson and said, "Apparently your daughter had too much to drink that night and the men they were with took things too far."

Carson didn't ask for details, and neither did I. We both knew what Brenden was insinuating. "Who were they with?" I asked

Brenden shook his head and said he didn't know. "Nora never said, and I only asked once because she made it clear that it was too dangerous for her to tell me. But I do know this: somehow they found themselves at Barry Tate's house and, at some point in the night, a fight broke out."

"Between who?"

Again, Brenden didn't know. He said, "Nora was scared and left."

Was this when she had left Jocelyne behind? I assumed it was.

As if reading the expressions on our faces, Brenden said, "What you have to understand is I only recently learned this about Nora. She obviously has wanted to keep this a secret for a reason."

"When did she tell you this? And did she tell anyone else?"

"Just recently. Like, a week before Barry's car was found." Molly was begging for her stick to get tossed but Brenden didn't seem to recognize her panting at his feet. He continued, "And just the other day she said since Barry was now for sure dead, she was going back to the sheriff with evidence proving who killed him."

"Are you suggesting Nora was scared of Barry?"

"Like you wouldn't believe. I always got the feeling Nora was looking over her shoulder as if Barry was coming after her." Brenden then said to Carson, "She never saw your daughter after that night."

"Why did she tell you all this?" I asked.

"She trusted me. We both love art, the mountains, bluegrass. Everything that makes living out here worthwhile. Nora could be bubbly and full of joy, but there was a dark side to her. A damaged past. She found refuge in me because I was the only one who believed she had something great to share with the world. I encouraged her to end her nearly two decade grief and stop living in fear. So maybe I'm partially responsible for what happened."

"What do you think happened to her?"

Brenden turned his head and let his gaze travel deep into the forest. "I really don't know. I've checked everywhere Nora likes to hike, sit, and get away from it all. I've even left numerous voicemails hoping she'll surprise me and call me back. But the longer she's missing, the more responsible I feel for her disappearance."

I stared at Brenden, getting the sense I could trust what he said even if his words could be interpreted as an admission to guilt. Without question, his concern was genuine and I felt bad for him. He'd lost a friend and blamed himself for something he had no control over. These wheels were set in motion years before he arrived in the county. I couldn't help but think, *Barry might be dead, but whoever killed them all certainly wasn't.*

Carson asked, "Can you prove what you said today is actually true?"

Brenden didn't seem offended as he told us to wait outside. A minute later he came back with a house key. He put it in Carson's palm and said it was a key to Nora's house.

"I can't promise you'll find anything," Brenden said, finally tossing Molly her stick, "but Nora led me to believe she's kept proof of what happened, evidence inside her house she planned on giving the sheriff. Maybe you'll find what you're looking for there."

CHAPTER SEVENTY-ONE

IT DIDN'T TAKE MORE THAN TEN MINUTES TO MAKE OUR way back to Nora's house. The silvery sedan was still parked out front, looking lonely and cold, and the neighborhood was as quiet as before.

I hadn't noticed it earlier, but I did now. Back with a fresh set of eyes, Nora's house was the exception on the block—the only house that seemed to not be falling apart. Whoever her landlord was took care of the place, and it showed.

I was nervous to be here. All roads kept bringing us back. I suspected Brenden knew what he was talking about, but I didn't like how Carson was so close to the person who had once put a restraining order on him.

"We don't have to do this," I said to Carson.

"Yes we do."

I heard the determination in his voice and I wasn't going to argue. This was Carson's decision, something he had been waiting for, a long time. I wanted to get inside as badly as he did and, if what Brenden suggested was true, the key to finding out what happened rested on the other side of those walls.

Carson stuck his fingers into his pocket and retrieved the silver house key. He held it between his fingers, stroking the metal as he stared, seeming to come up with a plan to do this right. There was a lot happening inside my head as well. I wanted to clear Jocelyne's name as much as he did, but we couldn't make a mistake that would stop our pursuit.

I asked Carson, "If Brenden knew Nora was keeping proof of what happened, and had the names of the men she was with, why hasn't he bothered to look himself after he learned Nora was missing?"

Carson lifted his gaze and met my eye when he said, "Would you have?"

It wasn't an easy answer. I was used to taking risks, regularly putting myself in the path of danger. Could Brenden be as courageous? It didn't seem likely, especially when considering this might be the reason people were getting killed.

"He's scared," Carson murmured. "Knows people have been murdered over this."

"He didn't look scared."

"Men don't give visual clues like women do."

I raised an eyebrow and asked, "Do I look scared?"

Carson shook his head no, but said, "You sound scared."

"Because I am," I admitted. "What if this is a setup? A part of me thinks it is. Another part of me wants to go to the sheriff and tell him what Brenden told us. I'm assuming Brenden hasn't told the sheriff everything."

Carson shifted in his seat and squared his shoulders. "You do remember the conversation we just had with the sheriff, don't you?"

"How could I forget? He threatened to charge us with trespassing. It's like he knew we would be offered Nora's house key and would come back here." Carson was staring into my eyes when I said, "We're already being watched. If we go inside that house, there is no turning back."

"It isn't against the law; we have the key. And it's not like we're robbing the place," Carson reasoned.

"No, it's not. But if someone sees us and the town finds out about it, everyone will think we're responsible for her disappearance."

Carson opened his car door and said, "Then let's just hope she isn't found dead."

CHAPTER SEVENTY-TWO

I COULDN'T LET CARSON GO IN ALONE, BUT WE HAD TO BE smart about this. My heart was pounding loudly in my ears as I inhaled a deep breath to steel my nerves before they managed to get the best of me.

"Let's at least try to make it seem like we were never here," I said, zipping up my jacket and tucking my hair inside the collar.

We both put on winter gloves and Carson tossed me a dark, knitted winter hat to wear.

As soon as I closed the car door, I glanced around to see who might be watching. Was anyone? I couldn't tell, but it was safer to assume we'd been seen. It felt like we were dressed in tactical gear and were here to rob the place.

I followed Carson to the front door where he quickly unlocked it with the key Brenden had given us. Carson looked me in the eye and turned the doorknob. I was the first to enter the house and, as soon as Carson was inside, we shut the door and took a look around.

Nora lived comfortably. The inside was as nice as the outside. On the surface, she didn't own anything fancy or expensive looking, but her house wasn't empty, either. There was a pair of nice vinyl couches and modern furniture, including a flat screen TV mounted onto the living room wall. The paint looked as fresh as the carpet and, ironically, it didn't smell like cigarette smoke. Did Nora own these things, or did she rent this place fully-furnished?

With my back against the door, I thought how this was what I had wanted—to get inside, conduct a quick sweep, then get out with whatever information we could gather before anyone knew we were ever here.

"You take the living room, I'll take the kitchen. We'll meet somewhere in the middle," Carson said.

"Let's just be sure to make this quick."

We went to work and it didn't take me long to see that Nora's house hadn't been searched or treated as a crime scene. It was encouraging for our purposes, but I was also worried that no one had bothered to search her place for clues to where she might have gone off to. Was that done on purpose, or were we barking up the wrong tree?

As soon as I began searching through Nora's things, a strange feeling fell over me. Something about it didn't feel right, but what choice did we have? This was our best option at learning more about the person who seemed to know everything. I kept searching, ignoring the feeling that we were doing something wrong.

I heard Carson in the kitchen, opening and shutting draw-ers. I slowly padded through the living room, appreciating the home Nora had built for herself. It was simple but cozy with a few house plants growing up the walls near the windows, and lots of paintings and artwork to fill in the empty white space. If she had done these, she was extremely talented.

I paused to look over my shoulder. The house seemed lived-in but there was no sign of a struggle, like if she had been attacked. Nothing of value seemed to have been taken—

her electronics were all in plain view. Women's magazines had been left open, the TV clicker on the coffee table next to a smudged water glass. What happened, Nora? Where did you run off to? She may have left in a hurry, but was she taken?

Carson said from the kitchen counter, "She kept your business card."

I turned to look, wondering if I should take it back, but it was useless. The sheriff already knew I had talked with Nora. Was that why he was following us today? Had he come here and seen that as well?

Carson continued opening drawers as I checked out Nora's bathroom. The counters were filled with beauty products, a hair drier and curlers. There was a half-empty tube of toothpaste and a single tooth brush. There weren't any signs to lead me to believe she had a boyfriend or anyone staying with her. The more I got a feel for the woman she was, the more I hoped she would just come home, proving to us all it was only a misunderstanding. But when I left the bathroom and turned to her bedroom, I stopped dead in my tracks.

"Carson," I called behind me, "you're going to want to come see this."

CHAPTER SEVENTY-THREE

CARSON HURRIED TO THE BACK OF THE HOUSE AND CAME into Nora's bedroom. He stopped just as fast as I had and, without looking at him, I pointed to the adjacent wall. Carson's eyes immediately began to water.

It was a watercolor painting, perched on an easel, of two young women sitting on the mountainside watching the sunrise with an outcropping of granite off in the distance. It was of Nora and Jocelyne. There was no doubt in my mind that's who it was, but was this the evidence Brenden had spoken about? It couldn't be; there had to be something more concrete.

Carson stepped around me and skirted around the queen sized bed tucked into the far corner of the room. He stood in front of the painting for a minute, just staring at it, before taking it off the easel and into his own hands. I didn't object. He was grieving and deserved to do it his way.

Carson took a step back and sat on the edge of the bed, continuing to mourn over the painting. After another minute, I watched him gently touch the woman we both believed to be Jocelyne with the tip of his index finger. Then he broke my heart when he whispered, "Please, Samantha. Can I have a minute alone?"

Quietly, I turned and closed the door on my way out. As I walked back to the kitchen, I heard him start to cry. It was a painfully awful sound that had my own insides bursting with sadness. As difficult as it was to listen to him hurt so bad, I knew there had to be more than this.

Who were the men Nora had told Brenden about? Was Brenden even telling us the truth? If so, how many men were there? Two? Three? Maybe more? Just when I thought this case couldn't get more complicated, it did. If there were more than two men linked to the murders that night, it could explain why the town wanted us gone. Too many people were working against us to keep the truth hidden.

I kept looking for something to light my path. No matter where I looked or how deeply I dug, I kept coming up with nothing. Nora didn't keep a journal, or at least I couldn't find it. There were no photographs like the one Jocelyne had sent Carson to give us at least an idea who was at that same party —or who, if anyone, was currently in her life. Not even Brenden.

I was growing frustrated as I stuck my head deep into a cupboard, finding it strange she lived in such a nice place for someone believed to only be scraping by. I needed to find something more than a painting. Carson come into the kitchen and said, "It reminds me of the view from Brenden's place."

I knew he was referring to the sunrise in the painting. I fell back on my heels and said, "Yeah, it kind of does, doesn't it?"

"But it doesn't prove anything."

I shook my head and told him about my failed search efforts. We were both starting to worry about the time. We'd been here too long already and knew we should get going.

Carson agreed and, just when I was about to give up, I received a text message from Erin saying she would be arriving later than expected.

On our way out the door, I promised to email my notes to Erin later tonight for her to review. I then put my cellphone back into my pants pocket and relayed her message to Carson.

"Erin won't be here until tomorrow morning at the earliest." Carson's eyes drifted from my face and his mouth drooped into a frown. "How about I take you out to dinner?" I said. "Maybe get a beer at the bar and grill?"

"That's nice of you, but I need to make some calls and let my family know I've finally found Jocelyne."

CHAPTER SEVENTY-FOUR

"DADDY, KEEP YOUR EYES CLOSED."

"They're closed," Lefty insisted, squeezing his eyes shut.

When he felt the brush touch his bottom lip he puckered his mouth and listened to his two girls giggle. They had convinced him to have a tea party with them, leaving out the part about dressing up—and that included wearing makeup.

Lefty sat patiently on the floor, wrapped in a brightly colored shawl, and several beaded necklaces dangling around his neck. Now his oldest daughter applied lipstick to complete the look.

"Now, can I open my eyes?" he asked.

"Almost."

Lefty's wife walked into the room and stifled a laugh. Lefty peeked one eye open and said to his wife, "Please. Don't shatter my confidence."

"You look great honey."

Lefty smiled and knew his wife was the only woman he'd ever truly love. He said to her, "I'm really beginning to feel like my true self."

His wife beamed with happiness. She was a family woman

who loved her husband and daughters more than anything—
even if she had to forgive her husband sometimes for working
so much. But she was grateful for all he provided and knew he
worked so much to give his daughters the childhood neither
of them had had.

"All done," his daughter said, turning to her mother.
"Doesn't daddy look nice?"

"Very pretty," her mother said.

Lefty reached for a plastic tea cup and brought it to his
lips, making sure to stick his pinky finger straight into the air
as he pretended to sip his imaginary tea. There was more
laughter and it didn't stop until the dog started to bark.

Lefty immediately stood and turned his attention to the
front door. The dog was still barking when Lefty peeked
through the curtains.

"Who is it?" his wife inquired.

"It's only Rip." Lefty told his dog to be quiet. The dog
whimpered in protest, his tail swishing through the air.

"You going to let him see you looking like that?"

"Like what?" Lefty tilted his head to one shoulder. "A
princess?"

His wife laughed. "Never mind." She turned away. "Girls,
time to get ready for bed."

The girls protested their bedtime as Lefty wished them a
goodnight before stepping outside to meet Rip near the front
step. Rip moved to the edge of the floodlight and gave him an
awkward look but didn't say anything.

Lefty hurried to him. "Jesus, what the hell is the matter
with you? My wife and kids are sleeping."

Rip opened his mouth but nothing came out. His eyes
followed the necklace to the center of Lefty's chest and Lefty
began laughing.

"I'm only kidding with you. Christ, lighten up, will you?"

Rip was giving him a funny look when he asked, "Are you wearing lipstick?"

Lefty made a fist and set his jaw as he lunged in front of Rip's face. "Do you have a problem with it?"

Rip stepped back and stared before lighting up a smoke. Pulling at his collar, Lefty motioned for him to follow. They moved away from the house and Lefty tipped his head back to gaze up into the sky.

"The stars are out tonight," he said.

"So what is it you wanted to tell me?" Rip asked.

Still staring up into the sky, Lefty thought about the text message he had sent and said, "Remember how I told you about that reporter, Samantha Bell?"

Rip blew out a cloud of smoke. "I remember."

"Well, I've come up with a plan to get rid of her."

"I told you, I'm not doing this anymore." Rip inhaled more smoke. "And didn't you tell me earlier you would be doing the heavy lifting from now on?"

"Would you just listen for one second?" Lefty cursed. "Shit, I swear, you're worse than a woman." Lefty stared for a beat, then said, "Now listen, this is how it has to get done." After explaining his plan to Rip, Lefty asked, "Do you understand?"

Rip's eyes sparkled beneath the starry sky. He flashed a big toothy grin and said, "Lefty, you're a bloody genius."

CHAPTER SEVENTY-FIVE

I WOKE SUDDENLY IN THE MIDDLE OF NIGHT TO THE SOUND of a large truck revving its engine just outside my bedroom window. Too afraid to move, I didn't lift a muscle. It continued to roar as loudly as a jet engine, shaking the windows in their panes. My heart pounded and my eyes blurred as I tried to decide whether or not to look out the window.

No doubt they were here for me, but who was it?

I twisted onto my stomach and reached for the window sill. As soon as my fingers curled over the ledge, I pulled myself up and peeked out the window. It was as dark as a blackhole and impossible to see. The engine revved louder and then suddenly headlights flicked on as if knowing I was there.

I quickly ducked behind the wall as my entire bedroom was lit up in a bright white light. I laid there debating what to do next—asking myself if there was anything I could do. Had they seen me? It didn't matter, they obviously knew I was inside. But who were they? Was I right to assume they knew

Carson and I were getting close to finding out their secret? It seemed likely.

As I looked for my clothes, my thoughts jumped to Brenden, Nora's house key, and his blue Ford F-150. It was a big, mean truck. Possibly the same one that had visited me the night I arrived. If it was Brenden outside, why was he stalking me?

Another loud roar of the engine shook the walls and I rolled out of bed. I quickly put on my jeans and slipped a t-shirt over my head. The room was still lit up and, when I peeked outside again, I squinted into the lights hoping to see who was behind the wheel.

"Who are you? What do you want from me?" I said aloud.

The wall of light was impenetrable. I couldn't see who was driving, nor what color or type of vehicle it was. The engine kept revving, roaring like a lion. Then, as if knowing I was staring, the engine thundered and the truck aggressively lurched closer to the house.

Thinking they might drive through the front door, I instinctively crouched down and crawled across the floor until I found my cellphone on the nightstand. Leaving the bedroom, I kept my head down as I hurried into the kitchen. It occurred to me there might be more than one person outside and I remained on the lookout for signs of someone on foot.

The stove clock was off, so was the microwave. The power seemed to be out. Was it cut on purpose? I pressed my back up against the wall and flicked on a light switch. Nothing happened. Feeling trapped, the only light I had came from the truck outside. When I saw my cellphone was dead too, I cursed.

Feeling like my options were running dry, I was scared someone was coming after me. If I didn't do something about it quickly, I could meet the same fate as Nora. Then, to my surprise, the headlights clicked off and I heard the truck kick up dirt as it sped away from the cabin.

CHAPTER SEVENTY-SIX

LEFTY WAS PARKED UP THE HILL AT ONE OF THE EMPTY cottages, waiting for Rip to message. He'd since washed off the lipstick, shed the shawl and necklaces, and changed back into his flannel shirt. It was nearly three in the morning and the world around him was quiet.

Hunting hours, he thought as he yawned.

Palming his cellphone, he expected to hear from Rip any minute. His wife didn't ask questions when he said he was going out. She knew the business, knew that sometimes work had to be done at night. There was nothing unusual about him leaving the house tonight, but what he was hoping to accomplish was extraordinary.

Hoping his first plan would work, he then had to do something about Nora. He couldn't hang on to her forever, not when the entire town was looking for her. It wasn't going to be easy, certainly not like it had been with Barry Tate's Aston Martin. Lefty had a plan to get rid of her, even if it was a risky one.

Lefty unlocked his cellphone and navigated to Samantha's blog, Real Crime News. The last post hadn't been since last week, but Lefty knew that could change at any moment. Samantha was hot on his trail. Since meeting with Rip a few hours ago, Lefty's mind had become obsessed with this reporter who couldn't keep her nose out of other people's affairs. He'd be happy to see her gone and hoped that tonight she'd finally get the message that it wasn't safe for her to stay.

Another yawn and stretch, and Lefty cast his gaze to the cottage he knew Carson Reynolds had rented out for the week. He suspected he might be staying here, and it was easy to confirm once he made a few phone calls. Everyone in Idyllwild always knew where the outsiders were staying, especially in shoulder season—a time when tourists were an increasingly rare sight.

He still couldn't get over the irony of Carson's striking resemblance to the late Gavin Bell. That couldn't be coincidence. Lefty wondered if there was an attraction there. If perhaps Carson was the reason Samantha stayed in California to investigate the case? Even if it was a stretch of his imagination, Lefty knew the type of woman he liked and rarely strayed too far. Was Samantha the same? He was counting his luck she was because, if Samantha proved him wrong, Rip would be the first to strike down his genius.

Lefty's cellphone buzzed. It was a message from Rip.

Scared the mouse out of the house. Hopefully she comes your way.

Lefty grinned when he reached for his digital Canon camera with telephoto lens and prepared to catch the little mouse in his trap.

CHAPTER SEVENTY-SEVEN

I KNEW I DIDN'T HAVE A LOT OF TIME. I WASN'T convinced my tormentor had left the cabin. A part of me worried they were luring me into a trap where they would then surprise me just when I thought I was free. But I couldn't stay here, either.

Taking my chances, I got up off the floor and quickly packed everything up, preparing to leave, planning to never come back.

The house was pitch black and I kept thinking I was going to leave something important behind. I tried the lights but there still wasn't any power. Minutes later, I was outside, tossing my luggage into the backseat of my car. It was quiet and I was sure I was alone. There was only one way off this mountain and I was afraid of what lay ahead.

As soon as I was behind the wheel, I locked myself inside my car and plugged in my cellphone to charge the battery. Then I backed out and sped down the hill, heading into town.

I was still trying to make sense of what happened, trying to put a face to who kept coming up the mountain to torment me. Keeping my eyes peeled, I wondered where they'd gone, if they were waiting for me or had decided they had done enough to scare the shit out of me.

I flicked my gaze to the rearview mirror, expecting headlights to suddenly appear, but nothing was there. It was just me and my thoughts drifting back to the day Hineman set up my stay at the cabin. Questioning everything, I wondered who owned this place, who else knew I was staying here?

There was no doubt tonight's experience was connected to the tracks I saw in the driveway dirt the other day, but was it also who nearly ran me off the road the first night I was in town? As much as I didn't want to admit it, it seemed likely. Whoever was here tonight had been on me long before I knew they even existed.

Soon, I came within sight of the town streetlights. I turned on my phone and called Carson as I drove.

"C'mon, answer your phone," I said as the line rang and rang.

Carson never answered. I got his voicemail, hung up, and dialed again. I wondered if something had happened to him, if the person who was just at my house went to his next. I hoped he was just a deep sleeper, but my mind was running wild.

"Pick up. Carson, please pick up. It's important."

Relief swept over me when a sleepy Carson finally answered.

"They came after me," I said.

"Who came after you?"

"I don't know, but they were just at the cabin." Dale Tanner crossed my mind as I told Carson what happened. I was speaking a hundred miles per hour, trying to catch up to my thoughts. "It's totally insane, but have they come for you?"

Carson perked up and I heard him moving through his

rental cottage. "Listen to me, Samantha. You need to drive straight to my place. Got it? Come here where it's safe."

I stomped on the gas and couldn't get there quick enough. I checked my mirrors and said, "Thank you."

"Don't thank me yet. Just get here as quickly as you can."

CHAPTER SEVENTY-EIGHT

As soon as I was off the phone with Carson, an eerie feeling fell over me. I had a strange sense I was being followed but, when I checked my mirrors, they were clear. I was certain I was alone—the only one on the road—as I kept thinking about Brenden and his truck. Though I didn't want to believe he was responsible for tonight's scare, I had to at least think it was possible.

I wound my way up the hillside and found Carson waiting outside his one bedroom cottage. I parked behind his Cruiser and, as soon as I opened my door, Carson reached for my luggage. He took a bag under his arm and then reached for my hand. He pulled me out of the car, I locked it with the fob as he led me inside the cottage. Carson locked the front door and immediately asked if I had been followed.

"I don't think so," I said.

"Tell me again what happened."

I rehashed the same story I had told him on the phone. Carson hit me with a series of questions that didn't seem to stop. What did the engine sound like? How high off the ground did the truck sit? What color was it? Did it have an open or closed bed? I kept shaking my head, wishing I had an answer to give him, but I lacked the detail we both knew we needed.

Carson glided across the floor and peeked behind the front blinds. As he leaned forward, his shirt lifted above his waist and I saw that he was carrying. I didn't want it to have to come to that, but I liked knowing we had something to defend ourselves with if the need ever came.

Feeling lightheaded, I found my way to the couch and sat down with my elbows rooted onto my knees. I stared at my feet, wishing there was something more I could have done. Whoever came tonight spooked me pretty good. I was thankful to have Carson invite me in where we could find safety in numbers.

Carson held still at the window for another fifteen minutes before he stepped away and opened the closet, bringing a spare pillow and blanket to the couch. He said, "You can have the bed. I'll sleep here."

"No," I said, reaching for the bedding. "You stay where you are. I'll sleep on the couch."

CHAPTER SEVENTY-NINE

BRENDEN DONALDSON KEPT MOVING, ONE FOOT IN FRONT of the other, as a way to fight off the shiver threatening to move up his body as he hiked in the cold morning air. His dog, Molly, was out in front of him and the last of the night's stars shone above them.

He tried to not think about last night but it proved to be impossible. Each step closer to the high mountain meadow had him thinking about Nora. He knew she was dead and would never be coming home. It was tough for him to accept. He wished it had never come to this. Now that it was over, his eyes watered as he marched forward in a final tribute to a friend he dearly respected.

Molly zig-zagged on and off the trail. Brenden moved faster as a way to distract his tired thoughts. He needed to get to the meadow before the sun reared its face over the distant ridgeline, but fatigue was settling in. It had been an especially emotional twenty-four hours. He kept on marching, inhaling the scent of earth and pine and deep seeded memories of hiking with Nora.

He knew the search for his friend had concentrated their

efforts in this area without anything to show for it. There was no denying a weight had been lifted when he decided to hand Nora's house key off to private investigator Carson Reynolds, but at what cost? He relinquished his rights and was now wondering what about his own past had Carson dug up.

The trail curved over the hillside and Brenden meandered through the trees. Once at the top, Brenden spotted the meadow he had remembered from his time hiking with Nora. Some time had passed since he was last here, but it looked the same as he remembered.

Molly darted through the golden grass that reminded him of Nora's beautiful hair and, as Brenden called Molly to his side, he said, "We're here, girl. This will be our home for the next few hours."

Molly's tail wagged. He set his pack down, retrieved his water bottle, and poured a cup to give to his dog. As Molly licked up her drink, Brenden unzipped his pack and took the camera out. Holding it with his right hand, he found an area near a flat spot and clicked the camera base onto the tripod. Six years in Idyllwild had all come down to this. Capturing a single impression on the morning he'd never forget.

It felt good to be outside; good to be alive, inhaling clean air with Molly sitting next to him. He put his arm around her neck and pointed across the valley. "You see that, Molly? That's Suicide Rock."

Molly panted and stared, her tongue dangling out the side of her mouth.

"It's important to our story," Brenden said, informing Molly of the details. "If anyone asks, you can tell them this is where it started."

Molly barked and Brenden laughed.

As the sky faded from black to morning pastels, his anticipation grew. Brenden was on his feet, preparing the settings on his digital camera to capture the perfect shot. He couldn't miss it. When the sun crested the horizon, Brenden's shutter clicked furiously, making sure to capture the entire sunrise.

"I'm here, Nora," he whispered into the breeze. "This meadow, this mountain, will forever me *ours*."

Brenden closed his eyes and soaked in the warmth from the sun as he said a prayer inside his head.

Shine down upon me. Forgive me, for I have sinned. Tears fell from his eyes as he thought the words. *It wasn't supposed to be like this. I wish I could have done more. I failed you and I'm sorry for that.*

Brenden's knees buckled and he collapsed forward. With his face in the dirt and the sun warming his back, he unzipped the breast pocket of his coat and reached for the photograph of Nora and Jocelyne sitting in the exact spot where he was now weeping.

CHAPTER EIGHTY

I WOKE THE NEXT MORNING TO THE MUFFLED SOUND OF MY cellphone vibrating in my pants pocket. The sound worked itself into my dreams before I remembered how I ended up sleeping on Carson's couch. It had been such a wild night, one I wouldn't forget no matter how hard I tried.

I tossed my feet to the floor and pushed myself into a sitting position, quick to notice I was still wearing the same clothes I had arrived in. Combing my fingers through my tangled hair, I felt a bit groggy as I fumbled to retrieve my phone as I glanced in the direction I knew Carson to be sleeping. His bedroom door was closed and, judging by the light pushing past the edges of the curtains in the living room, I assumed it to be early morning.

I glanced at the device still buzzing in my hand. I didn't recognize the California number when I answered with a whisper, "Hello, this is Samantha Bell."

"Samantha, it's Brenden. Sorry to be calling so early; I hope it's not a problem."

My expression pinched with worry at his tone. Because he

was calling me at such an early hour, I assumed something bad had happened.

"It's fine," I said. "Tell me what's going on. Is everything all right?"

"I don't know how to say this, but I found Nora."

I sprang to my feet, feeling optimistic Nora might still be alive. "You found her? Where?"

When he told me, a funny feeling moved to the pit of my stomach. Then Brenden started to cry when he said, "She's dead, Samantha. Someone killed her."

CHAPTER EIGHTY-ONE

IT WAS AWFUL.

Our worst fear had come true.

If Brenden was right.

Nora had been murdered. But it was where Brenden discovered her body that had me most worried. What was he doing out there at such an early hour? How could we have missed the clues ourselves? It didn't add up. I hated to predict what the sheriff would think of us now.

I stood and raced across the floor, banging my fist on Carson's bedroom door. "Carson, wake up. I just received a call from Brenden." I heard him stir awake. "Hurry, wake up. We need to go *now*."

Heavy footsteps traveled across the floor and then the wooden door swung open. Carson stood in only his white boxer briefs with sleep in his eyes. "What did you say?"

Doing my best to keep my eyes above his shoulders, I told him what I just learned and watched his eyes light up. He hurried to dress. A minute later we were leaving his cottage and jumping into my car.

"Brenden's still at the scene," I said, backing out and

turning my wheels toward the main road. "The police just arrived. If we hurry we can catch it all before they close the road."

Carson asked for details and I gave him only what I knew. It wasn't much, but it was enough for us both to question why and how Brenden was the person to find Nora.

"He said he was in the area to take photographs of the sunrise, and on his way down the mountain Molly got ahead of him. That's when he discovered Nora's body."

Carson was quiet for a beat as he thought. Then he said, "He didn't see her on the way up? How is that possible?"

It didn't make sense to me, either. "Too dark I guess."

"But Molly would have picked up the scent."

I kept a firm hand on the steering wheel as we debated what might have happened. Either Nora's body was dumped after Brenden had already headed up the trail, or he was the one responsible and was making it look like he wasn't.

That same strange feeling I had last night was back. All I could hear myself asking was: was Brenden responsible? Had he led us astray on purpose?

If he'd never given us Nora's house key, I wouldn't believe he would be capable of murder. But he did, and that simple act changed everything I originally thought about him.

Worse, apparently Nora had been found in the exact location we had searched only days prior. This was no accident. But how did the killer know?

Carson seemed to read my mind. "The sheriff isn't going to like us being there."

"Maybe it's exactly what he wants," I said, thinking how it was only yesterday the sheriff called Carson out to the scene to tell him his daughter was a murderer.

My mind raced to understand what was happening. All I could think about was the black sneakers I saw marked in the grass as evidence. Were they Nora's or someone else's? It was early and my brain was a little foggy from my lack of sleep but we had to assume the location of her body wasn't exact.

Carson said, "If Nora was there yesterday, she would have been found."

"Why didn't we see anything?" I asked. "Why didn't the sheriff?"

Carson didn't have an answer, and neither did I. We couldn't explain it. Soon, Carson shifted the conversation to what happened to me last night. "Let's say Nora's body wasn't there yesterday, then whoever was responsible for her murder needed to know they could dump the body without anyone seeing."

"Okay," I said, thinking of last night's incident and how frightened I was to be out at the cabin all alone. I caught on to what Carson was thinking and said, "They would need to make sure we were together. And nowhere near that trail."

Carson gave me a knowing look. "Exactly. Which makes me think that whoever killed Nora scared you straight to me. Why? So they could keep tabs on both of us to make sure they could kill Nora and dump her where everyone knows we've been searching, without any witnesses."

"Which then means there might not be one killer, but two."

Carson inhaled a deep breath and said, "Let's hope it's not more."

CHAPTER EIGHTY-TWO

IT FELT LIKE FOREVER SINCE ERIN HAD BEEN TO IDYLLWILD. Nearly thirteen years, to be exact, and she had thought at the time maybe she wouldn't ever be back. Then the news of her father came and Erin knew she had little choice but to come and read the reports herself—maybe even sign off on his death and make it official.

She was nervous and far too anxious to be traveling for hours on end just to get to her destination. First, the plane ride from Denver, then the overnight in Los Angeles, and now the two hour road trip east. At least the sky was clear, Erin thought, wishing she could enjoy the incredible views. Instead, her mind was stuck on her father's supposed murder. She wasn't sure if she should cry or be afraid of all the things that weren't being said.

The tires hummed on the pavement and Erin soon zoned out to the mantra in her mind.

She still couldn't believe how Samantha had found her way to Idyllwild and managed to work her way into the investigation of her father's murder. Erin knew it wasn't by mistake. Some power greater than themselves had brought her full circle, knowing that she could only do this with someone like Sam.

But Erin knew her presence would complicate things and worried what old baggage would be waiting for her upon her arrival. There was a lot of it—secrets Erin hoped had been long forgotten. It was naïve of her to think they'd be gone. She'd never mentioned any of it to Sam before because of all the baggage and emotions that came with it. Now, Erin was thinking maybe that had been a mistake.

Erin turned on the radio, hoping music would distract her cluttered mind. It didn't work. When she couldn't find a station she liked, she went back to driving in silence.

Again, she thought about what Samantha had written in her report and still couldn't believe her father's Aston Martin had been discovered. In a complete turn of fate, after all these years, her father's car was practically hiding in plain sight.

Erin recalled her own search many years ago and wasn't at all surprised to learn her father's car hadn't gone further than a few miles from home. But Lake Hemet was the last place she would have thought to look, and now she wanted to know how his car ended up there. She supposed that was the reason Sam stayed to investigate. Erin could only hope that now that her father and his car had been found, she wouldn't continually be blamed for something she didn't do.

The sun crested the rugged mountain horizon and reminded her of the beauty of this place. A part of her wanted to see her father's old house, take a trip down memory lane; another part told her to convene with Samantha and get on with the investigation so they could get the hell out of here as soon as possible.

But Erin wasn't naïve. She knew this wasn't going to be as

easy as ticking off a few check marks. There was more to this story than most knew—including her—but maybe if they pooled their resources, they could close the chapter on what had been the nightmare of her life.

When the road descended into Mountain Center, Erin stopped at the light, turned left on Green, and continued traveling north to Idyllwild.

The butterflies in her stomach fluttered. Only a few miles to go before she'd have to deal with the other obstacle Samantha had warned her about: Carson Reynolds.

All Erin could remember was how poorly they got along. When her father had first disappeared, Carson blamed her for not telling him the truth about her father. He accused her of doing things she didn't and said a lot of nasty things, things that were simply not true. Then again, so did the town. But when trails went cold and nothing was ever found, Carson then accused her father of murdering his daughter and Carson led Erin to believe that was the real reason Barry had disappeared—suggesting he skipped town to avoid getting caught.

"How the tables have turned," Erin said aloud.

Would she ask Carson to apologize? Or could she forgive and forget like Samantha had asked her to? Was it even possible Jocelyne was someone who could murder? Erin couldn't decide. Two people were dead—had been dead for a very long time—and only now was the truth coming out.

As soon as she got into town, a sheriff's vehicle sped toward her with its lightbars flashing and siren blaring. Erin pulled to the side of the road and watched as the vehicle turned onto a side road, heading off in the direction of Suicide Rock. Her instinct was to follow, to see what news was breaking. Then she remembered the notes from Sam and, with Suicide Rock looming in the distance, Erin's gut told her this had something to do with her father's investigation and the woman Sam said had disappeared.

Erin stomped her foot down on the gas and raced to catch up with the sheriff, even if she wasn't ready to face the department who apparently still blamed her for her father's murder.

CHAPTER EIGHTY-THREE

CARSON WAS STARING OUT HIS WINDOW AS I FOLLOWED THE road up the mountain. I kept my speed up around the corners, making sure we arrived before we missed anything important. Neither of us spoke as we mentally prepared ourselves for the worst. The last thing either of us wanted was for someone else to die for something that should have ended long ago.

Around the next bend, Carson moved his hand away from his face and straightened his back. We both saw it at the same time. Up ahead, a deputy's pickup truck was parked behind the sheriff's. It was clear by the lack of detail they hadn't expected news to reach the town, let alone the media. We decided to park only close enough to get out on foot to see what happened.

I parked on the opposite side of the road off to the side, making sure we didn't lose visual of the scene. I unbuckled my belt and leaned forward, looking over the dash. The bar lights on the deputy's truck were still flashing and the coroner's van was backed up near the edge of the road with its back doors open.

Death was never easy, and this time was no different. I kept asking why Nora had to die. It seemed so senseless. I didn't know her well, but what I did see was a woman who had a lot of life left to live. To make matters worse, I felt responsible for bringing unwanted attention to her quiet, secluded life.

Carson pointed to his left and murmured, "There."

I followed Carson's gaze and caught movement of two heads near the edge of the trees. The coroner and sheriff stood over a depression in the dry grass near where the shoes were marked as evidence only yesterday. The way they were working, I knew they were looking at a body.

"What would you like to do?" Carson asked.

I stared at the crime scene, filing through my thoughts. I had been at scenes like this too many times to count, but had never felt responsible for what happened to the victim like I did with Nora.

Was Nora's knowledge of one night in the past so detrimental? It appeared so. A killer was amongst us and I liked to think we had them running scared as they tried to stay one step ahead.

Inside, I was a mixed bag of emotions. I was coming to terms with the idea that we seemed to be the only ones to have uncovered the killer's secrets enough to have them come after us, and I certainly didn't like how they knew an awful lot about Carson and me. Was this person—or persons—toying with an inexperienced sheriff's department, or were they playing games with us?

I said, "The sheriff really needs to bring in outside help."

Carson didn't disagree and, conveniently, we were the only people outside the department who knew about yesterday's evidence in the meadow.

"It's like we're being set up to fail," I said.

Carson gave me a knowing look and said, "Then let's make sure we don't."

We stepped out of the vehicle and gently closed our doors before making our way to the edge of the dirt road. Carson paused mid-step and was the first to see him. I followed his gaze and saw that Brenden was speaking to a deputy fifty yards up the road from where we currently stood. Neither of them noticed we were there. I deliberately ignored what was happening with the coroner and instead chose to study Brenden's body language.

His posture was straight, his chin held high. Every few seconds he shifted his weight to the opposite leg. He didn't hold back whatever he wanted to tell. But I was still confused about one thing: why had he decided to call me, an outsider, to tell me about Nora? Was it out of kindness? Was there an ulterior motive? We'd only spoken twice before that call, and I doubted that was enough of an opportunity to create the kind of trust to be the first person to notify of Nora's death. He must have had others he could have called besides me. Besides, I would have found out about it sooner rather than later, just like everybody else. So, what was his motivation?

Brenden's posture suddenly changed. He was surprisingly still as he stood with his hands buried deep in his coat pockets. I wondered what had caused that change. His expression was tight, his eyes steady on the deputy's face, and even from this far away, they didn't look like eyes that had been crying.

Was he making himself out to be some kind of hero? The thought crossed my mind. Maybe he wanted me to write about him, have his name get in the paper so he could become some sort of local celebrity. I'd seen it before. What I really wanted to know was if Brenden had been on Erin's list of suspects. It was unlikely—he'd only been in Idyllwild six years, according to his story.

Carson turned his back and mumbled, "I hate how he gave us Nora's key."

"Me, too," I said, hating even more that we went to her house as soon as we got it.

Though neither of us stated it, we both knew it was going to come back and bite us in the tail, and for what? A painting that told us nothing about what had happened.

Sirens rang in the distance, echoing off the hillside, and everyone turned to look in our direction. No one seemed surprised we were here, not even Brenden who met my eye with a look that said he was happy to see me.

I didn't like it. It was too confident for having just discovered your murdered friend. When the sheriff's detective arrived on scene, it was the car following that caught my attention.

Was that what Brenden had been smirking about?

It was a silvery sedan like the one Nora drove. When I squinted into the windshield, hoping to catch the face of the driver, they suddenly stopped and turned the car around before I had a chance to see who was driving it.

CHAPTER EIGHTY-FOUR

I SAID TO CARSON, "TELL ME YOU SAW THAT."

Carson said he had, then asked, "Did you see who was driving?"

"I didn't, but was hoping you did."

He shook his head no and we agreed it looked like the same make and model Nora owned—a silvery sedan we last saw parked in front of her house only yesterday evening.

"What the heck was going on?" I said. "If that is Nora's car, then who the heck was driving it?"

We both turned and looked in the direction we believed Nora's body was lying. Strange things were happening that couldn't be explained. When I flicked my gaze over Carson's shoulder, Brenden was gone.

I jogged ten feet up the road and stepped to the side, spotting Brenden climbing into his Ford F-150 pickup truck. Feeling I should chase after him and speak to him before he left, I was stopped by a voice telling me, "Members of the media aren't welcome."

I spun around and came face-to-face with the sheriff's detective who had only just arrived. He was a tall, imposing man with a set jaw and long nose that slanted his eyebrows into a scowl. I'd never seen him before but apparently word had spread about who I was.

"There isn't anything to see," he sneered.

"Nothing to see, yet we aren't welcomed to stay?" I responded.

His eyes narrowed. He clearly didn't like to be challenged by a woman. "Get any closer and I'll have the deputy arrest you."

"On what grounds?" I asked. Before the detective could answer, Brenden drove past us. He nodded his head in my direction. I thought it strange that he had called me here only to leave as soon as we arrived. Apparently his statement to the police was enough and nothing further needed to be discussed, but I'd make sure to change that.

The detective said to me, "Obstruction. Now leave before I *make* you leave."

As if things weren't tense already, the detective's presence certainly complicated matters further. Before we followed his orders to leave, I wanted to get a visual on Nora's body. We had every right to be here, and had nothing to hide. I didn't see a problem. I just wanted visual confirmation, but knew how it looked. I could guess what would come next if I pursued it.

Carson gripped my arm just above the elbow and gently pulled me away from the officer. He seemed to have more restraint than I did. I appreciated that he could keep his wits about him even when threatened with a bullshit charge like obstruction.

As we headed back to my car, all I could hear myself asking was, *Did we lose our only witness who knew what happened the night Barry and Jocelyne died?*

I thought we had, and was sure Carson did, too.

CHAPTER EIGHTY-FIVE

IT WAS FIVE MINUTES BEFORE NINE A.M. WHEN RIP TURNED into the restaurant and parked his rig in the back. Before getting out, he angled the rearview mirror on his face and straightened his eyebrows. His eyes looked puffier than normal, but nothing too unusual for him. A long night on the road, working his rig, and then out early again. It was the life he chose and he was happy to be doing it. What he was happiest about was Lefty's plan to finally end their dreaded worries.

Rip kicked his door open and the autumn air hit his face, further invigorating him. What he needed was a black coffee and a hot breakfast to wake him up and fight off the chill. There was no better place to get them than at the restaurant where Nora once worked.

He entered the restaurant through the front door and, before finding a seat, he assessed the few faces inside to see who he might know. Swiping his right hand over his head, he took off his winter cap and inhaled the heady scents of bacon, sausage, and egg, thankful the restaurant was open again.

Spotting an open table in the back corner, Rip nodded to

people he knew. Their responses to seeing him, here, at the restaurant where Nora had worked, had Rip feeling like they knew what he had done.

What, you don't like seeing me here? At least I'm not drunk. He smirked.

Instead of caving to their stares and side glances, Rip held his head high and stared back to show he wasn't afraid of them, was afraid of no one. His gaze hardened and they quickly looked away as if pretending not to have noticed him arrive at all.

That's right you, sumsofbitches. Look the other way. If you've got nothin' good to say, don't say nothin' at all.

He liked putting fear in people's eyes. They respected him for it. That was what he chose to believe, anyway. But one thing was certain, and always had been: Rip could count on their silence. They knew that if he learned they had said something he didn't like, he would do something about it.

Six feet deep. That's where you'll go. They don't call me R.I.P. for nothin'.

Just as he was about to take a seat, swift movement from the kitchen caught his eye. It was Rachel. He smiled as she approached, but Rip wasn't stupid. He could see she didn't want him here, either. *Was this about Nora?* He assumed it was. What else would it be about?

"Honey, it might not be a good idea to eat here today," Rachel said by way of a greeting.

"And why is that?" Rip said it loud enough to garner the attention of others.

Rachel's cheeks tinged a deep, embarrassed red and said, "Quit making a scene."

"Am I making a scene?" Rip cocked his head to the side and squinted his eyes as if warning Rachel to change her tone, or else.

"If you're here about," Rachel lowered her voice to a whisper, "Nora. We've already heard."

"Heard what?"

"Please, Rip. Not now."

"Not now? I don't think so. Rachel, what about Nora?"

"That's why you're here, isn't it?"

A blonde, Rip hadn't noticed until now, was eating near the window when she lifted up her head and turned just enough to make Rip think she was eavesdropping on their conversation. He kept his eyes on her as Rachel murmured, "Word is they found her body up near Suicide Rock."

"What are you saying? She's dead?"

Rachel's eyes widened as she saw Rip react to the news. It was as if he was excited to learn Nora had died. Not wanting to poke the bear, Rachel said as confidently as she could without exposing her fear of him, "I'm afraid so."

"Well, I'll be damned." Rip slammed his hand onto Rachel's shoulder and he felt her entire body recoil and tense. Feeling energized by the news, he pushed past Rachel and moved toward the attractive blonde he knew wasn't from around here. He wanted to be the first to welcome her to Idyllwild.

CHAPTER EIGHTY-SIX

As soon as we were inside the car and driving toward town, I asked Carson, "Now what?"

Carson didn't answer right away, but I had a feeling I knew what he was thinking. Nora was the only witness we knew was there the night Jocelyne and Barry were killed. My thoughts kept circling back to Brenden. What was he hoping we'd find at Nora's? Anything?

I turned my head to Carson and said, "Brenden said his dog found Nora."

"That's right. That's what you told me."

"Except, when Brenden drove by, I didn't see Molly anywhere."

Carson turned his head and we locked eyes. "Now that I think about it, I didn't either."

We didn't know what that meant, if anything. It was just an observation at this point. Worse was that we had found ourselves in the thick of this investigation that kept getting more deadly. We had been inside Nora's house only yesterday, and since I went to Carson's last night, our alibis—if accused of her murder—were each other. Was that the plan? To pin Nora's death on us, knowing no one would believe our story?

I believed it was only a matter of time before the sheriff was back at our doors asking us where we were and what we were up to last night. It wasn't looking good for us but, until then, we had to get answers, at least for ourselves.

Once we were back in town I circled around, driving up and down the street looking for Brenden's truck. He couldn't have gone far and I wanted to make sure he hadn't stopped in town before driving all the way out to his place.

It didn't take us long to find him, but I was surprised where, having missed him on our first pass.

His dark blue truck was parked in the back of the parking lot of the breakfast restaurant. While I knew we needed to hear his story in person to see if it matched up with everything else we knew about Nora, I didn't think it was appropriate to do it here.

"Maybe the owner has a private office we could use," Carson suggested.

I recalled my conversation with Daniel Mahoney and thought better of it. I didn't think he would be too keen on having us interview a patron of his restaurant as if we were the police.

"No, there is a better option," I said.

"Which is?"

"I'll tell you when I figure it out."

We entered the restaurant together and a part of me hoped Daniel would be here, perhaps shed light on Brenden. It was busier than I expected and, though it felt wrong to have it open after learning Nora had been murdered, I guessed it was because news of her death hadn't yet spread.

The cook gave Carson the side eye from behind the kitchen partition and I listened to the whispers swirl around us, neither of which knocked us off kilter. I swept my gaze to the back and caught sight of Brenden moving away from a young blonde who looked visibly upset. I wondered if he was the cause of her anguish, and if it had to do with Nora's fate. Was that why he was here? To tell her Nora was dead? If so, who was she and could she tell us something we didn't already know?

Rachel came out from the kitchen and we immediately locked eyes. She briefly stopped at a table to check on her diners before meeting us at the door.

"I can't say I'm surprised to see you two here," she said. "Will you be staying long?"

"No, I don't think we will," Carson said.

A local at a nearby table turned his head and said, "You're smarter than you look."

Carson ignored the man and kept his focus on Rachel. I was starting to hate this place. Who was spreading rumors about us? It wasn't like we were getting in enough people's hair to make them all want to hate us.

"I assume you're here because of me," Brenden said, joining our circle at the front.

"Mind if we speak somewhere private?" I said.

Brenden nodded and said, "I think it's best we take this outside before things get ugly."

It felt like the entire restaurant had stopped what they were doing to stare. I flitted my gaze around the room, feeling like we weren't welcome. Was it something Daniel had said? Or did people just consider us to be bad luck?

On our way out the door someone yelled, "Your daughter has been found. Now go home. You aren't welcome here."

Carson stopped and turned his head. I reached for his arm and felt his muscles flex. There was a man with tired looking eyes in his thirties staring back from beneath a knitted winter hat. I remembered him being the tow truck driver who pulled the Aston Martin from the lake.

"C'mon. Forget him," I said.

Carson let it go. As soon as we were standing along the outside of the building, he turned his attention to Brenden. "What the hell was that about in there?" he asked.

Brenden said, "Don't worry about it. It's nothing personal."

"Except they made it personal by referring to Carson's daughter," I said.

Brenden sighed and said something under his breath that sounded like, "And it will be dealt with."

I didn't know what he meant by it, but I kept looking to see if Brenden was noticeably upset about Nora's death. There weren't any signs. I thought it strange how he chose to come here after finding his friend dead. "What are you doing here, Brenden?"

Brenden said, "Excuse me?"

"We saw you speaking to the sheriff's deputy; what did you tell him?"

"What I told you."

I didn't ask the obvious. Instead, I said, "Who else knew Nora was going to go to the cops?"

Brenden's expression pinched and he looked visibly upset by me asking. "You're misunderstanding my phone call this morning, Samantha. See, I was doing *you* the favor, not me."

"What do you want from me?"

"What? Nothing."

"Then why send us out to Nora's house?"

Brenden's eyes perked up. "Did you go? You did, didn't you? What did you find?"

"What were you hoping we'd find?"

Brenden chortled and looked away. He turned back and said, "You don't get it, do you?"

Either Brenden was in shock or he wasn't as close to Nora as he had led us to believe. I couldn't understand why he wasn't more upset by her death. I asked, "Do you even care what happened to Nora?"

The twinkle in his eye vanished. "Maybe the people of this town are right about you two."

Carson said, "What the hell does that mean?"

Brenden snapped his neck toward Carson and sneered. "We don't need you to tell us how to feel, or who we should miss, and we certainly don't need any outsiders like you to solve our problems for us."

Carson stepped in Brenden's face and jabbed his finger into his chest when he said, "Let me remind you of something: now that Nora's dead, we're the only friends you've got."

CHAPTER EIGHTY-SEVEN

BRENDEN DIDN'T FIGHT BACK AND DIDN'T HAVE ANYTHING else to say. But he did make me want to go back to Nora's house, believing the answer he wanted us to find was still hidden somewhere inside.

We watched him go back into the restaurant as I wondered if Carson had pushed him too far. "What did we miss?"

"Probably nothing," Carson said walking toward Brenden's pickup truck.

I followed one step behind, checking my phone along our way. I had a constant worry about Diaz suddenly going quiet. What was he up to? Should I be concerned about what he had coming down the barrel?

Carson stepped up to the dark blue truck and cupped his hands around his eyes as he peeked through the glass. A dog barked and Molly lunged at the window. Carson jumped back and said, "I found Molly."

I tried not to laugh, but I was so happy to have found Molly, too. Now I was second-guessing everything I had thought about Brenden when trying to learn what he was hiding. Had Brenden been telling us the truth? It seemed he was, but his behavior had definitely changed. Why was that?

Peeking through the back window, I spotted an expensive Nikon digital camera and a set of lenses tucked safely away in an unzipped carrying case. Molly recognized me and started wagging her tail. I asked Carson, "What do you think he's taking pictures of?"

Carson was still staring at Molly as he circled the vehicle, making his way over to me.

"Could be anything," Carson said.

"Do you think he took pictures of Nora?" I asked when I heard the sound of someone approaching.

Boots crunched on gravel and we both turned and looked at the same time. It was the tow truck driver who had told Carson and me to go home now that Jocelyne had been found. He hesitated a second when he saw us and had the look of someone who knew he'd picked a fight with the wrong man.

Carson must have noticed it too, because he squared his shoulders and stared the man down as if challenging him to a fight. Before I allowed that to happen, I gripped Carson's arm and said, "He's not worth it."

Carson held still but I could tell he wanted to put the man in his place. As much as I would have liked to see it myself, now wasn't the time.

"C'mon, we've got work to do," I said, reminding Carson what was at stake.

We turned away from Brenden's truck and headed toward my car. Walking past the tow truck driver, he kept his eye on us but never moved.

"Remember this face," Carson said, pointing at the man as we walked past. "Because I'm not going to forget what you said about my daughter."

As soon as I unlocked my car, I received a call from Erin. "Hey, are you here?"

"I'm at the public library. Where are you?"

I told her where we were and I asked, "Ready to get to work?"

"Wouldn't be here if I wasn't."

I grinned, happy to be back working alongside my partner in crime. "Great. Stay put. We're coming to you."

CHAPTER EIGHTY-EIGHT

As soon as I was off the phone with Erin, Carson locked eyes with me and gave me a skeptical look. I asked him, "You're still okay with this, right?"

"Fine."

"You don't sound fine."

"Where is she?" Carson asked.

"When was the last time you two saw each other?"

"It was a long time ago."

"I'm assuming it didn't go well?"

Carson held my eyes for a beat before dropping into the passenger seat. I settled into my own seat, buckled my belt, and assumed his lack of response told me everything I needed to know.

I started the car and said, "Just answer me this, was it as bad as your encounter with Nora?"

"No," Carson said.

I put the car in reverse. "Then there is nothing to worry about."

A couple minutes later I turned into the branch library and parked in the back so our car wouldn't be seen from the road. Sheriff Graves was on the back of my mind and I was still convinced he had pegged us as possible suspects to Nora's murder.

I stepped out first and Carson followed my lead. It was smart of Erin to come to the library; very appropriate for what we were doing. When I glanced at Carson, he pointed to a silvery sedan.

"It can't be, can it?" I said.

Carson looked over each of his shoulders as he approached the vehicle, needing to get a closer look. I followed and we were both thinking it could be Nora's. Making matters worse, neither of us had written down the plate number when we were at her house, knowing she was gone. But if she was dead like we were made to believe, whose car was this?

I stood over the hood and found the same green inspection sticker I saw on the car I witnessed leave the crime scene earlier. Life was full of coincidences, but was this just one of them?

I snapped a few photos with my cellphone when a familiar voice said from behind, "Is there a problem?"

I turned to find Erin. She was wearing a stallion black leather jacket and had her blonde hair tied up in a ponytail. I said by way of greeting, "Please tell me this is yours?"

"It's mine," Erin said, wrapping her arms around me. "Well, it's actually a rental."

I laughed and wrapped my arms around my friend. It felt like I could finally breathe again. I was so happy to be reunited with a friend in what felt like the longest week of my life.

Erin turned to face her rental car and said, "You're not actually thinking of finally getting rid of that old car of yours when you get back home to Denver?"

"Never," I said. "But you were at the crime scene this morning."

"I was." Erin flicked her eyes to Carson, then brought them back to mine. "I saw you there, too. I would have stayed but, truthfully, I'm afraid of having to face Sheriff Graves."

"I get it," I said, sharing the irony of how today's victim, Nora Barnes, had owned a similar compact car.

"It's a common car, Samantha. Neutral color, too. If you haven't noticed, they're everywhere."

It was clear Carson found her response too convenient to be believed. Erin felt the tension, too. Her expression changed, and an awkward silence encircled the group. Staring into Carson's eyes, he was the first to break the ice.

"I'm sorry about your father," he said calmly to Erin.

Erin's shoulders released with a breath. "I'm sorry about your daughter, too."

With the air cleared, I reminded them both we were all here to learn the truth. When everyone nodded their heads and agreed to the terms, I turned to Erin and asked, "Did you read my notes I sent you?"

"I did."

"Good," I said, turning to face the library entrance. "Now, let's get you caught up with what's happened since. Things are moving quickly and we don't have a whole lot of time."

CHAPTER EIGHTY-NINE

ERIN SILENTLY STARED AT HER HANDS AFTER I TOLD HER how Nora had been found dead. She didn't react as I expected. However, Erin did think Brenden's actions were certainly suspicious but he wasn't on her list of suspects. That comforted me some but I still had a feeling that Brenden was hiding something from us. What was it and was I right to think it was hidden at Nora's house?

We were seated at a table in a secluded section of the library. Things between Erin and Carson seemed to be going well until she ruined it by playing devil's advocate. "Let's say Jocelyne killed my father. Any idea why?"

Carson leaned back and sighed audibly. "Not this again."

"What? Did I say something wrong?" Erin looked at me and pointed to the notes spread out on the table in front of her.

"You're wrong. Always have been," Carson said.

Erin shot back, "How? My father was in the trunk of his *own* car. Your daughter was in the driver's seat. I bet that was a surprise to you, but not me." She turned to me and said, "Did you know Carson accused my father of murdering his daughter and then saying I helped my father disappear so he wouldn't get caught?"

Old wounds were opening up and I needed to correct course before losing them both. "I don't claim to have all the answers, but can we try to at least stick to the facts?"

Carson ran his hand over his face and murmured, "Then let's talk about the party your father had that night."

"There was no party," Erin insisted.

I said, "I believe you, but isn't it possible there could have been a party?"

"Impossible. Where are you getting this? From him?" Erin pointed her accusatory finger at Carson.

I said, "Multiple sources, the most recent from Brenden. He was Nora's friend and told us yesterday that Nora also said something about a party at your father's house. She was with Jocelyne. We don't know how they ended up there, or why, but we do believe they weren't alone. At some point that night a fight broke out that Nora may have been witness to."

A flash of recognition caught Erin's eye and I caught her up on the strange things happening to us since we started our investigation. I told her about the impressive effort the town took in their search to find Nora, then how it seemed the same people did a complete one-eighty by turning against us.

Erin wasn't surprised, said it had happened to her as well. "First they like you, then they learn you're not one of them."

I asked, "When you were looking for your father, did you ever speak to Nora Barnes?"

"Of course I did. I heard a similar story to the one you just told me, but when I approached her about it she denied it."

"And you believed her?"

"I was at my father's house that night."

"You were?"

Erin nodded. "And so was my father."

Carson shifted in his chair and brought his elbows to the desk. He had a knowing look on his face that said he knew something I didn't. Thankfully he let Erin talk.

Erin looked him in the eye and said firmly, "There. Was. No. Party. Not that I planned, and not that my father had either."

Thinking of Dale Tanner, I asked, "What about friends? Did he have many of those?"

"Not in Idyllwild. He moved here to get away. People were nice to his face, but they said nasty things about him behind his back."

We knew about the rumors too, but I still wanted to hear what Erin had to say. I asked, "Why is that?"

"I assumed they were envious of his money and perceived influence, but I think it had more to do with my father building that huge eye sore on the side of a mountain. Have you seen it?" I nodded and Erin continued. "Not exactly what artists and people wanting to get back to the land like to see. They prefer mountains and forest, not development. Perhaps things are different now. I don't know."

I told her about my visit to San Quentin and Dale Tanner's confession to murder. Erin responded by saying, "I don't know how Tanner got his fixation on my father but, if I had to guess, I would say he linked my father's name to the many articles written about him. Which, by the way, are also bullshit."

"You don't think there's a connection?"

"If there was, I didn't see it."

I sat quietly for a minute, just thinking. Was it possible Tanner wasn't even in Idyllwild like he claimed? If so, how did he learn enough to fool Diaz into arranging an interview?

I turned and stared at Carson.

During the time Erin was looking for her father, she was also listed as a suspect. Now I couldn't help but feel like someone was trying to set me and Carson up with the disappearance and murder of Nora Barnes. Were these two experiences linked? Was that even possible? In each of the two instances, Carson was looking for answers to his own questions and there seemed to be a lot of competing interests. Once again, all roads led back to Nora.

I asked Erin, "And that was your only encounter with Nora?"

Erin shook her head. "I didn't like how she was saying one thing and others were saying something different; I followed her, hoping she'd lead me to her secret."

"And?"

"Nothing. Nora lived a completely boring life. A life without many friends or boyfriends. It was strange to see because it was the exact opposite of what I expected to find."

Carson nodded and agreed. Erin had done everything Carson had, except she never had a restraining order placed on her.

I asked, "What did you expect to find?"

"A young woman enjoying her youth."

"You mean partying?"

"And with boys."

I asked, "If there wasn't a party, then what happened? How did Jocelyne find herself at your father's house, inside your father's Aston Martin? It doesn't add up. She had to get there somehow, yet you and your father both saw nothing. What am I missing?"

Carson narrowed his eyes and asked Erin, "What is it you're hiding from us?"

I could see the fire in Erin's eye but, before she launched her attack, I asked Carson, "Is there a reason you thought Erin helped her father skip town?"

Carson nodded. Still staring at Erin, he said, "I know, for a fact, Erin left her father's house that night in a hurry."

CHAPTER NINETY

"EVERYTHING ALL RIGHT HERE?"

Rachel hovered over the table, trying not to look Rip in the eye. The blonde, Rip had been hitting on, lifted her head and forced a smile.

"We're doing just fine," Rip answered for both of them. He was sitting on the opposite side of the table, but Rachel suspected that would change as soon as the opportunity presented itself.

"There's fresh coffee at the counter. I just put it out," Rachel said, hoping to lure Rip away from the blonde who she could see didn't know how to get rid of Rip. But nothing Rachel said could break his attention. He was focused on the blonde, making it uncomfortably clear he was interested in her.

The blonde said to Rachel, "Just the check, please."

"Leaving so soon?" Rip smiled at the blonde. "We're just getting started. I haven't even eaten."

Rachel put a menu in front of Rip and said she'd be right back with the check. Then she hurried to the register and requested the blonde's check from the cashier. Keeping an eye on Rip, she pulled her cellphone from her pocket and dialed Lefty's cellphone.

Rachel had a bad feeling about Rip, and it certainly didn't help when thinking about the last time he had come here to speak to Nora. Unfortunately for her, the shift manager had called in sick today and Rachel was it until Daniel came in. She hoped it wasn't soon.

"C'mon," she whispered. "Answer."

Rip got up and moved to sit next to the blonde. He had her trapped against the wall and she looked extremely uncomfortable by his advance. Rachel muttered something to the blonde about telling Rip to leave, to stand up for yourself, but she knew the blonde was too nice to tell Rip. Besides, she doubted he'd get a clue unless it was spelled out for him.

"Hurry up with the tab will you?" Rachel said impatiently to the cashier.

The line clicked over and Lefty answered. "Candy cane."

"It's Rachel, you dummy."

"Oh," Lefty laughed. "I thought it was my other girlfriend."

"Real funny, mister. Now shut up and listen. He's here again."

"Who? Rip?"

"Yeah," Rachel said when Daniel walked through the front door. He stopped mid-step and glared, disappointed to see her talking on her cellphone while on the clock. Rachel ducked her head and cupped her hand over her mouth. "This time he's harassing some poor blonde from out of town."

"Has he bothered anybody else?"

"No. but it won't be long before he's asked to never step foot inside again."

"Put him on the phone."

Rachel turned to the cashier, retrieved the tab, and

hurried across the floor to hand the phone to Rip. "For you," she said.

Rip stared at the phone and said, "Tell whoever it is I'm busy."

"You tell Lefty yourself."

Rip's eyes widened and he took the phone. Pressing it to his ear, he headed for the front door. Rachel turned to the blonde and apologized. Handing her the check, she said, "Thanks again for coming in."

Rachel turned back toward the kitchen and she could see through the front window, Rip pacing as he talked. Then she had a moment of clarity when remembering the conversation she had with Samantha and Carson.

Rip had always been a problem, but was he the cause?

Rachel wasn't sure she knew, but maybe Lefty would. Perhaps she was just too afraid to admit Rip could have murdered Nora, but it made sense. Didn't it?

She turned and looked for the blonde, but she had already left the table. Then Rachel's stomach sank when she saw the blonde speaking to Daniel. She knew they were talking about her, about Rip. As if today wasn't stressful enough, Rachel knew this was going to be a problem.

A second later, the blonde hurried past Rachel without looking and, outside the restaurant, she turned opposite Rip so she wouldn't have to face his harassment again. Rip saw her leaving and tossed up his hands. When Rachel stepped outside to get her phone back, Rip blamed Rachel for the blonde leaving.

"What did you say to make her leave? I really liked that one."

"Just give me my phone back."

Rip held it above his head. "I don't think so."

Rachel stared into his wild eyes, thinking about his last visit here with Nora and how upset she was afterward. What was it about him that had her thinking he could be the killer the police would now be looking for? She couldn't place a finger on it, but her sixth sense was keeping her alert—just a feeling, one she didn't like.

"Quit that," Rip said. "Quit looking at me like that. Here's your damn phone back."

Rip turned and walked away but Rachel didn't move. She squeezed her phone as tightly as she could, waiting for the plastic to crack. After a beat, Rachel went back inside the restaurant only to find the cook whispering something into Daniel's ear. She couldn't catch a break.

Rachel tried to ignore them, but she knew they were talking about her. It didn't take long until Daniel pulled Rachel to the side and said, "Next time someone is drunk and harassing one of my employees, you better let me know about it."

"He wasn't drunk."

"I'm not talking about today."

Rachel's throat constricted and tears welled in her eyes. "I'm sorry."

Daniel said, "Not as sorry as Nora."

CHAPTER NINETY-ONE

ERIN SUDDENLY WENT QUIET. SHE HAD THE LOOK OF A guilty person. Her expression tightened as she stared into Carson's eyes. It was hard to make sense of what Carson was saying, so I asked Erin straight up, "Is he right? Did you leave your father's house in a hurry that night?"

"Yes, but it's not what you think."

I wasn't sure what I was thinking, or why it took Erin so long to come clean. "I thought you were there," I said.

"I was—"

"But not the entire night."

Erin shook her head, no.

Again, I thought about Erin becoming a suspect to a murder, how it seemed we had, too. I was certain there was something here but I couldn't put my finger on what exactly that was. I stared into my friend's eyes. As if anticipating the question I was about to ask, Erin said, "My father and I had a fight."

Carson turned to me and said, "Are you hearing this? This must be what Nora told Brenden."

Instead of getting upset, Erin just looked confused. She

said, "What are you talking about? What did Nora tell this guy?"

I quickly caught Erin up, mentioning the rumors that said her father had kicked everyone out of his house, but kept Jocelyne. It was the first time Erin had heard such a story. I wondered if the fight Nora had heard was the one Erin had with her father.

Carson said, "Apparently, your father was kicking everyone out of his house that night, including you."

"My father wasn't like that. He didn't hurt your daughter."

"How do you know; you weren't there?"

Tensions rose and, after calming everyone down, I got our conversation back on track by asking Erin, "What did you two fight about?"

"It was a heated discussion," Erin corrected me. "My father wanted to lend money to a person I thought was taking advantage of him. Dad disagreed and told me to leave. I did."

Erin gave us the time and details of her departure, but mostly to prove her innocence to Carson. This was the first any of us were hearing this, but I didn't see any red flags to suggest Erin was involved with any crimes. From the look on Carson's face, neither did he. But her departure did open the door to the possibility of having Nora and Jocelyne somehow find their way into Barry's home. Did he invite them there? Or had they invited themselves?

I asked Erin, "Who did your father want to lend money to?"

Erin gave us a name I didn't recognize and said the man lived on the East Coast. "I know what you're thinking, and there's no connection to Riverside County. He couldn't have murdered my father."

"Then is it possible your father used your fight as his excuse to kick you out so he could have a few friends over?"

"My father wasn't like that. He was an honest man. He didn't need an excuse to have people over. We didn't always see eye-to-eye, but we had a great relationship. Those articles of him being a drunk gun nut are completely false. That night was the last time I saw Dad, and I regret not putting up more of a fight to stay. Maybe if I had, we wouldn't be here now. "

Carson leaned back; he seemed to relate to Erin's regret. Perhaps it was what they had in common. They both wished they had done more.

As the conversation settled and the air grew silent, I wrestled with the puzzle I was piecing together inside my head. I didn't think Erin was hiding anything, but I suspected she didn't know as much as she thought about her father, either. There were too many rumors—too many he-said-she-saids— to sift through to uncover the truth from eighteen years ago. But one thing was certain: Barry had been murdered. Whether it was at the hands of Jocelyne or someone else, it was the only truth we had.

I asked Erin, "Can anyone vouch for your whereabouts that night?"

Erin shook her head. "Unfortunately not. I was alone."

I shared a knowing look with Carson. It was like the other night when I was driven out of the cabin and into Carson's cottage. Our alibi was each other, a story I was certain no one would believe if we were ever accused of murdering Nora. Like Erin, our alibi was weak and difficult to prove.

"What we haven't told you," I said, "is that Nora was found in an area we had searched the night she disappeared."

"What does that mean?"

"It means someone knew where we had searched and maybe planted Nora's body there to make it look like we were responsible for her death." I locked eyes with Erin and said, "If we can figure out who might have done that, we might be able to find the person who knows who killed your father."

CHAPTER NINETY-TWO

My cellphone buzzed in my pocket. One glance at the screen was all I needed to know I had to take the call. It was a number from the *LA Times* newsroom. I thought I might know who it was. "Samantha Bell."

"Samantha, it's Jeffrey Hineman."

Thoughts of Diaz and the interview Hineman wanted me to get from Erin came crashing to the front of my mind. I still hadn't given him my decision even though I was certain I knew what it was.

I looked Erin in the eye when I said, "Hi."

Hineman said, "I'm calling because I just received word that the cabin you're staying in seems to have been...what's the word the property manager used...ah, yes, abandoned."

My brow pinched. I knew by Hineman's tone I had made a mistake. He had every right to be angry. As much as I didn't want to get blamed for what happened, I couldn't explain my way out of this mess.

I listened without speaking as Hineman filled me in on the details. He said the property manager had found the house lights left on and the front door wide open. I was certain I had locked it on my way out, but maybe in my rush to leave, I hadn't.

Hineman then asked me, "What the heck is going on?"

The terror of being woken up by someone threatening to drive their truck over the house flashed across my mind when I said, "If I told you, you wouldn't believe me."

"Then you better get up there and explain it to the property manager, because the paper can't afford to have an unexpected bill come at us for damaged property."

"I'll take care of it," I said.

Hineman ended our call without ever asking about how I was doing, if I had been hurt, or if this had to do with the story I was researching. I sat there quietly for a moment, thinking about Ryan Dawson—my empathetic Denver editor at the *Colorado Times* who was always concerned about my safety, the same person who seemed to have my back, no matter what.

Erin said, "What was that about?"

I started packing up my things and said, "C'mon. I'll tell you all about it in the car."

CHAPTER NINETY-THREE

WE LEFT THE LIBRARY AND PILED INTO MY CAR. CARSON was in the front and Erin in the back. I reversed, turned the car around, and drove past Erin's rental, not concerned with leaving it here. No one knew she had arrived and I preferred to keep it that way.

"What's going on, Sam? Did you catch a break?" Erin asked.

Heading south, I kept checking my mirrors, expecting to find the sheriff following us. I wondered if he had been tipped off by the same person wanting to frame us for Nora's murder. The more I thought about it, adding up all the coincidences, I was convinced either the sheriff was part of the cover-up or friends with the man who was.

By the time we reached the outskirts of town, I told Erin where we were going and shared the story of why I had left the cabin in such a hurry. I caught her eye in the rearview mirror when she said, "Whoa. I'm glad you're all right. Seems to me like you two are ruffling the right feathers."

I drove fast and steady, one hand on the steering wheel, telling Erin how this was another instance on the long list of strange things that began happening to me since starting to research this case.

Erin wanted to know more about Brenden Donaldson, beyond what she already knew, and I told her about Rachel Sweeney and the rumors of Brenden dating Nora.

"Rachel's the one that told us to talk to Brenden, and he's the one who then sent us to Nora's," I said.

"But she was already missing by this time?"

I nodded. "Brenden gave us her house key. He said that Nora had evidence to prove that she wasn't lying about the party at Barry's house and was planning to take it to the sheriff."

"And, let me guess, you went inside Nora's house?"

Carson patted his chest with his hand as if feeling to make sure he was still hanging onto Nora's key. When he met my eye, he gave me a subtle nod to say he was.

I said to Erin, "Of course we did; we had the key. You never heard Brenden's name before today because he only moved here six years ago."

I could see Erin staring out the window, processing everything I was telling her. "If that's true, it's probably safe to assume he didn't kill my father."

"He's hiding something, but I don't know what."

"Do you think he has the evidence Nora said she had?"

"Maybe."

"You never found anything at Nora's house?"

I shook my head. "Nothing like what we expected to find."

"If Brenden knows what Nora had, why not just come out and say what he wants you to find?"

"Because he might have been the last person to see Nora alive."

Carson retrieved the photograph of Jocelyne and Nora

he'd been carrying and handed it back to Erin. "This was one of the last pictures Jocelyne sent me."

Erin said, "Sure, they're partying, but that's not my father's house."

"No, it's not," I said. "It's likely that picture wasn't even from the same night, but maybe they are with the same people Nora claimed to have been with when they found themselves at your father's house."

Erin said, "You want to know what I think? I think Brenden might not have killed Nora but knows who did, and they are covering their tracks by putting you in places they knew the sheriff would be looking."

It was a sobering assessment, and one I didn't want to hear. Not wanting to think of my own demise, I said, "If we can learn who started the rumors about Barry killing Jocelyne, then we can find who is responsible."

CHAPTER NINETY-FOUR

We wound our way up the mountain side and, as we settled into our own thoughts, I was reminded of everything that happened to me this week. Each bend in the road was a new twist in the investigation.

During my stay in California, I had felt completely out of my element, in over my head. I assumed it was because I was working in unfamiliar territory without any connections to call upon, but perhaps it was only this case that was making me feel inadequate.

As the car climbed further up the mountain, Erin said, "I can't believe the paper put you all the way out here. Why not get you a place in town?"

I didn't know; I assumed Hineman had his reasons. "That's a great question," I said, "and one I wish I had asked sooner. I assumed it was because it was a place they could afford."

"So, are you going to pack up and trade in the Mile High city for Hollywood, after all?"

"I haven't had time to give it much thought," I said, not wanting to have this conversation now. To get Erin off my back, I added, "They haven't exactly made the best first impression."

"So, is that a no?"

Erin turned her head and I caught her eyes in the mirror. She was giving me a knowing look that said she knew I wasn't about to leave her behind to work our blog and podcast alone.

I said, "One story at a time; but I should warn you, the editor asked me to interview you for the story."

"My side of the story?" Erin raised an eyebrow. "Umm... no. I don't think so."

"I think it's the reason they kept me on to freelance," I said, knowing Erin wouldn't be willing to consent.

Erin said, "Well, in that case, I'll do whatever you want, Sam. But just so you know, if we solve this case, you can write whatever you want *after* we put the story out."

I smiled, but it didn't last. As we rounded the next bend and came within sight of the cabin, my entire body tensed. Triggered by last night's events, I was surprised to see a black pickup truck parked near the front bedroom window. I wondered if my tormentor was back for more.

CHAPTER NINETY-FIVE

AFTER I PARKED, NO ONE SAID A WORD. I WAS STILL fixated on the truck when Carson reached his hand over and touched my forearm. I jumped, totally spooked. Carson reeled his hand back and knitted his eyebrows. I blinked and flicked my gaze to the rearview mirror. Erin was staring with a look of surprise on her face.

"Do you recognize the truck?" Carson asked.

It was a black Chevrolet Silverado. Six cylinder diesel engine and close to ten thousand pounds of muscle that looked like it could drive over anything. Was it the same truck I saw last night?

"It could be the same one," I said, asking myself what role Hineman might be playing in all of this, if anything. Just when our investigation was gathering momentum, it came to a halt so I could deal with this—a problem that should have never been an issue.

Erin unbuckled her seat belt and put her face between Carson and me. Together, we stared and watched the tall, lean cowboy-hat-wearing man approach.

"Anybody know who he is?" Erin asked, not taking her eyes off him.

Carson shook his head; I didn't recognize him but I knew who he had to be. "Must be the property manager," I said, telling them to both stay in the car while I tried to figure out what was going on.

Scattered clouds drifted lazily across the sky and, as soon as I stepped out of the car, the man raised his left hand and introduced himself as Property Manager, Ewing Clark.

"Are you Samantha Bell?" he asked.

I said I was and added, "I heard what happened. I guess I'm curious to know why any lights were on in the house."

"Yes, I found the entire house lit up and the front door wide open. Don't worry," Ewing smiled and waved his left hand, "it's cool. I'm sure nothing happened while you were gone."

I wasn't sure if he was being facetious or not, but I said, "I was certain I locked up when I left. I really am sorry for your troubles."

"Truth be told, Samantha, I was surprised to see you already gone. Thought you were planning to stay until the end of the week?"

"That's the plan," I said, eyeing Ewing. "Mind if I take a look inside?"

"Please do. By all means."

Ewing stepped aside and I could feel him watching me walk to the house. I entered through the front door, hearing Ewing take a call on his cellphone.

Wanting to make sure it was exactly as I left it, I pulled out the cabin key and inserted it into the lock. It clicked over; the door trim looked undamaged. I didn't think anybody besides Ewing had been here after I left. Opening and closing the door, I was now beginning to doubt I had locked it at all.

I entered the house, feeling strange to be back. I moved deliberately from room to room as I listened to the floor creak while taking in each feature, trying to remember the finer details. Nothing was out of place; everything exactly as I left it.

Once through the kitchen, I then traveled through the living room, flicking the light switches on and off as I passed. Everything worked as I remembered before last night's bizarre power outage.

I peeked out the window and heard Ewing's muffled phone conversation when I spotted Carson near Ewing's truck. I grumbled a quick protest as I headed into the bedroom but knew Carson was only doing his homework.

The bed was still unmade; everything was exactly how I remembered leaving it. Amazingly, I hadn't left anything behind. When I glanced out the window again, instead of seeing Carson, my eyes drifted to the truck, remembering the feeling of getting woken up by the sound of a big engine rumbling and feeling trapped by the headlights blinding my every move. When I blinked, I recalled how on my first night here, I was certain I had left the lights on only to return to a dark house. I wasn't sure what that said about last night, if anything, but I found it interesting, nonetheless.

A minute later I exited the cabin, satisfied with my inspection and found Carson talking to Ewing about his children.

"Two girls," Ewing said proudly as he looked me in the eye. Then he asked Carson about his own family as I checked to see where Erin was. She was out of the car, leaning against the hood.

"It's just me," Carson said.

Ewing turned to me and asked, "All good?"

I said, "Do you know if the electricity went out last night?"

"Not at my house. But, then again, I might have slept through it." Ewing smiled. "Why? Did it go out here?"

I nodded. "Anyway, again, I'm sorry for leaving the lights on. It's my fault entirely. I promise it won't happen again."

"Just happy we could clear this up. We have a bear in the area and the damage could have been much worse."

Damage? I hadn't noticed any damage. Had I missed something Ewing had spotted himself?

Then Ewing cleared things up when he said, "Just wish you didn't tear up the gravel driveway on your way out. You did quite the number on it. I'll have to get the grader out to fix it."

Carson said, "You're referring to these ruts over here?"

"That I am," Ewing said, following Carson across the driveway. I followed close behind and Ewing turned to me and said, "Must have been in quite the hurry."

I flicked my gaze to Carson, wondering what he was doing. He crouched down and traced his finger in the dirt, then side-stepped and repeated his actions in a second set of tracks.

"Couldn't have been Samantha who did this," Carson said to Ewing. "These tire tracks are much larger than the ones on her car."

Ewing tilted his head, took one step forward, then bent at the waist as he stood over Carson's shoulder. He narrowed his eyes as if studying the dirt Carson had traced. Then he said, "Would you look at that. I think you're right. You should be a detective." He laughed.

Carson raised his gaze and I knew he had his eye on something but I couldn't tell what it was. I watched him stand and casually walk ten yards before kneeling again and brushing some dirt away with his hand as he uncovered a broken plastic coffee mug.

Carson took the mug into his hands and read the logo

aloud, "Towing by Mack." He looked to Ewing when asking, "You know it?"

"Hot damn." Ewing slapped his knee. "You really are a detective. Yeah, I know it. That's Dave Mack's company. The only hook and chain tow truck in town." Ewing swung his head over his shoulder and asked me, "Did your car break down or something?"

"No," I said, staring at the mug in Carson's hands, realizing I knew exactly who Dave Mack was.

CHAPTER NINETY-SIX

EDGAR DIAZ WAS SITTING IN HIS CAR, STARING AT A photograph that made him think about Samantha Bell. Pinched between his meaty fingers, he couldn't stop staring at the people's faces, thinking how this was his ticket to proving he was the better journalist.

It couldn't have come at a better time. Just when he thought he was about to lose it all.

He had her face memorized to the point of it being an obsession. It was all he could think about. If he wasn't already anxious enough, this was fuel to the fire that this might be his last chance to get Samantha to pack her bags and finally head home to Colorado.

Edgar lifted his head and glanced in his mirrors, then at the clock. He couldn't sit still; time wasn't moving fast enough. He wanted it to happen now. To get it over with so he could finally receive the recognition he thought he deserved.

He lifted his eyes and cast his gaze across the street where he stared at the small house's front door, knowing for a fact this was where she was staying. It took some time to find out the details but, like always, Edgar persisted until he had the facts. Now that he was here, it was time to prepare the attack.

He calmly gathered his thoughts and things, checking to make sure there was no one around to see what he was about to do. Just as he went to open his car door, his cellphone buzzed on the dash.

Edgar reached for the device with his free hand and checked to see who was calling.

Hineman.

He decided to ignore the call. Edgar had a feeling he knew what his chief editor's call was about and didn't want to be bothered with it.

"Bad timing, Jeff," he said aloud.

Besides, Edgar was already annoyed by Hineman's constant need to handhold each of his steps since assigning him to show Samantha the ropes. He didn't like the idea from the beginning, but their trip to San Quentin proved to be enough of a disaster to get Edgar to break out on his own.

He checked his mirrors again, knowing he needed to get his message hung on the woman's door before his subject came home. He wasn't sure when that would happen, but he suspected it would be soon. Then his phone chirped with an alert and, though Edgar was tempted to listen to the voicemail, he chose not to. Instead, he preferred to let Hineman stew in his own personal regret.

"Don't blame me for the mistake you made. I told you from the beginning Samantha would be trouble."

Finally, Edgar stepped out of his vehicle and stared at the house as he stuffed the photograph he'd been looking at back into the envelope. Then he walked casually to the front door where he wedged the envelope next to the door handle, making sure it wouldn't be missed.

Satisfied with his work, Edgar turned around, made sure

no one had seen him, and hurried back to the car where he settled in to wait.

He had never been on board with Samantha's hire, but her connection to Erin Tate was something he couldn't get past. He knew that was the gold that would make this story great. Hineman knew it too, and Edgar was certain that was the only reason he kept her around, no matter the cost.

All night, Edgar debated how he could get what she had and kept coming up with nothing. He had no plan. There wasn't anything he could do to get Erin to agree to give him the interview instead of having Samantha conduct it herself. He was completely envious. It killed him to know Samantha had something he'd never get.

Until...he came up with a plan of his own.

He reached across the seat and switched the lenses on his digital camera, pointed it at the house, and fired off a few shots. Edgar hadn't got this far without a few tricks up his sleeve, and he had a few others if push came to shove.

"You'll never see this coming," he murmured, firing off a couple more shots, filling his memory card as he planned to beat Samantha at her own game by staying one step ahead.

He was feeling good about his plan. The one truth Edgar couldn't change was that he preferred to work alone. He wasn't sure what that said about himself but he knew how others perceived it, and he worried that it might be his one flaw that could get him caught.

The lone wolf that didn't play well with others, Edgar thought as he lifted the camera and closed one eye, saying, "My approach might be unorthodox, but it's guaranteed to get a reaction."

The shutter clicked in rapid fire as Edgar promised himself he wasn't about to go down without a fight, knowing that soon, everyone would know he was on the brink of something big.

CHAPTER NINETY-SEVEN

Dave Mack. I didn't know the name but I could see his face.

Dave was the person we needed to find—the person who came to my cabin to terrorize me in the middle of the night. The evidence was written in stone, clear as day. When I turned and looked Ewing in the eye, he had a bewildered expression as he questioned why Dave Mack would have come all the way out here if my car hadn't broken down. I didn't have it in me to explain.

Carson made his way to me and whispered into my ear, "Well, I think we know who came to visit last night."

"Let's go find him," I said. Turning to Ewing, I apologized again.

Ewing said, "Everything all right?"

"Yes. Not a problem. Just some business that needs attending to in town," I said, backpedaling to my car.

"Well, all right then."

By the time I reached the car, Erin was climbing into the backseat, Carson going around to the passenger side. We slammed our doors shut and I fired up the engine, wanting to tear out of here. I suspected Dave could be on to us. I couldn't race away with Ewing still watching.

"This is it, Samantha," Carson said to me. "The big truck stalking you. The man at the restaurant telling us to leave. I knew there was something off with that man."

It made sense. Even the hesitation I saw when Dave was leaving Daniel's restaurant only an hour ago. I recalled Carson telling Dave to remember his face. Dave had to be responsible for Nora's murder.

A mile away from the cabin, I stomped my foot on the gas and Erin asked, "Anyone care to fill me in on what just happened back there?"

Without taking my eyes off the road, I said, "Look up the address to Towing by Mack."

Erin got out her phone and began plugging in her search. I then told her that we were followed by a tow truck on our way to Climbers trailhead, adding, "That's where we searched for Nora, where her clothes were found the next day, then her body this morning. It's how he must have known where to leave Nora's things."

"Okay, it's loading," Erin said.

"It's also the same company that pulled the Aston Martin from the lake."

Carson turned his head to me and said, "That had to be what sparked his worry."

"And the reason he's coming after us."

Carson agreed. The most concerning piece of all this was that his mug ended up in the dirt just outside my bedroom. It meant he got out of his car. Was he planning to kill me, too? It was possible, but I couldn't understand why he'd want to take the risk. I supposed with Nora dead he had nothing left to lose. But what had stopped him?

Then I thought I figured it out. I said, "He must have

gotten to the breaker box and been the one to cut the power."

"Then who flipped the switch back on?" Carson asked.

Neither of us knew. Though Ewing was the obvious answer. I'd asked him about the power outage and he'd seemed clueless about it.

"Okay, I got it," Erin said, mentioning an address in town. She tried calling but no one answered.

"Don't worry about it," I said. "I know where he might be."

"Daniel's restaurant," Carson and I said at the same time.

My heart was racing as fast as I was driving. Carson told me to watch my speed, but I didn't care. It felt like we had finally found our killer and I didn't want to let him get away. I had made far too many mistakes this week and couldn't afford another. I was ready to end this investigation and get back home to my son. But when we arrived at Daniel's restaurant, the wrecker we had our sights set on was already gone.

CHAPTER NINETY-EIGHT

As much as I wanted Dave to be at the restaurant, I'd known he would already be gone. When I turned to look at Carson, neither of us was surprised Dave had left. We had assumed earlier that he was leaving, but now we wondered where could have gone from here.

As we went around in circles trying to make heads or tails of this mystery, Erin reminded me of the address she had pulled up for Towing by Mack. Then Rachel Sweeney surprised us with a hard knock on my window.

"I was about to call," Rachel said as soon as I powered down the window, "but then I saw you arrive. And thank God you did."

Rachel's brow furrowed with worry and she kept looking over her shoulder like she was hiding from someone, or just didn't want anyone to know she was talking to us. I wondered if this was about Brenden—what he might have done after our conversation earlier.

"Rachel, what is it?" I asked.

She snapped her neck and stared at me with wide eyes.

"Remember how I told you that all the missing persons aren't from here?"

I nodded, thinking back to Brenden making the blonde woman visibly upset. Was that what this was about?

"Did something happen?" I asked. "It was the blonde, wasn't it?"

Rachel said, "You saw it, too?"

"Christ, what did Brenden do?"

"Brenden?" Rachel's face scrunched. "No. It's not about him."

Rachel seemed offended by my accusation, maybe because she'd led us to believe they were friends. I asked, "Then who is this about?"

Rachel glanced to the restaurant and crouched lower, hiding behind my car. She seemed nervous and afraid. It had all of us worried, too. In a low voice she said, "I stopped it before something could happen, but it got me thinking."

She was hesitating. I needed to get her to spit it out before she had a change of heart. I said, "Rachel, Nora is dead. Do you understand that? Whoever murdered her, also killed his daughter." I pointed at Carson. "If you know something, you need to tell us *now*."

She closed her eyes for a second and sighed. "I can't believe this. If something happens to me—"

"Things will keep happening to you, and everyone else, the longer this town makes excuses for whoever is responsible."

Rachel's eyes lit up. "His name is Dave Mack and he owns the only towing company in town. He was the one pushing himself on the blonde."

Erin mumbled something in the backseat and Carson drummed his fingers on his thigh as I wondered if Brenden was friends with Dave.

I looked Rachel in the eye and said, "Dave Mack?"

Rachel nodded.

"You're sure?"

She nodded again.

"Why haven't we heard his name until now?" I didn't mean to sound skeptical, but I was. She saw Dave hitting on the blonde woman, but I was certain I'd seen Brenden do the same thing. Had they both hit on the blonde? Were they working together?

Rachel said, "It might be because people around here know him as Rip."

CHAPTER NINETY-NINE

BRENDEN FOLLOWED THE BLONDE TO A CORNER STORE ON the opposite side of town, making sure to stay back just far enough to not be made. Then, when she entered the store, he parked two empty spots to her right.

He put his cellphone on vibrate and watched through the front windows, as she moved between the aisles, deciding he'd wait a minute before going inside himself. He had to be smart about this. He could get close, but not too close. As he kept his eye on her from the safety of his truck, the blonde reminded him of Nora. The thought worked its way into his mind, and he quickly pushed it out. The memory of this morning was too fresh to think about now. It felt like a dream, a dream he hadn't yet woken up from, and perhaps that was why he followed the blonde.

Molly whined and danced on her paws. She was staring at the store's front door, her tongue dangling out of her mouth, pleading with her eyes to go inside with him.

Brenden put his hand on her shoulders and said, "Watch the car while I'm inside. Can you do that for me?"

Molly smacked her lips and wanted to get out with him.

Brenden put on a Dodgers ball cap and walked past the blonde's car, taking a quick look inside. There was an empty soda bottle and GPS on the dash. She had California plates but he was certain she wasn't from Riverside.

Inside the store, he nodded at the clerk and headed to the refrigerated drinks on the back wall, completely avoiding the woman he was stalking. He knew she might recognize him from the restaurant and he had a plan for what he would say if she did. Brenden hoped he wouldn't have to confront her because he was more curious to know where she was going next than what she was buying here.

He picked out a soda, the same kind he saw in the woman's car, and quickly put it back. Then he browsed the deli while keeping one eye on the blonde. She seemed to be picking through snack supplies, maybe something for lunch. None of it was interesting to Brenden, so he kept his distance, thinking Rip sure knew how to pick his women.

She was young, attractive, and clearly alone. Why had she come to Idyllwild? To get away like the rest of them? If so, get away from what? It seemed to be the common denominator for what Rip wanted in a woman. A person without ties, new to town that no one else knew. Like staking a claim before others had a chance to plant their flag. Brenden thought he might be onto something.

He left the store first without purchasing any items and climbed back into his truck.

"Any troubles while I was away?" he asked Molly.

Molly sniffed his hand, expecting to receive a treat. She licked his empty palm, regardless, as Brenden reached under his seat and wrapped his fingers around the Glock 42, the perfect option for concealed carry. He preferred not to have to use it today, but something told him he might need it.

Molly yipped and, when Brenden lifted his gaze, he locked eyes with the blonde. With her car door open, she stood still, staring at Brenden. Recognition flashed over her eyes and neither of them smiled. There was a split second of hesitation, then she quickly got into her car and drove away.

Brenden remained seated with his hand on his gun, the truck engine off. He said to Molly, "Don't worry, girl. If we could find her once, we can certainly find her again."

CHAPTER ONE HUNDRED

DAVE MACK.

Rip.

It didn't matter what people called him; all I wanted to know was where I could find him.

I asked Rachel, "Where is Dave now?" She was biting her lip and I was losing my patience. "Did Dave go after the blonde?"

"I don't know," Rachel mumbled.

"I don't have a good feeling about this," Erin said from the backseat. "We need to find him, Sam."

Rachel told us that Rip came into the restaurant the morning before Nora disappeared. I asked what about. She said, "I wasn't there to see it, but the shift manager did."

"Does he know what Rip said to her?"

Rachel shook her head. "I just know it made her feel extremely uncomfortable."

I thought about my conversation with Daniel, how the entire town was looking for Nora that night. Rachel's information that Dave was an alcoholic who seemed to have relapsed as soon as the Aston Martin was found, assured us he was our guy.

"Is Daniel aware of this?" I asked.

"He is now," Rachel said. "And is taking care of it."

She didn't say how, and we didn't ask. Minutes were ticking by and all we wanted was to speak with Brenden and Dave. I glanced towards where I had last seen them both parked and asked Rachel if they left together. She didn't know.

"Rachel, listen to me," I said. "This is really important. Did you ever hear who murdered Jocelyne Reynolds?"

Erin held her breath. Carson's fingers stopped drumming. Rachel reminded us she wasn't from here, but said, "Yeah. I heard."

"Who was it? Who murdered Jocelyne?"

Rachel said, "Barry Tate."

I asked, "Who did you hear that from? Do you remember?"

"Hell, I don't know. Everyone said it."

I kept thinking about Brenden and Dave; how they both seemed to be up to something suspicious. Could they have started this rumor? It seemed possible. Especially since Dave had it in him to scare me away from the cabin in the middle of the night.

Carson leaned into my seat and asked Rachel, "But who said it first?"

"I don't know. Maybe Rip."

"Then that's who we need to ask," Carson said.

Rachel told us where Dave lived and warned, "Be careful. I know for a fact he's armed and doesn't take accusations lightly."

CHAPTER ONE HUNDRED ONE

ALL SIGNS WERE POINTING TO DAVE MACK. WE DIDN'T know if Brenden was also part of the equation. Who murdered Nora? One of them? Both of them? Who started the rumor suggesting Barry killed Jocelyne? It couldn't have been Brenden; he wasn't here then.

Rachel left and went back to the restaurant. Erin asked if we should be worried about her.

"I think she'll be safe here," I said, turning to Carson. I asked him, "Do you have your piece with you?"

Erin said, "Wait one hot minute. Gun? What are you planning to do with that? Kill Dave?"

"We might need it," I said, catching the sheriff pass by in my rearview mirror. I was certain he saw us but he didn't stop. I started the car, backed out, and turned my wheels south. Not more than two minutes into our drive, I caught the sheriff riding our tail.

Erin said, "All I'm saying is we should try diplomacy first."

Carson responded, "We will. This is for the just-in-case scenario." Then he turned to me and said, "To answer your question, no. I don't have it. It's back at the cottage."

"Good. Then we'll stop to pick it up."

I kept my eye on the sheriff, wondering if we should get him involved. I didn't know who to trust, if anybody, and instead worked a plan in my head. I gave Erin the task of learning more about who Dave Mack was.

"See who his friends are, if he has any close relatives we could speak to," I said.

Erin nodded as she stared into her cellphone's screen.

Carson was staring in his side mirror and I knew he had spotted the sheriff, too. He said, "We have to believe Rachel and go in assuming Dave's armed and dangerous. He's already proven he's willing to go to great lengths to keep his secret from coming out. Who knows what he'll do when we come knocking on his door."

"Here we go," Erin said, scrolling through Dave's social media.

I asked her, "Do you recognize him?"

"No. But he's a year older than Nora and they attended the same high school."

Once we turned toward Carson's cottage, the sheriff pulled back and disappeared. I parked out front and was the first to spot an envelope wedged into Carson's door.

"What do you think that's about?" I asked.

Carson stared but didn't seem to be in a hurry to leave the car. I opened my door, then Erin followed, and by the time we were standing at the door, it was all three of us. We stared down at a picture of Carson holding my hand, leading me into his cottage in the middle of the night.

"Do you remember seeing anyone last night?" I asked Carson. He shook his head no. "Dave left the cabin before me; he could have taken this."

"It's possible, but I think he had help."

Carson was speculating but it made sense. We were all

thinking about Brenden when I flipped the picture over and couldn't believe who it was addressed to.

Carson asked, "Detective Alex King? Who is that?"

Erin met my eye and said, "This isn't good."

CHAPTER ONE HUNDRED TWO

EDGAR DIAZ SMILED WHEN HE SAW THEM ARRIVE. Concealed by the tinted windows of his car, he powered down the opposite window just a crack, lifted his camera, focused his lens, and began taking pictures.

There were three of them but he only cared about one.

One by one, they made their way first to the steps, then to the front door. Edgar followed each of them in the view finder of his camera and, as anticipation grew, he looked over the eye piece, waiting for them to find the envelope he had placed in the door a few minutes before.

"Take it. I left it for you," he said aloud.

Then he watched her go for it and he took pictures of it all. Though he couldn't hear what was being said, he knew they were debating what it was and who put it there. They looked confused and curious, all tightly wrapped into a single package of interest.

"Go ahead, open it up."

Then she did. When she pulled out the photograph stuffed inside, Edgar snapped a couple more shots before lowering his camera to his lap to study their reaction. The woman's face went pale and Edgar grinned, knowing he finally got her.

CHAPTER ONE HUNDRED THREE

"How do they know who King is?" Erin asked me.

I was still staring at the photograph of Carson leading me into his cottage in the middle of the night. Though I looked scared, it could easily be misinterpreted as a face that said I was about to do something I shouldn't.

"I don't know," I said.

Carson asked again who Alex King was.

Erin said, "Her boyfriend, a homicide detective in Denver."

Carson said nothing and I suspected he didn't care. Nothing had happened between us. We only had each other to account for our whereabouts. But I did care. Cared that King knew I hadn't cheated on him.

Erin pulled me aside and said, "What the hell happened between you two?"

Carson sensed the tension and headed into his cottage. He left the door open and I listened to him rummage around a bit before opening and shutting what I assumed to be his gun case.

Erin said, "Sam, did you and Carson..."

"You can't be serious."

"I didn't think so, but you have to understand how it looks," she said, pointing to the photograph.

"I know exactly what it looks like," I said, wishing I knew who took it.

Now I understood why I was scared out of the cabin. It was to set me up. All week we had been getting set up. I couldn't wait to test Dave Mack's intellect because whoever was behind this was certainly a cunning individual. How did he know I would come here? It had to be just a guess. I regretted my own predictability.

Erin took the photograph into her hand and said, "He looks like Gavin, you know?"

"I know," I said, thinking about my day, beginning with the phone call from Brenden saying he found Nora's body. I couldn't believe it was ending like this. Again, I questioned if he was in on this somehow, too.

"What am I missing?" Erin cast her suspicious gaze into the cottage.

I knew that look; the look that suggested I was being played at my own game of seduction and betrayal and doing whatever it took to get the story. Though Carson wasn't a journalist, a private detective used similar tactics. Erin's own history with Carson made it hard for her to trust him. But I did. I reminded her that it wasn't Carson who had done this, but Dave.

I said, "After I left the cabin last night, who did you think I called?"

Erin was staring into the cottage and I knew she didn't want to see anything happen to Alex and me.

"Relax, Carson is on our team," I said, assuring her all was going to be fine.

But I did shoot off a quick text to warn King of what might be coming his way.

CHAPTER ONE HUNDRED FOUR

I DIDN'T EXPECT KING TO MESSAGE ME BACK IMMEDIATELY but I wished he would. If only to clear my conscience so I could fully concentrate on how we were going to get Dave Mack to talk.

"King has been through similar situations," Erin reminded me. "I'm sure he'll understand."

I knew he would but it still felt like I was having to admit guilt before getting caught. And it didn't help that Carson looked so much like Gavin. My shoulders were weighed down by an imaginary sandbag when Carson stepped outside and said, "Are we ready to roll?"

I locked eyes with Erin. She nodded and I said, "This is how it's going to go down." I laid out the plan I had been working and told them, "The sheriff has us pegged as suspects. We have to assume it's because someone has led him to believe we are. Whether that was Brenden or Dave or someone else, I would prefer the sheriff not follow us to Dave's."

Carson said, "The sheriff is already onto us today."

"I saw it, too," I said. "That's why Erin is going to drive my car and pretend it's me."

"And you, Sam?" Erin asked. "What are you going to do?"

"I'm going to take your car, drive to Dave's, and see what I can find out."

"I don't know. Rachel said he's dangerous. Maybe it's a good thing the sheriff is following us."

I said, "But if we involve the sheriff too early, we might never know who killed your father."

"I'll shake the truth out of him," Carson said, referring to what he'd like to do to Dave. That got me to smile.

Erin was still expressing her doubts, even after she'd once been blamed for her father's murder. She said to me, "If we lead the sheriff to Dave and he runs, then we know he's guilty. Isn't that enough?"

"I'd rather scare him myself," Carson said, not willing to risk Dave getting away before asking him about Jocelyne.

I said, "If the sheriff follows us, fine. But we have to surprise Dave. And the only way to do that is by me taking your car." Erin didn't look like she wanted to be alone with Carson, but I thought it would be good for both of them. Then I added, "You two stay back and act as backup. If Dave gets violent, Carson can step in. And if Dave decides to run, you two can follow. Either way, if he thinks I'm alone, he might do something stupid—like admitting to killing Nora."

Erin was still staring, thinking things over, when Carson clapped his hands and said, "Time to face the music."

Then, as I turned to the car I heard Erin tell Carson, "Just promise me you won't shoot anybody if you don't have to."

CHAPTER ONE HUNDRED FIVE

At the library, Carson offered me his weapon but I refused to take it.

"In case we get separated," Carson said.

I didn't want to ask him why we would get separated but it was definitely possible with the wildcard of the sheriff. I said, "Just make sure you get there shortly after me."

Erin handed me her car keys and climbed into the driver's seat of my car. Before I shut her door, she said, "We'll see you there."

I smiled and closed her door, then walked to her car hoping my plan would work and that Dave would be where Rachel said. If he wasn't, I'd have to assume she'd tipped him off and accept that she might be deeper into this than I thought.

As soon as I was behind the wheel, I adjusted my mirrors and watched Carson and Erin leave the library parking lot. The plan was for them to circle through town, giving me just enough time to draw Dave out of his house and for him to think I was alone before surprising him with the entire cavalry.

Dave lived in a middle class neighborhood surrounded by trees on the south end of town. It took me ten minutes to find his place and, when I arrived, I parked across the street and one house down. I hid my car behind an old growth pine. I had a clear visual on his modest house, as well as his wrecker parked in front of the garage.

I thought about what I was going to say, how I could fool him into thinking I knew more than I did. My heart was drumming loudly in my chest when I opened my door to step out. Before I had a chance, I heard an engine rumble behind me. I checked my mirrors and instantly dipped down into my seat to hide my face.

A dark blue Ford F-150 drove past without noticing me and I watched with surprise as Brenden turned into Dave's driveway and parked behind his tow truck.

"I knew it," I said, watching Brenden leave his truck and confidently walk to the front door where he opened it without knocking.

I took a couple photos with my cellphone but I was too far away to capture any detail. I needed to get closer to see why Brenden was here.

I got out of my car and hurried to the house, keeping myself low and out of sight so as not to be seen. I kept one eye on the house and the other on the two trucks.

Molly barked at me through the window as I passed Brenden's truck.

"It's just me, girl," I whispered as I crouched alongside Dave's vehicle.

I turned to look toward the road, hoping Erin and Carson wouldn't be too much longer. But I couldn't wait, either. I feared if I didn't look inside his truck now, I might not get another chance.

Not entirely sure what I was looking for or what I expected to find, I reached for the handle and opened the driver's side door to begin my search—worried that the interior light might give me away. The floor was littered with discarded food wrappers and an oily scent clung to the inside of my nostrils. But when I dove my hand beneath the seat and touched a plastic bag, I froze.

Without pulling it out or having to open it up, I angled my head to the side and could see a navy blue hooded sweatshirt tucked away inside. Remembering the list of what Nora was last seen wearing—*a navy blue hooded sweatshirt with the Dodgers logo on the right breast*—I was sure it was hers.

My breaths shallowed and I decided to leave the bag where it lay in case it eventually became evidence. Then I checked the inside door and found the driver's license of a blue eyed beauty from Venice named Scarlett Moss.

Who was she? Why did Rip have her license?

Suddenly, I heard the two men fighting inside. I hurried to the front windows to see what was happening and, when I got to the door it swung open in a flash. I watched a hand quickly grip my coat and pull me inside.

CHAPTER ONE HUNDRED SIX

My nose was pressed into the cold wall when I felt the barrel of a gun press between my shoulders. I immediately raised both hands to show I wasn't armed when Brenden said, "I told you to stay out of our business."

"Where's the blonde?" I asked, slightly turning my head.

"Are you alone?"

I turned my head further and found myself staring into the eyes of an obviously frightened Dave Mack. He had his hands raised in the air as well and was giving me a look that said I might have just saved his life. When he dropped one hand below his waist, Brenden took the gun off me and pointed it at Dave.

"I'm not done with you," Brenden said to him. "Put your hands up, and keep them up."

My mind raced to understand what I had walked in on; it seemed the boys were about to settle a dispute on their own terms. I was thinking of a way I could get out of this before getting caught in their crossfire, when Brenden said, "Since you're here, Samantha, I assume you've also concluded that Rip's the one who murdered Nora."

I flicked my gaze to Dave and he stared as if waiting for me to answer. His eyes glistened, looking scared. I said nothing and kept my hands out in front of my face as I slowly turned to face them both.

"Yes. Yes. Yes," Brenden said, still aiming his Glock between Dave's eyes. "I know you killed her."

"You don't know shit," Dave said.

"Shut up," Brenden snapped. "You don't get to talk."

I took one small step to the left, then another. No one seemed to notice my retreat and I kept heading toward the hallway wall, moving further away from Brenden who kept telling Dave to shut up. Something told me bullets were about to fly and the hallway was my only shot at keeping myself alive.

"I don't know how they did it," Brenden said. "But they knew you and Carson had hiked Climbers trailhead. They planted Nora's body in the exact spot you searched so I would be the one to find it."

I kept one eye on Brenden, the other on Dave. Neither of them moved, but Dave was swaying back and forth as if he had been drinking.

"You're delusional," Dave said to Brenden.

Brenden barked out a laugh and I watched as his trigger finger tightened its squeeze. I listened as Brenden shared his theory with Dave, allowing my thoughts to travel to the painting Carson and I had discovered at Nora's and how Dave had come to my cabin last night. I was trying to make sense of it all, when I realized Brenden was right.

"You're crazy. Everyone knows you had a thing for Nora. If I had to guess, I'd say you were the one who killed her," Dave said to Brenden.

"Go ahead, say it again," Brenden tempted him. "Go on. Say it."

Dave shifted his eyes over to me and said, "What he's not telling you is that he was the last person to see Nora alive."

"Bullshit," Brenden shouted.

Dave was still looking at me. He continued, "It's true. Ask him."

I shared a quick look with Brenden. I could see it in his eyes. He was with Nora the night before she disappeared.

Brenden said to me, "I didn't kill her. I loved her."

"Romeo and Juliet." Dave laughed.

"Were you with Nora that night?" I asked.

Brenden never answered the question. Instead, he looked Dave in the eye and said, "That's when I started putting the pieces in place. Nora knew things were about to change when they found Barry's car. She knew it was you who killed him."

I kept waiting for Brenden to reveal why he had sent Carson and me to Nora's house, but he never did. I still didn't know what he expected us to find. One hole I found in all of this was how Dave knew Brenden had been at Nora's. When I asked him, he was too busy taunting Brenden to answer.

Dave narrowed his eyes and said, "How many more have you killed? Two? Three more?"

I could see Brenden was losing his temper and I was afraid he was going to pull the trigger. I wondered if Dave was trying to get killed. It certainly seemed like he was.

"Brenden, don't listen to him," I said. "If you're innocent, don't listen to him. He wants you to shoot him."

"Maybe I should." Brenden's arm flexed. "Do it for Nora."

"No. Don't give in," I pleaded.

"He's the one who killed Nora and if I don't do something about it, no one will."

As Dave further instigated Brenden to pull the trigger, I kept hoping Carson and Erin would show up and be smart enough to come looking for me inside the house.

"Don't make a mistake you'll regret," I said to Brenden.

"No one believes me," he said.

"I believe you."

"I told the sheriff everything Nora shared and nothing happened. Rip will get away with murder if I don't do something about it."

"Give it time. Investigations are complicated."

My forehead beaded with sweat as I pleaded and begged for him to stop, hoping to buy enough time to walk out of here alive. Then Brenden's eyes welled with thick tears of sadness and, as he swiped at his face, I could see he was losing concentration. Just when I thought Brenden was going to put his gun down, a shot went off and Brenden hit the floor.

CHAPTER ONE HUNDRED SEVEN

I DIDN'T SEE IT HAPPEN BUT I KNEW WHERE THE SHOT came from. One quick glance at Brenden was all I needed to see that he was dead. It was a perfect shot—straight through the heart. Dave pointed his gun at me and I dove across the floor, landing on my knees in the hallway just before another shot was fired.

"Oh, Samantha," Dave called. "Where oh where do you think you can run to?"

I pushed myself up to my feet and darted down the hallway, slamming a door along the way with hopes of confusing Dave. Then I slipped into a closet to hide, hoping to buy enough time until Carson and Erin arrived.

I was breathing too fast, too noisily. My heart pounded loudly in my ears with no plan of what to do next. I felt trapped, walled off, not knowing where to go from here. If I ran, he'd certainly shoot me. But if I stayed, maybe I had a chance.

I listened to Dave's footsteps between breaths. I was certain he was still in the living room and I imagined him stopping to make sure Brenden was dead. That's what I would have done, unwilling to risk having Brenden take another breath before moving on to the next person I was hunting down.

"Holy shit," Dave said. "Talk about a shot. Straight through the heart, Samantha. Can you believe it? I can't. I'd say it was luck, but a man creates his own luck. Don't you agree?"

I tipped my head back and closed my eyes, regulating my breaths as best I could. It was a failed effort. I was too scared. As long as he kept talking, I could gauge where in the house he was, how much time I had before he forced a fight. If he went silent, there was no way I could keep him talking without revealing my location.

It was silent for a long beat as I openly stared at the light pouring in at the bottom of the closet door, listening. I wondered what he was doing when suddenly Dave said, "You know, he was right."

He was closer this time. Probably at the end of the hallway.

"I did get Nora killed."

The hairs on my arms raised and I made a fist with my hand.

"She was getting too brave."

One step closer to me.

"The Aston Martin was supposed to stay buried."

A door slammed and made me jump. I bit down on my knuckle and held still.

His footsteps were getting closer. Caron and Erin were my only hope. Where were they? When I heard him open the door I had slammed shut, I squeezed my knees tighter to my chest.

"You should have got a clue, Samantha, and gone back home to Denver." He paused and I imagined he was waiting for me to reveal myself by mistakenly making a sound. "This was never supposed to be your story. But here you are, about to become part of it."

My left leg started to tremble and I pressed my heel deeper into the floor.

"All alone at the cabin, and now all alone here." He laughed. "But it's the ironies that make me really laugh. Shall I tell you what they are?"

Another door opened and slammed shut. My insides lurched but I held still.

"First, it was the irony of being asked to retrieve the same car I had put into the lake eighteen years ago. Then, it was you being partners with Barry's daughter. What were the chances? But when I saw Erin with you today, I knew something had to be done. Never did I think I'd have the pleasure of killing you in my own home."

A shot was fired and I heard the bullet crash through the sheetrock on the opposite side of the hallway. I clamped my teeth down on my knuckles until the skin broke. My eyes were wide, round and dry as I continued to stare at the light pouring into the dark closet from beneath the door.

"What did you do with Carson? Will he be joining our little party, too?"

Dave knew too much about me. In an instant, I relived my conversation with Dale Tanner, my work with Edgar Diaz, and how I had discovered Erin was connected to this beautiful place with an extremely dark past. I did anything to take my mind off of feeling like I was about to die, but it was only a temporary escape. Dave made sure to keep me tuned in and afraid.

Everything inside me went still the moment he stopped just outside the closet door.

I held my breath and stared at the door handle, waiting for it to turn.

Without moving a single muscle, I prepared myself to

lunge forward and throw my shoulder against the door with hopes of hitting him square in the face.

Seconds felt like hours. When everything but my heart went quiet, I got scared.

Where was he? What was he doing? If he knew where I was hiding, would he just shoot through the hollow door? The thought of getting shot went through my head the moment I heard a knock on the front door.

I watched Dave's shadow move to the tune of his feet.

Another knock on the front door vibrated through the walls behind me and I pictured Carson there with gun in hand.

Finally, Dave moved past the closet and hurried to answer the door. I slowly stood and pressed my ear to the door to listen. Dave was doing most of the talking, but then I heard a male voice say, "Well, that might be fine and well any other day, but unfortunately I have reason to believe you may have spoken to Nora Barnes at the brunch restaurant a couple days ago and, because of that, I'd like you to come to the station with me and answer a few questions."

Dave said, "I'm not going anywhere, Sheriff."

I kicked the door open and screamed, "He's armed and just shot Brenden Donaldson. Help, Sheriff! He's bleeding out in the living room. Come quick."

Guns were drawn and both men began shouting. Then another shot was fired and everything went quiet again.

Too afraid to look, I crouched back down into a ball and hid in the closet once again. This time I put my head down and started praying. If the sheriff was dead, there was no way I was getting out of here alive. Dave would kill me, too.

The sound of heavy boots traveled closer and I felt my entire body tense, except for my arms that wouldn't stop shaking. When the door opened, I looked up into the sheriff's eyes and began to cry.

CHAPTER ONE HUNDRED EIGHT

THE SHERIFF HELD ME IN HIS ARMS AS HE LED ME OUT OF the house. He told me not to look as we passed near both Brenden, then Dave, but I couldn't help myself. I needed to see it with my own eyes, know with absolute certainty that Dave was dead.

Dave lay not far from Brenden, neither being attended to. Once outside, I squinted into the light and heard sirens in the distance. Standing near the street were Carson and Erin. When Erin saw me emerge from the house, she ran toward me.

"Easy," the sheriff said to Erin. "Your friend has been through a lot."

"I'm fine," I said.

"That may be," the sheriff said, "but I'm still going to order you get checked out once the ambulance comes."

Erin held Sheriff Graves's eyes and he nodded his head before letting me go. I was happy to see they had put things behind them—at least temporarily. When Erin put her lips next to my ear, she said, "You couldn't have waited one minute longer?"

I told her that Brenden arrived shortly after I did and then shared what I saw in Dave's truck. "I wasn't looking for trouble, and certainly didn't expect any of this to happen."

"You never are," she said, wrapping her arms around me. We hugged and when Carson joined our circle I told him what happened.

I said to Carson, "I'm sorry. I never had a chance to ask Dave if he killed Jocelyne."

"His actions speak for themselves."

I thought so too, but something about how today ended didn't feel complete. We had always believed there was more than just one person responsible for Jocelyne and Barry's deaths, but Dave made me believe he acted alone.

The house was soon taped off and a team of detectives began working the scene. The sheriff asked me to come to the station so I could give a statement and, once there, I told the sheriff everything I knew, including the sweatshirt I thought to be Nora's in Dave's wrecker. Then I asked him, "How did you know to come to Dave's?"

"Just a feeling, I guess."

I knew he couldn't say, but I suspected it was Rachel who called.

I hated that Dave got off without being judged by his peers. It didn't feel fair. Not to Jocelyne, and certainly not to Barry. There was still the question of whether he was guilty of their murders burning in the back of my mind, and it felt like there was nothing I could do to know for sure.

The sheriff walked me to the door but, before leaving, I asked, "Who is Scarlett Moss?"

The sheriff shook his head and said he didn't know. "Why?"

"No reason. Just a name I came across that I thought might be linked to Dave."

CHAPTER ONE HUNDRED NINE

EDGAR DIAZ APPROACHED THE DUPLEX TOWNHOUSE cautiously, thinking about what he needed to say to break the ice. He knew he had to be gentle in his approach and not scare her away before he had a chance to ask her about her experience. At the door he turned the knob, more out of curiosity than with an intention to enter, and wasn't surprised to find it locked.

He knocked a little rhythm and glanced over his shoulder.

A minute later, the lock clicked over and the door opened.

The young, bright-eyed woman he had photographed only a minute ago answered with a curious look on her face. Diaz said, "Scarlett Moss?"

The woman said nothing, but Edgar swore he saw recognition flash over her eyes. He introduced himself and said he was a reporter from the *Times* when a male voice asked from inside the house, "Scarlett? Is everything okay?"

Scarlett looked into Diaz's eyes and Edgar hoped he'd smoothed out his rough edges enough for her to trust him—at least today. Scarlett swallowed and took a deep breath of air before saying over her shoulder, "Yes, everything is fine."

Scarlett stepped outside and closed the door behind her. "What's this about?"

"Your car—the Mazda."

"What about it?"

"Well, I'm curious to know what happened to it."

Scarlett folded her arms across her chest and asked, "How did you know I drive a Mazda?"

"Is it here?"

The front door opened and a man's head poked out. He sized Diaz up. Scarlett stepped back and whispered something into her friend's ear that got him to go back inside. The man gave Diaz a questioning glare and, as soon as the door shut, Scarlett said, "It's not. The car broke down and I haven't been able to get it fixed."

Diaz flitted his gaze around the window trim before landing his eyes on the house's address. He knew this wasn't her home, that she was only staying here until she found a place of her own. He said, "Did that happen on your move to Idyllwild?"

Scarlett held his eyes with a suspicious look and Diaz could feel her getting nervous. He decided to come clean before he lost her completely.

He said, "I'm not here to frighten you, Scarlett. I just want to know what happened because I think you were extremely lucky to escape Idyllwild alive."

Scarlett looked away, tucked her hair behind her ear, and Diaz watched as her eyes filled with tears. "It was a mistake," she said. "I didn't know what I was getting myself into. It wasn't until after, that I learned Idyllwild was a hot bed of missing persons."

"Will you tell me what happened?"

Scarlett told Diaz that she was planning to move there, get away, and have a fresh start. "Then I got a flat tire and it changed everything."

"What do you mean?"

"For starters, I hit a pile of rocks in the road. It was like they had been placed there on purpose."

"Do you think they were?"

"I don't know how else they got there."

"Then what happened?"

"When I changed my tire, the spare was flat. It was just one of those days, you know? Like the universe was telling me this wasn't what I was supposed to be doing. I started having doubts I had made the right decision. Eventually, a truck stopped and I got a lift into town."

"What did you do with your car?"

"I left it there. The man who gave me a ride said he had a buddy who owned a tow truck who would pick it up for me. It was late and I didn't see anything wrong with the plan. When he asked where I was staying, I said I didn't have a place, so he offered me a bed for the night, free of charge, at a small apartment he managed."

"And did you accept his offer?"

"Of course I did. He was nice, I trusted him. After the day I'd had, I just wanted to take a hot shower and go to sleep."

"Then what happened?"

"The next day, he picked me up just like he promised he would, and took me to where my car had been towed."

"And had the tire been repaired?"

"I don't know. When we got there, I could tell his friend was on edge. He seemed nervous about something, maybe suspicious of me being there. I don't know what it was, but I got a bad vibe from him and thought it was about me, so I let the two of them talk. On my way back to the truck, I over-heard them talking about some car that had just been pulled from a lake and how two people had been murdered. It scared the shit out of me and I didn't know what to do."

"Did they say they did it?"

Scarlett shook her head. "No, but something about it made me think they did."

"What did you do?"

"I left. Hitched my way home. I didn't even care that I left my car there. Whatever happened, whoever those men are, I want no part of it." Scarlett then asked Diaz, "That's why you're here, isn't it? You know who they are and what they did."

"I'm working on it," Diaz said. "Do you remember either of their names?"

"I never caught the name of the tow truck driver, but the friendly man who picked me up called himself Lefty."

CHAPTER ONE HUNDRED TEN

CARSON AND ERIN WERE WAITING FOR ME IN CARSON'S FJ Cruiser outside the sheriff's department. I spotted them and climbed into the backseat. "Anyone else hungry?"

Erin twisted around in her seat and asked, "Samantha, did the sheriff say whether or not Dave Mack was responsible for my father's murder?"

I shook my head no. Erin frowned and looked disappointed. It was a difficult conclusion for all of us, but we had to accept this outcome. It seemed like it was the best we were going to get.

Carson put the car into gear and said, "I know a place that serves excellent tater tots."

"Perfect," I said, leaning my head back against the seat.

I wasn't in the mood to celebrate, but I didn't want to be alone either. There was a lot I was still processing. I kept touching the bandaged knuckle I had bit when hiding in the closet. I stared out the window, thinking about the week I had.

It was a quiet night at the bar. There were a few locals drinking. They gave us one passing look but then went on with their night. It was a nice change from the experience this morning at Daniel's restaurant and I assumed it was because word had spread about what happened at Rip's.

When I saw Rachel come out from the back, I said, "You two find a table and I'll get us some food."

I met Rachel at the bar and she greeted me with a smile. "Tater tots are on the house tonight."

"You don't have to do that," I said.

"I heard what happened," Rachel said, stepping forward. "I'm glad you're okay."

"Thank you," I said with a knowing look. "The sheriff arrived just in time."

"Don't thank me, honey. It was Daniel who called him." Her eyes sparkled then she stepped back and said, "Beer?"

"No. I'm not planning to stay long."

She spun around to the grill and took the basket of tots from under the lights. "Will you at least take this to Carson?"

"He'll be thrilled," I said, popping a cheesy tater into my mouth.

Erin and Carson sat quietly at a back table and, when I joined them, the mood was somber. We didn't have anywhere else to go, but it seemed better than sitting alone in a hotel room somewhere.

Erin asked me, "What did the sheriff ask you?"

"Typical questions. Gave me nothing in return. You know how it goes."

"So, you're no longer a suspect?"

"I wasn't arrested, was I?"

"I guess it's over then."

"It doesn't feel over," I said, mentioning Scarlett Moss's driver's license.

"It's no longer in our hands," Carson said. "We did everything we could. Now it's up to the sheriff to finish the job."

I knew what Carson was implying. I had already been

thinking about it, too. I needed to write this story and blow it up to keep the pressure on the sheriff's department to see this investigation to the end. But what about Scarlett?

I said, "The sheriff didn't have a clue who she was when I asked him about it. What if Scarlett is another girl gone missing that Rip still has hidden somewhere?"

Carson answered confidently, "I'm sure they're working on finding out who she is now. If Scarlett is somewhere inside Rip's, they'll find her."

No one said anything for a long time, giving me time to wonder what happened to Edgar Diaz. It seemed he missed what could have been the biggest story of his career.

I asked, "Are you two happy with the outcome?"

"Do we have a choice?" Erin said.

I kept thinking about what Rip said as he hunted me down inside his own house about how the Aston Martin was supposed to stay buried. Was that his own admission to guilt? I wanted to believe it was, but there was something about it I couldn't accept.

"So, what are you going to do now?" I asked Erin.

"Depends."

"On?"

"You."

Erin held my eyes. I knew she expected me to have an answer for her tonight. I said, "I can't imagine telling this story without you."

She leaned back and smiled. "In that case, I'm going to stay here a couple more days and make sure we have everything we need to publish an award-winning story."

"You want me to stay with you?"

Erin shook her head no. "You go home to Mason. I'll take it from here."

I shifted my eyes to Carson and asked, "What about you, Mr. Private Eye? Where do you go from here?"

"I guess I'll get back to investigating cases of adultery." Carson smiled when he looked me in the eye. "Not nearly as exciting as what you two have going."

Carson stood and said he was calling it a night. "You two take care of yourselves."

"If we ever need a private detective, we'll give you a call," Erin said.

Carson said, "That's generous, but I think you two will do just fine without me."

I stood and gave him a hug. "It was great working with you."

"Good luck," Carson said, pushing Nora's house key into the palm of my hand. "I'm not going to need that anymore."

I slipped the key into my pocket, wondering what I was going to need it for. "Promise to stay in touch?"

"Promise." Carson held his hand over his heart and I remembered how perfect his social media profile was. He was a good man and I was going to miss him. Then, just like that, he was gone.

CHAPTER ONE HUNDRED ELEVEN

TOGETHER WE WATCHED CARSON LEAVE THE BUILDING and, once he was gone, Erin said to me, "This might come as a surprise, but I'm going to miss him."

It already felt different without him. Like we'd lost a member of our group. I said, "Something tells me we'll be seeing him again."

Erin perked up like I knew something she didn't.

"It's only a guess."

"Do you have his number?"

"Would you call if I did?" I asked, surprised to see that Erin actually seemed interested in the man she once viewed as an adversary.

"Maybe." Erin shrugged.

I laughed and couldn't believe what I was hearing. "Yeah, I have his number," I said, thinking about King.

Rachel brought us another basket of taters and said, "He didn't even say goodbye."

She was thinking about Carson too, and suddenly Mr. Private Eye had become the man of the hour with two single women in the bar swooning over his charm and good looks.

I said to Rachel, "I'm sure he meant nothing by it."

"I liked him." Rachel frowned.

Thinking of my own escape, Rachel went back to the bar and Ewing Clark walked through the front door. Erin tapped me on the arm to let me know of his arrival and we watched as Rachel stopped to say hello. He said something that made her laugh and then she directed him to us. Ewing adjusted his cowboy hat as he strode to our table with a friendly smile.

"Ladies," he greeted us.

"Don't tell me I left the lights on again," I teased.

Ewing chuckled. "No. Nothing like that. In fact, I'm here to apologize."

"Apologize for what?" Erin asked.

"The town's knee-jerk reaction. Some of our community can sometimes forget how our local economy works. They shouldn't have treated you the way they did."

I looked around, noticing that no one seemed to pay us any attention tonight. "I think they've moved on. What do you think?"

Ewing hooked his left thumb into his belt and looked behind him toward the juke box. Then he said, "We all knew Rip, but none of us could have predicted he was capable of murder."

"The jury is still out on that."

"Is it?" Ewing raised a single eyebrow. "About earlier, I didn't mean to put you in danger. If I would have known—"

"You were only trying to help," I said.

Ewing nodded and gave me a sincere, apologetic look.

"But I'm afraid I won't be staying at the cabin after all."

"Something told me you might change your mind."

Ewing turned his head and asked Erin, "Are you leaving, too?"

"I think I'll stay."

I said to Erin, "Maybe you could stay at the cabin?"

"Ha. No thanks," Erin said. Then she asked Ewing, "You manage any properties in town? Perhaps a place with two beds?"

"Planning to have company?" I asked her.

"In fact, I am." Erin looked at me and smiled.

I said, "I guess I'll be staying one more night."

Ewing grinned. "Shall I show you what I've got?"

Erin stood and said to me, "Sam, are you coming?"

"You go ahead, I think I'm going to sit here for a little while longer."

"Are you sure?"

"Go," I said. "I'll be fine."

Ewing charmed Erin out the door, leaving a thick scent of cologne in his wake. It lingered until I remembered it was a scent I had smelled before.

Thinking of where I last smelled the cologne, I cast my gaze to the bar and Rachel locked eyes with me from behind the counter. Her unsuspecting look took me back to the day she told us about Nora seeing Brenden. I suspected it at the time, but now I knew she wasn't alone that day. She had a man inside her house and I was certain it was Ewing she was cuddled up with that day. Was he the one who warned her about me?

I stood and hurried out the door, knowing I had one last stop before my day was through.

CHAPTER ONE HUNDRED TWELVE

NORA'S HOUSE WAS DARK AND EMPTY WHEN I ARRIVED. I parked behind her silver car and thought about the key Carson had given me. I dove my hand inside my coat pocket. Instead of reaching for the key, I retrieved my cellphone and called a friend.

"Before you say anything," Allison Doyle answered, "please tell me, who exactly am I speaking with?"

"A *Times* writer."

"Which *Times* would that be?"

"Samantha Bell with the *Colorado Times*."

"What can I do for you?"

I could hear Allison smile at the news of my decision, and said, "You up for some last-minute sleuthing?"

"You know I can't say no to that kind of offer. What do you have for me?"

Allison was one of my best friends in Denver, and a computer genius who ran her own internet marketing agency. She absolutely killed it at stuff I couldn't even begin to wrap my head around. What I was about to ask her to do was one of the easier tasks I assigned her and I knew she'd be able to complete it far quicker than I could myself.

"I need a title search on a property in California."

"I'm ready when you are."

I gave her Nora's address. Not more than two minutes passed before Allison came back with an answer. "And the winner is...Mr. Ewing Clark. Anything else I can do for you?"

I stared at the perfectly kept house, finally putting a missing piece in place—Ewing had to be the reason Brenden told us to look here. "That's all. Thanks for playing along."

CHAPTER ONE HUNDRED THIRTEEN

THE NEWS OF EWING OWNING THE HOUSE NORA RENTED had me suddenly worried about Erin.

I turned back to my car and dialed Erin's cell. The line rang but she didn't answer. Everything inside me buzzed and I hated to think I sent her alone with a monster like Ewing. But worse, I didn't have a clue where they were.

I opened my car door and felt my cellphone buzz with a call.

I went for it. It was Diaz.

"Where the hell have you been?" I answered. "You missed everything."

Diaz said, "Listen to me, Mile High. I've got something for you that is going to blow your socks off."

I listened, trying to keep up as best I could, but he was speaking too fast when telling me about Scarlett Moss and what had happened to her. I asked, "Did she give a description of what the men looked like?"

"Just a name. Lefty."

"Lefty? Is that a first name or last?" Before Diaz could answer, I had figured it out.

"Hang up the phone, Samantha," a voice said behind me.

I spun around and squinted into the trees. A figure stood in the shadows but I knew it was Ewing.

Diaz was still talking when Ewing stepped into the moonlight and pointed a gun at me. "Hang up the phone, *now*, Samantha." When I hit the end call button, Ewing said, "Good. Now toss it to me."

I lobbed the device in the air and watched it hit the dirt near the toe of his boot. Lefty kneeled and picked it up, making sure to keep his gun pointed at me as he unsuccessfully attempted to unlock the screen.

"Who were you talking to?" he asked.

"Where is Erin?"

"She's not far," he said, sliding my phone into his left coat pocket.

"How did you know I would come here?"

"You've been here before." Ewing looked at the house with pride in his eye. "It's a nice place, isn't it?" When I didn't answer, Ewing continued, "I let Nora live here rent-free in exchange for her silence."

I thought back to earlier and remembered that Rip said he got Nora killed. I thought it was a funny way to phrase things, but now I understood why he had said it that way.

"You killed her, didn't you?"

Ewing's eyes glimmered in the moonlight. He stepped forward and I stepped back.

"Where are you going to go, Samantha? I know these forests and mountains better than anybody. You can run, but you won't get very far." He smiled. Then, after a silent beat, he asked, "You know why Brenden sent you here?"

"Because he knew you owned it."

Ewing made a face and bobbed his head. "Yes, but also because Nora told him I killed Barry and Jocelyne."

"Did you?"

"Is that what Rip told you?"

I didn't respond.

"I thought you would have figured it out then. I couldn't understand why Brenden just didn't tell you, but after what happened today, I think I understand why he chose to keep that secret to himself."

"Because he wanted to kill Rip himself."

"You're showing me why I couldn't just let you go." Lefty glared. "But you're right. Brenden wanted to kill Rip himself, but he forgot that Rip wasn't working alone."

"Maybe he was planning to kill you next?" A knowing look flashed in Ewing's eyes and I said, "But you made sure he went after Rip first."

"Was that mean of me?" Ewing laughed. "I needed to get rid of him. Rip was losing his cool. After I learned what he did to that sweet blonde girl today, I knew something had to be done. Rip was making too many mistakes. It was only a matter of time until he was going to get us both caught."

"Yet, here you are making the last mistake," I said.

"I don't think so. You don't know the full story. If not for Rip, I would have never had to send that rich man's car plunging into the lake."

Ewing took a giant step forward and I screamed, "Erin!"

Lefty clenched his teeth and growled, "You do that again and I'll have no choice but to plug that hole with a bullet."

With nostrils flaring, I said, "Take me to her."

Ewing squinted his eyes and stared. Then he said, "This way."

He walked behind me with the gun pointed at my back. After a short maze through the woods, we came upon a clearing where I saw Erin's car parked in a dark section of the street. Lefty popped the trunk and said, "Would you like to say hello?"

I peeked into the trunk and saw he had Erin gagged and

bound. Her round, scared eyes stared back at me. I felt like I had let her down.

"You're not going to get away with this," I said to Lefty.

"On the contrary, Samantha, I beg to differ." He slammed the trunk shut and I listened to Erin bang around for a bit as Ewing said, "I was going to let this go, but then Erin said something that made me think I shouldn't."

Ewing was looking at me as if he wanted me to guess what Erin said.

"No guesses? Well then, let me tell you. Erin said she believed Carson's daughter hadn't killed her father, and if you two could find who started the rumor, you could find who killed Barry."

Ewing walked up to me and tipped my chin up with the barrel of the gun. I made sure not to flinch. Then he said in a coarse whisper, "I'm not stupid. I knew that with Rip dead the rumors would eventually lead back to me. One thing would connect to another and an avalanche of past allegations would bury me before I had a chance to explain myself."

I made a wild guess when I said, "But the most damaging rumor was the one you fed to the sheriff about me being responsible for Nora's disappearance."

"He believed it, too." A glimmer flashed in his eye. "You see, Samantha, I'm pretty good at starting rumors. And after tonight, everyone will believe you killed your own friend and I'll have nothing left to worry about."

"Except no one will believe you."

Ewing opened the driver's door and said, "I can be quite convincing."

Then he told me to drive.

CHAPTER ONE HUNDRED FOURTEEN

LEFTY KEPT A FIRM GRIP ON THE GUN AS HE DIRECTED ME where to go. I drove with both hands on the wheel, asking myself where he had left his truck and if Rachel was in on his game. With a tight jaw, feelings of betrayal burned in my gut as I kept wondering how we allowed this loose end to go untied.

When we approached Mountain Center, Lefty said to stay on the highway. I stayed left and, once we were through town, Lefty asked me, "Do you know where I'm taking you, Samantha?"

Of course I knew. Everything was pointing to Hemet Lake. I even suspected how he was planning to get rid of us. "You're sick," I said.

Lefty laughed. "Now, that's not a nice thing to say."

"You're one to talk," I said, accusing him of being the person who started the rumors about Jocelyne and Barry, and probably Nora, too.

Lefty kept his gun down by his hip when he began telling me what really happened that night eighteen years ago.

"The reason Barry had to die wasn't because he had some

sick teenage crush on Jocelyne. No. That was only a rumor I started to keep the heat off of me and Rip. Worked, too. Funny what people will believe when they already hate someone."

"I don't understand," I said. "How did you even find yourselves at Barry's house?"

"Somehow, we got it in our heads to go check out the house, spy on the rich asshole who lived there. But when we got there we saw Erin leaving and, soon after, Barry did, too. We decided to go in and check it out ourselves, seeing as we might not get another chance."

"You just wanted to see the inside of the house?"

"Exactly. Back then there wasn't a gate or anything and we were just stupid kids looking to score some high-priced booze."

"This all started because of booze?"

"Yes, but it all went to shit when Nora decided to take that bitch Jocelyne with us."

"Why did you call her that?"

"Because she's the one who started it all. If not for her, none of this would have happened." Lefty then told me how Jocelyne drank far too much. "It was clear she couldn't hold her liquor, and Rip was the idiot who couldn't keep it in his pants."

"What are you saying? He raped her?"

"And Barry caught him in the act."

"Where were you when this happened?"

"Nora and I were on the other side of the house when we heard a fight break out. I told her to leave so if anyone got caught it would be me."

"Did she?"

"Nora was a good listener. Always had been."

"So she left; then what did you do?"

"I saved Dave from that prick, Barry."

"You mean you killed him?"

"What choice did I have?"

I was thinking about the coroner's report when Lefty told me how they then decided to take Barry's car and put both of them at the bottom of the lake. What hurt most was learning that Jocelyne drowned for doing nothing wrong. She was a victim; just in the wrong place at the wrong time with a couple of goons who let things get way out of hand.

I said, "That's why Nora's story kept changing."

"She didn't know what happened."

"Except she did, and that's why you had to kidnap her."

"I hated to do it. I really did. Nora and I go way back. But that night changed everything."

"And you thought you could get the sheriff to believe it was us who kidnapped and killed her."

"I needed to kill her without it looking like I was responsible. It's the only way I know how. After eighteen years without anyone speculating I had killed Barry, I'd say I'm pretty good at it."

"Then why do this to me and Erin? You were in the clear. Home free. We were all about to go home and the evidence against Dave was indisputable. It was over."

Lefty took a long time to answer. Then he said, "I guess it was something about seeing Erin here tonight that I just couldn't pass up." He turned his head and we briefly locked eyes. "I've read about you two; what you're capable of doing. Eventually, something would surface and you'd once again be asking yourselves if you had caught the right guy."

A pair of headlights crested the knoll in my rearview mirror and they quickly turned off before Lefty noticed. I didn't know who it was, but their actions told me they were here for us.

I eased off the gas just a hair and, a minute later, turned into the Hemet Lake recreational grounds. Lefty told me to go to the same rocky point where the Aston Martin was found and I listened to the tires crunch over the gravel as I thought of ways I could get us out of this mess.

"I'm sorry, Samantha, but now that I've told you my life's secret, I have no choice but to kill you, too."

I checked my mirrors and caught a glimpse of Carson's cruiser following us. I felt a renewed sense of hope move through me as I navigated to the place where he told me to park. Lefty told me to keep the engine running and put my hands through the steering wheel. I watched him set his gun in his lap and, as he leaned over to tie my hands, he asked, "How many years do you think will pass before they find this car?"

"You're assuming I'm going to die."

Lefty stared into my eyes and burst out laughing when suddenly his door opened and a big hand landed on his shoulder. Lefty's eyes widened and then he was pulled from the car and thrown to the ground.

I unbuckled my seatbelt and ran around the car. Lefty sprang to his feet and immediately tackled Carson to the ground. A couple hard punches were thrown on both sides and both men were grunting and groaning as they fought for their lives.

I ran around them, searching the ground, looking for a gun. I knew both of them were armed but I couldn't find a single one. Did Lefty still have it? I thought he might. It was difficult to see and Carson was getting pummeled.

Then Lefty got Carson into a choke hold that Carson couldn't get out of. I knew if I didn't do something quickly, Lefty was going to kill him.

I spun around to face the car and fell to my knees. I crawled, patting the ground, miraculously finding Lefty's gun. As soon as I had it in my hand, I checked the safety and then immediately lunged forward and jammed it into Lefty's ribcage, firing a single shot.

Lefty collapsed on top of Carson and Carson pushed him off, catching his breath.

I fell back onto my rear and, after Carson lay there staring up at the sky for a long while, he finally said, "Good shot."

CHAPTER ONE HUNDRED FIFTEEN

LEFTY HADN'T MOVED ONCE SINCE I SHOT HIM, AND though I was certain he was dead, I wasn't willing to chance it. Finally, I pushed myself up off the ground and stood over him before nudging him with the toe of my shoe.

I cursed him, and I cursed myself.

None of this should have happened, but I didn't have any regrets. I'd kill him again if I had to.

I turned back to the car and set the gun on the hood. Then I popped the trunk and hurried to untie Erin. As soon as her arms and legs were free, Carson reached inside and helped her to her feet.

Erin looked around and, when she saw Lefty on the ground, she walked to where he lay, stood over him, and spit. "You bastard."

No one said anything. Erin was feeling what we all felt. Then she turned to the lake and something told me she was thinking about her father.

I slid my hand around her waist and pulled her into a hug. She wrapped her arms around me and asked, "How did we miss this, Sam? How did we not know he was the killer?"

None of us could answer that, but the bigger question that needed to be asked was how Carson knew we were in trouble. I turned to Carson and asked, "How did you know to find us, or even where to look?"

"I was just about to drive away from the bar when a truck I recognized pulled in."

"It was Ewing?"

Carson nodded. "But not the truck he had at the cabin; another one I saw parked at a nearby cottage the night our photo was taken."

I turned my head and looked at Lefty, thinking about the envelope and photo addressed to King left for us to find.

"It didn't occur to me until after I had already left. When I went back to the bar, everyone was already gone. I figured you might have gone back to Nora's since I gave you the key, and that's where I saw Lefty putting you into Erin's car."

"You're amazing," Erin said.

"What did I tell you? I knew we'd see him again."

Erin laughed and Carson looked confused.

Erin said, "So, what do we do now?"

I stepped away from Erin and dug my cellphone out of Lefty's coat pocket, preparing to call the cops, when I said, "First, I'm going to call the sheriff, then I'm going to call my lawyer."

CHAPTER ONE HUNDRED SIXTEEN

Two weeks later...

I was standing in front of my bedroom mirror finishing getting ready for my dinner date with King when the house phone started to ring.

"Mason, can you get that?"

"It's probably for you," he responded from the living room.

I grunted my frustration. I thought I knew Mason's reason for not wanting to answer. Besides the fact that his friends only communicated by cellphone, I had also learned when I got home from California that Ewing had called the house and spoken with Mason. Mason said it hadn't scared him but did admit to feeling bad for alluding to my relationship with Alex King. I was just glad it had all worked out and the danger I experienced in California hadn't followed me home.

I picked up the handset and said to Mason, "Can you please hurry up and get ready so we're not late? Alex is waiting for us."

"In that case," he said, jumping over the arm of the couch and hurrying to his bedroom.

I answered the phone and was surprised to hear Hineman's voice. "What can I do for you?"

"I'm just calling to see how you're holding up."

I leaned against the wall and cast my gaze to the floor as I thought how Hineman could have easily dismissed me once I declined his offer to come revamp the digital media arm of the *LA Times*. I suspected this was his subtle way of staying in touch in case I changed my mind. Though it wasn't an easy decision to make, I knew my heart belonged in Denver.

I said, "I can't discuss the details of the case, but I'm managing."

"That's good."

Since the night I shot Ewing, my life had been consumed by meetings with defense attorneys and long interviews with the Riverside detectives. As stressful as the past couple of weeks had been, I considered myself lucky, and not only because Erin and I survived Ewing's plan to murder us, but because Carson was there to witness that I acted in self-defense—and the Riverside district attorney's office agreed, deciding not to press charges against me.

"It is," I said.

Hineman asked, "So, that's it?"

I lifted my chin and checked the time, knowing he was curious what Erin and I were cooking up on our Real Crime News blog and podcast, our new episode about to go live. I told Hineman to tune in and said, "Her first guest is Carson Reynolds."

"Not Edgar?"

Thinking of Scarlett Moss, I said, "Perhaps sometime in the future."

"Samantha, there's something you should know."

I pushed off the wall and crinkled my brow.

"Word around the office is Diaz is actively pitching this story to publishing houses and movie studios with hopes of being the one to tell it."

I rolled my eyes, not at all surprised to hear what Diaz was up to. I also wasn't entirely concerned, either. I said, "I can't control what he does."

"No, but you should be the one they are talking to, not him."

Incredibly, I hadn't heard from Diaz since that random phone call to tell me about Scarlett Moss. I assumed it was because of the attention I had received in the aftermath, basking in Hollywood glory, a stage I knew Diaz craved to stand on himself.

Over the last couple weeks, Erin had kept tabs on Diaz and fed me the news. We knew he wrote and published the story of Idyllwild's missing persons and tried to link them to Dave and Ewing, but the evidence just wasn't there—even with Scarlett as his star witness—and things just fizzled out and moved onto something else.

Hineman asked, "Do you have yourself an agent? I know a couple good ones I could put you in touch with if you'd like?" When I didn't respond, Hineman continued, "Samantha, what you did in Riverside was incredible. The whole story is extraordinary. It should be in a book."

I whispered, "I'm sorry I let you down."

"You didn't let anyone down; that isn't what I'm saying."

"Then what are you saying?"

"I'm saying that you deserve your story to be told."

National acclaim, I thought when Mason came out wearing a jet-black collared shirt and pearl white tie. He had his dark hair combed back and was looking more like his father with each passing day. My handsome boy, all grown up.

I said to Hineman, "If that's what you think, you can begin the introductions."

"Happily."

My head was still spinning after the call and I couldn't stop thinking about what a publishing deal would look like. A book, I could do. A movie? I didn't know where to begin. Besides, I wasn't about to go back to Hollywood anytime soon so I let the thought go and turned my attention back to my boys.

"Ready?" I asked Mason as I texted King, telling him we'd be late.

"Just about."

Mason ran into his bedroom and came out carrying a big box.

He plopped it into my arms and I asked, "What's this?"

"Dad's old CDs. I told Alex he could borrow them."

"Does he really need all of them at the same time?"

Mason was already heading back to his room when he called over his shoulder, "There's another box I need to get. Take those to the car and I'll meet you there."

Not understanding what was happening, I didn't ask questions, letting this be *their* thing. I headed out the door and popped the hatch of my Subaru outback and released the cargo cover. It snapped and rolled up on itself. I jumped back, completely startled by the dull dead eyes staring back at me.

With my heart knocking, I turned and looked over my shoulder wondering if I was being watched. The streets were dark and quiet. A dog barked in the distance, but otherwise I was alone. I turned back to the trunk and felt a cold shiver move up my neck. It was Edgar Diaz's dead body but I couldn't explain how he ended up in my car without me knowing how it got here. I immediately flashed back to my trip to San Quentin and suspected Dale Tanner might be responsible for Diaz's murder. I couldn't explain how he could have done it, but if I was right, I knew I was in big trouble and that I might be next.

I hope you enjoyed the story. If you'd like to see more Samantha Bell mysteries, please consider leaving me a quick book review.

Never miss a new release. Sign up for Jeremy Waldron's New Releases Newsletter at JeremyWaldron.com

A WORD FROM JEREMY

Thank you for reading TO BELL AND BACK. **If you like the stories I'm writing, don't forget to rate, review, and follow. It really helps my books get in front of new readers.**

ALSO BY JEREMY WALDRON

Dead and Gone to Bell

Bell Hath No Fury

Bloody Bell

Bell to Pay

Burn in Bell

Mad as Bell

All Bell Breaks Loose

To Bell and Back

Never miss a new release. Sign up for Jeremy Waldron's New Releases Newsletter at JeremyWaldron.com

AFTERWORD

A special thanks to my editor and brilliant proofreaders for cleaning up the errors I missed. I couldn't do it without you.

One of the things I love best about writing these mystery thrillers is the opportunity to connect with my readers. It means the world to me that you read my book, but hearing from you is second to none. Your words inspire me to keep creating memorable stories you can't wait to tell your friends about. No matter how you choose to reach out - whether through email, on Facebook, or through a review - I thank you for taking the time to help spread the word about my books. I couldn't do this without YOU. So, please, keep sending me notes of encouragement and words of wisdom and, in return, I'll continue giving you the best stories I can tell. Thank you for giving me an opportunity of a lifetime.

Never miss a new release. Sign up for Jeremy Waldron's New Releases Newsletter at JeremyWaldron.com

ABOUT THE AUTHOR

Waldron lives in Vermont with his wife and two children.

Receive updates, exclusive content, and new book release announcements by signing up to his newsletter at: www.JeremyWaldron.com

Follow him @jeremywaldronauthor

 facebook.com/jeremywaldronauthor
 bookbub.com/profile/83284054

Made in the USA
Middletown, DE
31 January 2024